The Kansas NCO

D0873061

By Joe Campolo, Jr.

Library of Congress Control Number: 2014938985

ISBN: 978-1937958-63-3 Trade paperback

ISBN: 978-1-937958-64-0 eBook

Cover design and layout by Joyce Faulkner

Printed in the United States.

Dedicated to my mother, Vincenza Campolo, a voracious reader who encouraged me to write. (Finally started Mom!)

And to my good friends Tim and Larry...who made the trip through Nam tolerable

"I shall cast my jewels to the pigs so that they may swallow them, and die either of gluttony or indigestion."

Kahlil Gibran

Prologue

October 1970. What the fuck was he doing here? It was 23:00, and Sgt. Andrew Crucianelli was lying in a ditch next to a truck in a small convoy on a desolate road, somewhere in Binh Dinh province in the Central Highlands of Vietnam. Ten minutes earlier Crucianelli had been riding shotgun, on that same truck which was carrying cases of materials that he had helped off-load from warehouses at Phu Cat Airbase, where he was a buck sergeant assigned, at the time, to base supply. He was riding in a convoy with five vehicles; all manned by army and air force personnel, unofficially working for the Kansas NCO, a.k.a. Master Sergeant William Richards, U.S.A.F.

The first vehicle in the convoy had run over a booby trap, blowing it, and the two U.S. Army soldiers in it to kingdom come. The rest of the men in the convoy immediately evacuated their vehicles and were lying in shallow pools of rain water, nervously fingering the triggers of their weapons, listening to their hearts thumping through the thin fiber of their fatigue shirts. After the initial yelling, screaming and terror, they lay quiet, oblivious to the cold scummy water, waiting for one of the senior NCOs to tell them what the fuck to do. What remained of the destroyed vehicle lay beside them, upside down and steaming like an overturned rice beetle struggling to regain its feet. Watching and waiting, Crucianelli was cursing himself, for getting into such a position, with less than three months to go in country. The other men from the convoy were lying in their own pools of foul water, harboring their own fearful thoughts. Two of those men were assigned to Phu Cat Air Base supply along with Crucianelli; Alan, a big hillbilly from Tennessee everyone called Bear, and Redmond, a small tough airman from Northern Minnesota. Redmond had enough Native American in him to earn the title, Chief. Both of these guys could carry their water. Bear, though somewhat of a troublemaker, was big and strong and at base supply his non-commissioned officer in charge, took advantage of his size and strength, working him like a pack mule. Bear liked to screw whores, drink, smoke dope, and fight. The Chief, though slight of frame and unassuming, as it turned out was skilled with most any weapon available, a rare commodity amongst airmen assigned to base supply.

He had balls of steel, seemingly afraid of nothing and never giving quarter to anyone, Bear included. Cru really appreciated having him along on these night forays, he always knew what to do, and didn't take any shit from the army grunts. The ground pounders bullied airmen every chance they got; especially on the road where they would try to run the airmen into a ditch with their larger deuce and a half trucks. The grunts spent a lot of time out in the bush, and didn't cotton to those men who enjoyed the easier, less risky duty on the air base.

They didn't seem too comfortable in their current situation either, as they squirmed and glanced around tentatively. Finally the Kansas NCO's sidekick, whom Cru and Red knew as his personal bodyguard, rousted everyone out of their stupor. The remains of the dead GIs were put in body bags, and the salvageable materials from their vehicle were off-loaded into other trucks. They formed up again, and with no further incident continued on to their destination, a small army encampment about fifteen miles down the road. Cru and Red lamented the grunts killed that night, along with their friends and all the others killed as a result of their involvement with the Kansas NCO. Wasted in a dubious black market operation lining someone's pocket; not killed in an effort to free the world from communism, or even their nasty little corner of it. Years later after a reunion of sorts, they found their names on the Wall in Washington, D.C. But after spending thirteen months in Vietnam, the men realized that how one died in that miserable shithole made little difference in the grand scope of things. Since that time, Cru also thought of the Kansas NCO who although heavily involved in the black market, was like many other aspects of that war, sometimes evil . . . and sometimes good. He was complex, pragmatic, and he was a survivor.

Map of the Central Highlands of South Vietnam.

Chapter 1

"The end is in the beginning and lies far ahead."

Ralph Ellison

Just one year earlier Andrew Crucianelli was working as a supply specialist at Grand Forks Air Force Base, North Dakota, a cold, desolate place. Like many of his peers Crucianelli rapidly fell into the pattern of heavy drinking and seeking a way out of the undesirable location. Cru thought he found a way out when he became eligible for a transfer to nuclear weapons storage, which required extensive background checks and acceptability exams. The job would no doubt involve a transfer for at least six months while retraining. Cru was excited about the challenge the new duty would bring and looked forward to the possibilities it would open up for him. He did have some obstacles to overcome, however, some being derision from within his own ranks. "You ain't gonna be no fuckin' nuclear specialist," Sergeant Jimmy Johnston chided him.

Johnston, an Air Force lifer and longtime alcoholic, had been busted down in rank many times during his twenty-seven-year air force career. One of his few remaining pleasures was hassling new recruits. Tall, gaunt, and only in his mid-forties, as a result of years of heavy drinking and smoking, Johnston could have easily passed for a man of seventy. "Shut the fuck up, you old rummy!" said Sergeant Daniel Olsen, a first termer who worked alongside Johnston and Cru. Over the past two-and-one-half years Olsen came to hate the bitter old man who was often incapacitated as a result of his drinking.

Laughing, Cru told Olsen, "You know I don't pay attention to that old alky."

"Well, I can't stand the old bastard. How's the testing coming along?" Olsen inquired.

"Coming pretty well," Cru told him. "Sergeant Brunell thinks I'll find out next week." But as Cru was to discover, life often deals people

1

unexpected hands. Cru's mentor, Master Sergeant Howard Brunell, was the Non-Commissioned Officer-in-Charge of the nuclear weapons storage facility at Grand Forks AFB. He had encouraged Cru to apply for the program and helped him through the induction process. Then one day for some unknown reason Brunell stood at attention in the heavily secured area at the nuclear weapons storage facility where he worked, pulled out his sidearm, and blew his brains out. This stunned Crucianelli and threw him in doubt. He withdrew from the program, resumed his duties in supply, and as he had done almost every month since he'd been in Grand Forks, volunteered for duty in Vietnam. Within two months he had orders to proceed to Hamilton AFB California for extensive small arms training provided by seasoned army NCOs. From there he would be sent to McCord AFB Washington where he would board the Flying Tigers stretch DC-8 for the long flight to Vietnam.

At his going away party his Officer-in-Charge, 1st Lieutenant Myers Hagan, among others, wished him well. "You be careful over there, Cru."

"I will, thank you, Sir," Cru replied.

Hagan told him to look up a Master Sergeant Charles Prentice when he got there. "I know he went to Phu Cat, over there," Hagan said. "He's a good man, spent a lot of time training me when I was just a rookie. Taught me a lot about the supply function and a lot about the air force; also taught me how to drink, but you already seem to be good at that."

"Yes, Sir, thank you, Sir. I'll look him up," Cru replied

*　*　*

About the same time Crucianelli was winding down his duty at Grand Forks AFB, Airman First Class Arnold Redmond was finishing up his supply training at Lowry AFB Denver. A transfer from the Marines, Redmond was a curiosity among his fellow supply school trainees. Redmond paid little attention to his classmates; his only goal was to find his way to Vietnam and fight, as a warrior should. Back on the Ojibwa reservation in Minnesota, his family came from a long line of military men and Red, as he was called, wanted nothing more than to fulfill the family tradition, be it as a Marine or an Airman.

"Orders are in, Chief!" The barracks Charge of Quarters told Redmond as he came into the barracks. "They're gonna post 'em on the board in the next half hour." Upon hearing the news, Redmond and several others within earshot took off out of the barracks on their way to the first sergeant's office where the information board was located.

"Hope you get 'Nam, Chief … and hope I don't," one of his companions told him. Everyone familiar with Redmond knew he wanted to go to 'Nam and transfer into the security police or at least be assigned supply convoy duty out on the road.

"Thanks," was all Redmond said as they made their way to find out where their lives would soon take them.

* * *

"We got some new men comin' in," reported Master Sergeant Charles Prentice, non-commissioned officer in charge of the supply and storage detail at Phu Cat Air Force Base, Republic of Vietnam.

"FANGS Huh? Well, we could use some new guys, Charley," said Doug Montrell. He and Terry Hardy were working in the back of the steamy tool issue center, sorting tools when Sergeant Prentice went back to give them the information. Perspiration was running off their bodies like water off a duck. The tool center had been short of men for months and the tools, scattered all over the warehouse, were in total disarray.

Prentice gave Montrell a sharp look. "New men, Monty, and don't you two fuck-offs give 'em a hard time and run 'em outta here," he said. "We need to get this place up to snuff or it's your ass and my ass, so when they get here, you show 'em the ropes and treat 'em right."

Laughing, Hardy shot back,"You gonna show 'em your vodka stash, Charley?"

Now Prentice gave Hardy a bad look. "Don't you worry about my vodka stash," he said. "They'll probably want all that wacky tobaccy and other shit you guys get high on every fuckin' night, like all the rest of the damn hippies around here."

Laughing even harder, Montrell advised, "Okay, Charley, take a break, we'll take care of the newbies when they get here, don't worry about it. When you gonna get the Kansas NCO to let us in on a gig?"

At the mention of the Kansas NCO Prentice looked around the dismal warehouse as if someone might overhear them. "Don't you worry about him, Montrell. You got enough trouble keepin' me and the first shirt happy. Besides, you know Richards don't let hippies work for him. If he needs anyone to show him how to drip acid, he'll call you two goldbricks."

Montrell and Hardy were roaring laughing now.

"It's drop acid, Charley," he said. "*Drop* acid."

Looking exasperated as he headed out the door, Prentice replied, "Well whatever the fuck it is, he don't want any!"

*　*　*

"Did those new boots come in?" William E. Richards, the Kansas NCO, inquired of Prentice as soon as he walked in the door. Richards had sold several cases of GI issue jungle boots to the Montagnards and the original shipment that came in were all sizes 9 and up, much too big for the small foot of the stalwart, but diminutive warriors.

Nervous as always, Prentice stuttered, "The, the shipment came in but the damn things were the wrong size again."

"Goddammit, Prentice, this asshole Yard has been raggin' my ass for three weeks about those fucking boots. You're gonna go out there and explain it to him, get it?"

Richards didn't like mistakes. Mistakes cost time and money, and he hated losing both. The operation he was running, supplying goods and services to any and all that required them, was fickle. If he couldn't fill the bill, those in need would quickly seek other sources. "Denton, get in here!"

Technical Sergeant Thomas Denton slunk through the door, closed it, and leaned back against it. A chain smoker, he glanced derisively at Prentice and lit another cigarette off the one almost finished. Prentice never liked Denton, and Denton reciprocated the feelings. Prentice thought Denton was a sleazy little weasel, and Denton referred to Prentice as "that useless old alky."

"What's up?" he asked Richards.

"Call our boy in Qui Nhon and ask him how many pairs of boots he's got, size 8 and under. If he's got more than fifty have someone go pick 'em up. Prentice, when those boots get here, you take 'em to the Yards first thing . . . understand?"

Looking unhappy but not knowing what else to do, Prentice agreed to take care of it. As he was leaving Denton gave him a smirk. "Fuck you, Denton," was all Prentice could think to say.

Chapter 2

"To him who is in fear, everything rustles."

Sophocles

Andrew Crucianelli arrived in Vietnam at the Central Highlands coastal base of Cam Rahn Bay. The flight, filled to capacity, consisted of personnel from all branches of the military, most of whom were traveling on to other locations in that part of the country, known as the Central Highlands. There were four men traveling on to Phu Cat, and as they were to find out, they were on their own regarding those travel arrangements. All new arrivals in Vietnam were greeted by the stunning heat and humidity, as well as an exotic cornucopia of odors, which nothing they'd ever experienced had prepared them for. A kind of pungent smell comprised of rotting tropical vegetation, diesel fuel, sweat, fire, human waste, cordite, and the strong odor from Vietnamese cooking . . . And death . . . the smell of war.

"I hate this place already," remarked Clifford Canty, a big Airman 1st Class who was also on his way to Phu Cat. He stuck his hand out, "Cliff Canty from Missouri."

"Andrew Crucianelli, Wisconsin," Cru replied, shaking Canty's hand.

"You goin' up to Phu Cat too, huh?" Canty remarked.

"Yeah, hope to anyway, can't seem to get a feel for a flight heading up there," Cru told him.

Canty had heard all the rumors used to scare newbies before they even went over to 'Nam. "I ain't anxious to get there, I hear the place is crawlin' with VC and they get hit every day," he said.

Cru thought about it. "I don't know," he replied. "I heard it didn't get hit quite that much and it's still better than humpin' the boonies all day."

"Well, I won't be happy 'til I'm on a plane goin' home," Canty concluded. "Oh, and most guys just call me Flash."

Laughing Cru shook his hand again, "Just call me Cru."

Flash and Cru got to Phu Cat about two days later, arriving in the late afternoon. Tired from their long, tense journey, they slept straight through till the next morning in a tent where they would bunk until they got assigned to a barracks or hooch sometime after reporting in. After they woke up they showered behind the tent, changed into their newly issued jungle fatigues, and waited for someone to tell them what to do.

"Hurry up and wait, hurry up and wait," Flash complained. "What the fuck we supposed to do, hang around here till our DEROS date?" Unfortunately for Flash and Cru their date of estimated return from overseas was thirteen months away.

"What the fuck you new meats still hangin' around here for?" A buck sergeant with dirty jungle fatigues and the name "Stangl" on the nametag barked at them as he came into the tent.

"We were waiting for someone to tell us where to report, Sergeant," Crucianelli told him.

"Well, get your ass to the supply warehouse on the double and make sure you have your orders with you," Stangl barked.

Flash, never one to take much bullshit from anyone, barked back, "We supposed to have ESP or somethin' Stangl? You wanna tell us where the supply warehouse is, or do we have to find out right from the Old Man?"

"Don't get smart with me, new meat; I'll have your ass out on the perimeter for your first month in-country!" Stangl responded angrily. At that Flash stood up to his full height, intimidating the much smaller Stangl into retreating back to the opening of the tent.

Not wanting trouble from day one, Crucianelli stepped in between the two. "We will report to the supply warehouse with our orders, Sergeant Stangl," he said. "We just need directions."

Still looking up at Flash with concern in his eyes, Stangl told Cru, "Just take the road we're on and go right, follow it around to the flight line, and keep your eye open for a large metal warehouse. It's got a sign on it that says base supply." With that he quickly left.

At the supply warehouse Flash and Cru met Sergeant Prentice. He shook their hands and told them to wait outside. "Where're your duffle bags?" Prentice asked. Looking at each other Cru and Flash explained they left them at the tent where they bunked. Frowning Prentice said, "Damn, we better go get 'em quick if you have anything of value in them."

With a surprised look Cru and Flash started out the door to retrieve their possessions.

"Hang on, we'll take the jeep," Prentice said. After returning to the warehouse with their gear intact, the men met Arnold Redmond, who was sitting on his duffle bag outside the entrance of the building. "Damn, we got three of you," Prentice said, smiling. "Follow me."

"FANGS!" the three men in the warehouse were yelling. The men, shirtless and soaked in sweat, came over to meet the new personnel. "Charley make you buy him a bottle yet?" Montrell asked, looking at Sergeant Prentice.

Prentice, gave Montrell an angry look and shot back, "Men, I'm sorry you will have to spend part of your tour with these degenerates and hippies. Don't let them spoil your fine air force experience."

Laughing, Hardy interjected, "Okay, Charley, you can back off on the military bullshit, we'll take care of these guys."

Looking at him warily, Prentice replied, "That's what I'm afraid of . . . you fuckers will corrupt these new men before mail call tomorrow. I gotta go meet with Sergeant Richards, make sure these guys are quartered and see they understand the work details they will be a part of. I'll check in on you in a couple of days."

Happy for the interruption from the hot laborious work, Montrell and Hardy welcomed the three new men. After introductions they showed them around the warehouse and explained the duty they could expect.

"We work here ten to twelve hours a day six days a week. We usually get Sunday off, but if there's a backup of men waiting for tools, we may have to work Sunday, also. We have to pull perimeter guard every four to five weeks. That can be brutal, because it's an all-nighter and we still have to pull our day shift in this dump.

"We get a break every two to three weeks on convoy duty. We move material from here to Qui Nhon, or Phu Bai, or some other shithole out in the boonies. We drive either a pick-up truck or a deuce and a half, depending on the load. Besides the driver and the shotgun, there are usually one or two more men in the back with the load. We can hit a whorehouse if we're lucky, and once we even got to swim in the ocean while waiting for a load in Qui Nhon.

"But it can be dangerous, we've been attacked a couple of times since I've been pulling the duty. It's usually voluntary so if you don't want to take the chance, you don't have to. You guys got any questions?"

"Where's the chow hall?" asked Cliff, who was unhappy at eating nothing but c-rations since arriving in Vietnam.

"We'll show you around tomorrow, the chow hall, the post office, and the airman's club," Hardy said.

"You guys get hit here much?" Crucianelli asked.

"The first three months I was here we didn't get hit once, except for a sapper attack," Hardy replied. "Since they've been pulling the 173rd Airborne back, we've been getting hit more regularly; usually around once or twice a week. We've only had five guys killed, but there's been dozens of injuries and a lot of damage as well. It's scary and keeps us from sleeping too well."

"What are they hitting you with?" asked Arnold Redmond.

"Usually its Chi Com mortars," said Montrell. Maybe only five or ten; sometimes they throw in some 122 rockets. The mortars are bad, but the rockets scare the fuck out of everyone, even the goddamn dogs."

"Where can I get screwed?" asked Canty.

Laughing, Hardy said. "You're gonna get screwed every day you're here, buddy."

Chapter 3

"Render unto Caesar, that which is Caesar's."

The Bible

It didn't take long for the new men to settle into a routine. Crucianelli and Redmond quickly learned the warehouse and supply function at Phu Cat and were used to fill various jobs when other men were sick, injured, on R & R, or unavailable for any reason. Sergeant Prentice was happy with their work performance and was able to leave the tool issue center in the hands of Montrell and Hardy who oversaw most all of the duties involved there. Redmond, good to his word, pulled perimeter guard duty every chance he got, usually at least twice a week. Crucianelli also manned the post at least once a week, earning them both good reputations with base security. Clifford Canty, on the other hand, proved to be less reliable and somewhat of a problem for his NCOIC. Flash, as he was known, was not a quick learner or a good worker and he complained a lot. He appeared to be drunk much of the time and spent an inordinate amount of time sneaking off base visiting the local whorehouse. In addition, he often got into brawls at the airman club and found himself targeted by gangs of blacks who he constantly traded insults with. Rumor had it he was using and dealing heroin.

"You're gonna have to do something about Flash" Prentice told Montrell.

Montrell, looking at Prentice incredulously replied, "Damn, Charley, did they make me the NCOIC around here? I'm gonna have to see the paymaster cause I ain't getting no master sergeant pay. What the fuck!" Prentice looked at Montrell with narrowed eyes. Montrell called the shots among the lower-ranking enlisted men. They looked to him for guidance as well as entertainment. A reluctant but natural leader, Montrell had finished two years of college before deciding to join the service. He hoped to become a professional ball player some day and was just marking time, until that opportunity arose.

10

"You know he listens to you, Monty, though why I sure as fuck have no idea," Prentice said sarcastically. "Maybe he figures by listenin' to you he'll get to drink beer, smoke dope, and fuck off all day."

Laughing, Montrell conceded, "Okay, Charley, I'll talk to your boy. But he ain't the sharpest knife in the drawer, so if nuthin sinks in you're on your own."

"Just do what you can; things don't change I'll hand him over to Richards, and you know what that means."

At that, Montrell got serious. "Okay," he said. "I'll talk to him today."

Later that afternoon Montrell got Hardy and told him about the problem with Flash. He agreed to help.

"I'm not crazy about the dude, he's kind of a smart ass and a fuck-off, but I don't want to see him used as cannon fodder for Richards and his henchmen; he coming in?"

"Should be here any minute," Montrell replied. Not long after, Clifford Canty made his way to the back of the tool storage center.

"Damn, you guys got enough shit to open a fuckin' hardware store," he commented. "What's up?"

Montrell put down the tool chest he was carrying. "Let's go up front to Charley's office," he said. "We can suck up on some a/c and see if there's any beer lying around." The three men proceeded up to the small office where an ancient window air conditioner labored. It only kept the small area about five degrees cooler than the rest of Vietnam, but it was a welcome relief to all who got to use it. Reaching behind an old cabinet Hardy came back with a warm six-pack of Black Label beer. The three of them sat down and opened their beers.

"Damn, this ain't bad," Canty said with a big smile on his face. "You Tool Center bums live the life, don't 'cha."

Looking at him seriously Montrell replied, "Yeah, that's right, Canty, and from what we hear you been livin' the life pretty good yourself."

Suspicious now, Canty shot back, "Who the fuck's been bird-doggin' me?"

This time Hardy spoke up. "Seems like you got the attention of the wrong people, Flash," he said. "The first shirt and Sergeant Prentice aren't too happy with some of your habits."

Montrell jumped in. "They're saying you're a slacker, a trouble maker, and bringin' heat down on the squadron," he said.

Canty angrily replied, "I don't give a fuck . . . matter of fact that's good. They don't like it they can send my ass home."

"But they won't send you home," Montrell said. "They'll send you to Long Binh, where the grunts there will beat your ass every day. They'll keep you in tiger cages and piss on you all day and night." Canty's expression changed to one of grave concern.

"Or worse, they'll keep you right here and make you a permanent road rat for the Kansas NCO," Hardy interjected.

"Who the fuck is the Kansas NCO?" Canty asked.

* * *

The Kansas NCO was a USAF master sergeant in the supply function in the 12th Combat Support Group at Phu Cat Air Base, Republic of Vietnam. But that was his official title; unofficially he was the head of possibly the largest black market operation of the Vietnam War. Born during the depression in the Dust Bowl about half way between Wichita and Topeka, Kansas, William E. Richards had been hardened on those dusty, lean plains, where water, shade, and money were all hard to come by. Fatherless at an early age, the stringy, rangy boy learned to live off the land and his wits. Providing for him and his three siblings proved difficult for his mother, and the resourceful young William frequently brought in the only food and money the struggling family saw.

After finishing high school, Richards determined to leave the parched, desolate landscape of his youth, and enlisted in the U.S. Air Force. Soon, the Korean War broke out and Richards found himself a part of the 474th Aviation Construction Company, which included a group of army and air force personnel who built infrastructure for airfields on the hotly contested peninsula. Richard's reputation in acquiring materials and services for the war as well as the black market grew far and wide, even providing him with an opportunity to become an officer, an honor he refused. Airman Richards realized that as an officer he would not have the flexibility to buy, sell, and wheel and deal, so he respectfully turned the opportunity down.

After the Korean War ended, Richards decided to make the air force a career and moved around to various bases in the U.S. and Europe. At each base Richards developed a network of supply sources and new contacts. He honed his skills as the one who could always get things, and the profits he earned on the side purchased a 300-acre ranch for his mother back in Kansas, and fine college educations for many of his relatives and their children.

In Vietnam Richards found lucrative markets for the skills he had acquired. The practice of money laundering, loan sharking and a host of other illicit operations rounded out the activities of his thriving enterprise. The consummate opportunist, he always had his radar out for new operations, large and small. President Nixon's Vietnamization program had cut supply lines drastically for the American military charged with conducting the war. The Kansas NCO wouldn't need a blueprint or government order in three copies; a brief description of the product or service was all he needed to come up with whatever might be needed...for a fee of course.

The Kansas NCO filled other needs as well. Vietnamese civilians, squeezed by the VC, NVA, South Vietnamese military, various militias, and the U.S. military as well, were always hard pressed to just survive. Hunger, poverty, disease and terror were their constant companions. One could not attempt to paint the Kansas NCO as Robin Hood, but on several occasions he personally provided food and clothing, at no cost to some of the local villages. He also filled an important niche in supplying many hard-pressed U.S. military units. The failure of providing adequate supplies and equipment by the bureaucratic, clumsy U.S. military required flexible and timely solutions by those charged with carrying out the task at hand. The Kansas NCO was often ready, willing, and able to provide for those needs as well . . . though not so often free of charge.

Chapter 4

"Danger gleams like sunshine to a brave man's eyes."

Euripides

After a briefing by Sgt Prentice, Montrell and Hardy brought Crucianelli, Redmond, and Flash back to the tool issue center warehouse, where Montrell filled them in, "We're goin' out on the road tomorrow. We're takin' a load to Qui Nhon; we'll be taking the deuce and a half. Crucianelli will ride shotgun, the rest of you guys will ride in the back with the load. Bring your weapons, flack vests and helmets, five extra ammo clips, a full canteen and whatever C-rats you wanna eat. We'll leave at 07:00, should be back before evening chow. Any questions?"

"Will we expect any trouble?" Crucianelli asked.

"We expect nothing," Montrell replied. "We prepare for everything. The last three convoys I've been on have been quiet. The two before that both had trouble. No one killed, but one wounded and one lost load. The hot spot is usually the village of Binh Dinh; if we're gonna have trouble most often it's there."

"I hear they gotta whorehouse in Qui Nhon."

Montrell frowned; figure Flash to worry about getting laid instead of the detail. "Yeah, that's right, Canty," Montrell said. "But let's concentrate on the job at hand. Everyone has to keep their eyes open and their radar up; if we get a chance, and there's time, we'll stop at the Red Barn." The whorehouse at Qui Nhon was referred to as the Red Barn because the roof was made of red tin, and the girls also raised chickens and pigs. They were quite self-sufficient. "We leave at 07:00," Montrell went on. "And Cru?"

"Yeah?"

"There ain't much room in the cab to maneuver a -16, we'll be carrying a .38, check one out from the weapons locker."

"Got it." Cru replied. The next morning at 06:45 Montrell pulled the truck up to the warehouse. All the assigned men were there as well as Sergeant Prentice.

"Gotta be one of Richards' loads, otherwise Vodka Charley wouldn't be here," Hardy commented.

"Looks like it," Montrell agreed. "Okay, let's get it loaded and pointed down the road." Soon the truck was loaded and headed out the main gate. For Cru and Red this was their first trip off base since arriving at Phu Cat. Flash had been making regular visits to the whorehouse in Phu Cat, but had gone no farther than the outskirts of the village. Riding in the back Flash nervously clutched his weapon as they moved through the squalid village of Phu Cat and past it. Redmond was alert but not nervous. In the cab Cru took in the sights of the war-torn, poverty stricken countryside. The isolation on the air base had somewhat insulated them from the real war, beyond the rows of concertina wire and claymore mines all along their perimeter. Now, they were getting an up close view of the destruction, poverty and death the war had brought to the Vietnamese people.

"So what's the deal with this Kansas NCO dude?" Crucianelli asked Montrell.

"How do you mean?" Montrell casually replied.

Looking at him Cru said, "Well, he appears to have as much clout as the old man, but he's also enshrouded in this mysterious cloud — like some kind of guru or cult or whatever the fuck."

Montrell thought Cru would probably wind up on more of the Kansas NCO's operations so he might as well level with him. "He runs the black market around here," Montrell said. "Him and his buddies make money off the war; guess he figures someone's gonna make money off this fuckin' war, might as well be him."

"How does he make all this money?" Cru asked.

Glancing over at Cru and pursing his lips Montrell responded, "You look like a guy that knows when to keep his mouth shut, and since you'll probably be on more of these types of details I'll fill you in. But if it ever gets back that I told you this shit, I'll break your fucking balls."

"No sweat," Crucianelli replied. "I know when to speak up and I know when to shut up. You wanna tell me, fine, if not I'll find out sooner or later anyway."

"He's gotta lot of sticks in the fire, he doesn't depend on any one thing for his profit, but the primary source of income for the operation is money exchange," Montrell stated.

"How's that work?" Cru wondered.

"You remember what they told you about greenbacks when you got here?" Montrell asked.

"Yeah, no fucking greenbacks," Cru replied.

Nodding Montrell said, "That's because the dollar is worth around one and a quarter to one and a half the Vietnamese piaster at any one time. They issue us Military Payment Certificates or MPCs and hold the value of that to the 'P.' Richards acquires through various means large amounts of U.S. dollars. With those dollars he purchases the par value amount of piasters or MPCs. Say, for instance, he's purchased seven hundred dollars worth of MPCs for five hundred dollars in greenbacks. With his seven hundred dollars of MPCs he buys a seven hundred dollar money order, and off to the bank . . . with seven hundred dollars in greenbacks."

"Damn! That fuckin' simple . . . holy shit, I'm gonna get rich here," Cru exclaimed.

Glancing over at him, Montrell replied, "You can make a few bucks here and there at it, but if Richards finds out there's another big player in money exchange, you could end up on the endangered species list. This isn't someone you wanna fuck with, believe me."

As the miles rolled by Montrell filled Cru in on the other operations which Richards profited at as well; porno shows, animal parts marketing, souvenirs, etc. "Wow," Crucianelli commented. "I've got some relatives in the mafia and I think this guy could show them a thing or two."

"Probably" Montrell remarked.

The truck was coming around a bend several miles from the village of Binh Dinh. Just as they got to the outside of the curve, a huge boulder struck the front quarter panel of the truck nearly pushing them off the road and down the embankment.

"Fuck!" Montrell yelled, slowing down and wrenching the wheel, getting the truck back on the road . . . but not stopping. "Heads up . . . watch for an ambush!" he yelled.

The riders in the back were badly tossed around, banging against the walls of the truck several times. Flash, Hardy, and Cru were yelling and screaming; Montrell pulled the pistol out of his holster. When they regained their composure they were all scanning the surrounding countryside trying to see where the offending activity had come from.

Pop! Pop! . . . *Pop! Pop!* Redmond, quick as a whip began firing his M-16 at something on the top of the craggy hill.

"Fuck, you got 'em!" Flash shouted. Two Vietnamese, who had been attempting to set up a mortar to fire on the truck, tumbled down onto the road where the truck had passed just moments before.

"You gonna stop?" Crucianelli asked Montrell.

Nervously scanning from his seat Montrell said, "You never stop, Cru . . . first thing I should have told everyone this morning. There could be another bunch waitin' for us to stop so they can ambush us; and even the honest ones get ideas when they see an American truck loaded with goods sitting on the side of the road. You never stop."

The men were on hyper-alert the rest of the way to Qui Nhon, clutching their weapons and anxiously scanning the countryside for anything that looked like trouble. When they arrived at the main gate they finally were able to stop and assess the damage. They also had to report the attack to Qui Nhon base security and visit the dispensary. Hardy suffered a chipped tooth, and Flash complained of a sore knee, but for the most part the men were unharmed. The truck's left front quarter panel was smashed, along with the left front headlight and turn signal.

"Well, it's drivable and were gonna be back at Phu Cat suckin' Black Labels by dark, so I guess we'll be okay" Cru said.

Flash wasn't so confident. "Damn, I don't want to go back past that damn mountain again; those fuckers will try to finish us off this time!"

The lieutenant in charge of the afternoon security shift at Qui Nhon reassured the men. "Shouldn't be a problem, we're sending an APC and a patrol over there right now. By the time you guys get unloaded and laid at the whorehouse, the area will be secured. You can go back to your airman's club, get drunk and brag about your big adventure."

That information brightened Flash up considerably. "Yeah, Okay," he said. "Thanks, lieutenant. How much do they charge over there?

Looking at the big airman and smirking the lieutenant told him, "Depends on how much of a cheesedick you are." Looking over Flash carefully he added, "If I was you I'd take out a loan."

Flash got red in the face and stewed, as Hardy, Montrell, Cru and Redmond stood laughing at the lieutenant's joke. Soon the men found the Red Barn and spent about an hour there, leaving with smiles on their faces and warm beers in their hands.

"Okay, let's get moving, we've got about three hours before the sun goes down and I don't wanna get caught in Indian country after dark," Montrell told them.

The motor pool at Qui Nhon had repaired the headlight on the truck, and the men were soon on their way. As they got closer to the scene of the earlier ambush, they became tense. Upon arriving at the scene, they found several Vietnamese police in their white uniforms milling around the bodies that were still lying on the road as a result of Redmond's earlier handy work.

"Fucking-ass White Mice won't even clear the bodies off," Hardy said disgustingly, whistling thru his newly chipped tooth. An American patrol could be seen combing the area where the dead Vietnamese had staged their ambush.

"Let's get the fuck out of here," Flash urged.

"Relax, we're moving, we'll be alright," Redmond told him.

Later in the cab, Montrell said, "The Chief's gonna get a bronze for this."

"Yeah, I guess he might." Cru replied. "Sure deserves it, those gooks would have mortared our asses if he hadn't wasted 'em. Will you put him in for it?"

"No, I'll write up an incident report and give it to Vodka Charley. He'll approve it and give it to the first shirt, and then maybe he'll put him in for it. Don't think the Chief gives a shit one way or the other though." The rest of the trip was without incident and as the Lieutenant in Qui Nhon had predicted, the airman, juiced up on adrenaline got thoroughly smashed at the airman's club back at Phu Cat.

Chapter 5

"Change brings opportunity."

Qubein

"What's the story on this Redmond?" Richards asked no one in particular. Richards, Prentice, and McKay were having beers in the hooch that served as Richards' office. Looking at both men out of the corner of his eye, Prentice usually acquiesced to Master Sergeant Howard McKay, the first sergeant of the supply squadron at Phu Cat. As a matter of fact, Prentice usually acquiesced to almost everyone.

With Prentice silent, McKay spoke up. "He's an unusual guy. Indian from Minnesota, spent some time in the Marines, and volunteered for Vietnam almost every day till his squadron commander got tired of seeing him."

"Sounds like he's a stand-up guy," Richards replied. "What do you think, Charley?"

Prentice and Richards had been friends for a long time. They had served several tours of duty together at various locations around the world, this being their second tour of Vietnam. As a result of this close friendship Richards had always included Prentice in his business dealings, treating him like a younger brother, though in fact they were both about the same age. Richards was fully aware of Prentice's shortcomings that Denton and some others were quick to point out, but he usually overlooked them and ignored the comments. He knew Prentice had been troubled by the dissolution of his marriage, the death of his nephew to drugs, and the death of his bunkmate during his last tour in Vietnam. He also knew Prentice's quart a day vodka habit was impacting his performance. But, Richards always gave Prentice a chance to step up by including him in his operations as often as he could.

Prentice had an irritated look on his face. He didn't like having to make decisions, or stating opinions. He resented Richards' habit of pushing him all the time. "He seems okay," Prentice said. "He handles his duties fine, never complains. Understand he's pretty proficient with weapons. Guess he showed that pretty well on the last road trip to Qui Nhon."

After a moment Richards spoke again. "Well, let's get him more work in our projects," he said. "Redmond seems like the kind of guy we can really use. You think he should get a bronze for what he did, Mac?"

McKay, thinking about it, said, "You know, all these dudes that hear a shot fired in anger want a fuckin' medal. What happened to just do your duty and shut the fuck up?"

Prentice, looking at him irritatingly, replied, "'Cause he did something most of the cheesedicks on this base, me and you included, couldn't do. He ain't askin' for the medal, but it's the right thing to do."

Richards agreed, "I think Charley's right on this, Mac. Put him in for it. This Cru sounds okay as well. What's the deal on him?"

McKay said, "Crucianelli seems to have done a fine job since being here as well. He works like a mule and pulls perimeter guard once a week or more. He's been hanging out with some of the fuck-ups, but he seems to be a man of his own mind, and he doesn't fuck around with drugs, as far as I know."

Prentice agreed. "Cru's a good man," he said. "Proficient with weapons as well, and strong as a goddamn mule."

"Okay," Richards replied. "Let's get 'em into some of our other projects. We got a porn show coming up this week; let's start 'em on that. I'm sure they will enjoy it, and they can pick up a few bucks."

*　*　*

"A porn show?" Crucianelli repeated, with a puzzled look. "What kind of porn show?"

"Richards has fuck movies flown in from Scandinavia. He puts the word out and shows them on the side of the NCO barracks after dark, usually on Saturday. He charges a buck a head for the show, and two bucks for a cold bottle of Black Label. He makes a lot of dough on these shows," Hardy explained.

"What's our part?" Redmond asked.

21

"You guys are ushers and bouncers. You also collect the money. You seat the payees, and make sure there are no freeloaders around," Montrell said.

"What the fuck, someone could just stand behind the chairs and watch for nuthin," Crucianelli commented.

"Richards' man in security has a fence put up about thirty feet back from the chairs. It's pretty poor viewing from that distance, and if anyone jumps the fence they get tossed real fast," Hardy said. "You can also make extra money shaggin' beers and shit like that."

"Sounds like a much better gig than getting boulders dropped on you from the side of a mountain," Cru noted.

The porn show was another financial success for the Kansas NCO's operation. The show was well attended and with the exception of a brawl involving a member of the 173rd Airborne, it went off without a hitch.

The brawl involved a black airborne soldier, a huge spec 5, who had taken exception to paying two dollars for a can of lukewarm Black Label beer. He stood up and started throwing chairs around like matchsticks. Redmond grabbed one arm and Crucianelli the other, but it barely slowed him down. He eventually flung Redmond across three rows of chairs, and then proceeded to pound Crucianelli down on another chair like a hammer on an anvil. Redmond had made it back by now, and put a choke hold on the man's neck. Crucianelli started pounding the big man on the side of his head with his closed fist but they were merely fighting a holding action against the enraged giant. Fortunately base security soon arrived and subdued the man with repeated blows from their billy clubs. The man was shackled and thrown in the brig. Slightly bruised and battered, Cru and Red stuck it out, finishing up the evening and enhancing their reputation as stalwart and dependable troops.

"We're goin' off base again," Hardy told Cru and Red a couple of days later.

"Qui Nhon?" Crucianelli inquired.

"No, we're goin' to the army salvage yard at Phu Bai. It's another load for Richards."

"Phu Bai's only about fifteen miles away, this shouldn't be much of a detail." Redmond commented.

Looking at the two seriously, Hardy added, "This one will take place after dark."

Cru and Red looked at each other and said nothing.

Chapter 6

"Anticipate the difficult by managing the easy."

Lao Tzu

The difference in enemy activity between night and day in Vietnam was so profound that only missions considered absolutely imperative were conducted at night. Badly overmatched in firepower and technology, the Viet Cong and the NVA became highly proficient night fighters in an attempt to even the odds against the overwhelming superiority of the Americans and their South Vietnamese ally, the Army of the Republic of Vietnam or ARVN. Most night operations were thought to be futile, and hence night activity on the part of the Americans was mainly defensive. And though the countryside belonged to the Americans and the ARVN during the day, after dark the power dynamic shifted.

"Red, show Cru how to use the star scopes; we have two of 'em and they'll come in handy," Montrell said as he checked off the equipment for the trip. It was about fifteen minutes before dark and all the men were milling around, nervous and anxious to get moving. The star scopes, or night vision telescopes, could be mounted on a weapon or were hand held. Looking through them one could see an eerie whitish background with shapes of solid objects contrasted dark. It wasn't the same as normal vision but it was much better than the naked eye regarding night operations. There were also two men from the 173rd Airborne going along for extra firepower support, if need be. Hardy and Montrell had gotten last minute instructions from First Sergeant McKay, who then left.

"When we get there, I'm gonna hit the whorehouse first thing!" Flash hollered. He had appeared at the last minute, drunk or high or both, as he usually was this time of night.

Seeing him and frowning, Montrell told him, "We're manned up on this detail Flash. We don't need anymore men."

Flash became angry. "What the fuck, who cut me out?" he said. "I've been ridin' these fuckin' convoys since I got here. What's up, Monty?"

"You have to ask McKay," said Montrell. "He's the one who set this one up. You're too fuckin' stoned to go out on the road anyway, Flash."

"Oh yeah, like you don't hit it, right Montrell?" Flash replied.

"I don't hit it on duty, Flash. Besides it ain't my call," Montrell told him.

"Fuck it," Flash said and stumbled off, muttering under his breath.

"That guy's got problems," Hardy remarked.

"Yeah, he does," Montrell quietly agreed.

Driving slow through the darkened village of Phu Cat, things were quiet as few of the villagers ventured out at night, unwilling to risk getting killed by the VC or a trigger-happy American GI. The men, nervous and tense, drove slowly not wanting to create a lot of noise and bring unwanted attention to their presence. They were in two vehicles, both pick-up trucks. Montrell and Hardy drove with Cru and Red riding shotgun. The two airborne soldiers rode in the back with the load. Cru and Red continually scanned ahead with the star scopes, staying alert for anything that might be a sign of trouble.

Picking up a little speed outside the village, it didn't take too long to arrive at the Phu Bai army salvage yard. An army warrant officer they recognized as part of the Kansas NCO's network met them. The warrant officer checked the goods before unloading to make sure they weren't tampered with. When he was satisfied, the goods were off-loaded and taken away. Relaxing a little, he thanked the men and gave them each a bottle of Johnny Walker Black. The men were all grateful, for even if they didn't like the scotch, they could sell it for a nice price back at Phu Cat. Montrell and Red checked the vehicles' tires and undercarriage. VC occasionally clambered under slow moving vehicles and placed a charge, which would detonate later. Satisfied the vehicles were okay, they headed back to Phu Cat.

They pulled through the main gate around 01:30. They gave a quick report to Richard's contact. Exhausted, they finally hit their bunks.

The following day, the men were back to their standard work routines.

"How does he do it?" Crucianelli asked Montrell.

"How do you mean?" Montrell replied.

"He's moving all this material all over the place, through the country, and even back home in some cases. No one questions it? No one hassles him?"

Amused, Montrell looked at Cru in mild surprise, "Cru, you have shirt tail relatives in the mafia, you know how it's done. He bribes everyone. The local province and hamlet chiefs, the White Mice, the air force security detail, base ops, the 173rd Airborne, and even the fucking cooks. Everyone's on his payroll."

"Very impressive," Cru muttered.

Chapter 7

"Things do not change; we change."

Thoreau

It was 06:00 and almost like clockwork every two or three weeks, a barrage of VC mortars started raining upon the airbase. Prentice, half-awake, suffered a flashback of the attack that had killed his bunkmate and began screaming. "Get down! Get down, Lanard, get fucking down!"

McKay, his bunkmate in the NCO barracks, yelled, "Charley, get under your bunk! Charley!"

McKay, lying on the floor, then reached up and pulled Prentice off his bunk and under it.

Fully awake, Prentice mumbled, "Damn, what the fuck?"

"It's just a mortar attack, Charley. No rockets today, I guess. Think it's over now," McKay quietly said.

Embarrassed Prentice said, "Sorry; and thanks for dragging me under the bunk."

"No sweat," McKay replied.

The base took standoff rocket and mortar attacks on a basis regular enough to keep everyone tense. The first round to hit would get everyone's attention. The explosion and shock wave numbed your bones if you were close enough. After noting the range the attackers would start walking in rounds. The prize, of course, was taking out an aircraft or a direct hit on a barracks. Flash had been crawling back through the wire after a sojourn at the whorehouse in Phu Cat when the first mortar round hit. Panic-stricken, he froze, not knowing whether to continue crawling through the razor wire or retreat taking a chance that any nearby VC would make an easy target of him.

"Halt!" An alert perimeter guard had directed security to a shape he'd seen coming through the wire. If it were a VC trying to get into the base to place a sapper charge or something, he would immediately be shot. Fortunately for Flash the security detail recognized what appeared to be a large man in an American uniform, and hesitated.

"Halt and raise your arms and hands, palms forward," the guard ordered.

"Don't shoot! Don't shoot sir. I'm Airman First Class Canty from supply . . . don't shoot!"

*　*　*

"Charlie interrupt your sleep this morning, girls?" The "Charlie" Technical Sergeant Owen Mitchell was referring to was the Vietcong. Mitchell, an African American, was a member of the Phu Cat security team and was driving through the base checking on damage from the attack. While other members of security were checking the aircraft on the runways and the ammo dump, Owens was checking the enlisted men's quarters.

"Anyone killed, Sarge?" Hardy asked.

"No, no one killed, but a couple wounded. Airman Hilliard from Org maintenance got his big toe blown off, while lying in his damn bunk. He's on his way to the hospital at Qui Nhon. That'll get him a ticket home and a blowjob from his nice little white girlfriend."

"Damn!" Flash responded. "He'd only been here a couple weeks. I gotta find me a gook to blow my fuckin' toe off."

"VC be aimin' for your dick, Flash. VD gonna rot it off anyway one of these days, so it don't matter what happens to that little thang," Mitchell said. His remark brought a round of laughter and jeering from the others milling around after the attack.

"Fuck you, Mitchell," said Flash.

Mitchell was on duty when Flash was caught sneaking through the wire during the attack that morning. Flash was brought into the base security building and questioned regarding his reason and intentions for being off base. After getting grilled he was brought to his first sergeant. Master Sergeant McKay kept Flash in detention for several hours before releasing him. McKay let Flash know that his military career was in jeopardy and that he was on a short leash from here on out. In the future he had to report to McKay first thing every day; failure to do so could earn him a stay in the dreaded Long Binh military jail, where the actual conditions were even grimmer than the rumors.

The next day while going over the status on a shipment of electronic goods due in from Japan, McKay decided to speak to Richards about Prentice. "What's the problem, Howard?" Richards asked.

"You know I like Charley, he's a good guy and a good friend . . . but, he's weak. His drinking is way out of hand and he's not dependable."

Frowning Richards thought about it for a minute. "Well, let's just keep him off to the side. Give him little jobs that he can handle," he said. "I'd like to try and get him through till he goes home. Any ideas on who could take his place?"

"Denton's pretty solid," McKay said. "He's done well on all the jobs we've given him and he's always around when you need him."

"Well, I suppose he's the most likely candidate. We have to be careful here, he and Prentice don't get along, and I don't want him using Charley for a whipping boy." Thinking about it for a while, he conceded, "Okay . . . let's bring him up and see how he does."

* * *

"Fuckin' A," Crucianelli kept repeating "Fucking A." The mortar attack that had cost Airman Hilliard his big toe had also killed Noah, the barracks dog. Cru, Montrell, and especially Hardy had adopted the wily little canine. Crossing the road in an unlucky spot, a large piece of shrapnel from an incoming mortar tore through the small dog like a hot knife through butter, killing him instantly. Feral dogs had already begun feeding on his body when Cru discovered Noah's corpse and he shagged them off with rocks.

Although a major nuisance, Hardy would spend hours in the evening picking ticks off of the animal. Most other GIs would deliver a boot to Noah's ass whenever they had a chance, but the three friends from the supply detail felt compelled to look after him. Now he was dead.

"Whatta we gonna tell Hardy?" Cru asked looking at Montrell.

Frowning, Montrell thought maybe they should just throw the body out in the swamp and not say anything. Hardy would figure the dog ran off, or got caught and eaten by Vietnamese. The practice of eating dogs and cats, though repugnant to Americans, was merely a survival technique with the Vietnamese. Always on the verge of starvation, a dog or cat fed many people and was a welcome boost of protein for villages in most of the countryside.

Cru agreed, "Yeah, that's probably the best way to handle it, if he finds out what happened he'll probably freak fucking out."

"Yes, he will," Montrell replied.

* * *

"I ain't taken orders from that asshole," Sergeant Prentice told Richards.

"Charley, I'm not asking you to take orders from him, just some communication," Richards said in an attempt to console Prentice.

"Denton's a lyin' fuckin' weasel, a bully and a snake. I'd just as soon get assigned to a grunt patrol out in the damn boonies."

Now Richards felt compelled to speak frankly, "Charley, I love you like a brother, but I can't take a chance on a questionable link high up in the organization compromising our operation."

Prentice's face flushed red. "What the fuck you mean by that?" he yelled.

"Okay, Charley, you leave me no choice," Richards said. "I wanted to smooth this over so you could finish out your tour and go home, but that's gonna be up to you. At one time you were among the best in the air force, a top-notch airman and then a top notch NCO.

"But those days are gone. You are just a shell of the man you were even five years ago. I understand you had some personal setbacks, your nephew, your marriage . . . your friend in Ben Hoa . . . but you needed to move on. You needed to and you didn't, Charley. We all have stories, issues, problems; but we move on . . . we move on or we go down with our past. You have chosen to go down, Charley. And you're gonna have to sink alone."

Prentice sat listening to Richards with a look of fear. Richards was right about his performance, of course he was right; Prentice knew it more than Richards, but he had never been forced to deal with it before. His previous OICs and NCOICs never challenged him, never pushed him. It was easier to move him out than to face reality and deal with Prentice's failure as a non-commissioned officer in the military . . . his failure as a human being. Now the chickens were coming home to roost.

* * *

"Any of you guys seen Noah around?" Hardy asked.

The men were sitting outside the Tool Issue Center having lunch. C-rat canned wieners and beans, or motherfuckers as they were known, were the fare of the day. Hardy and Flash had come over from the warehouse where they were stacking crates and joined them. It was about 93 degrees and the humidity was around 97 percent. The men were soaked through and through with sweat. The green towels they often carried around their necks were soaked as well.

Not getting a response, Hardy asked again, "Haven't seen Noah for about a week, you guys hear of anything?"

Finally Crucianelli spoke up, "Probably ran off after another bitch in heat, knowing that old hound."

"Yeah . . . surprised you didn't go with 'im, Flash," Montrell added.

Laughing along, Flash said, "Fuck you, Monty, at least I don't fuck the old washerwoman in the shower stall."

Now everyone was laughing. A village woman named Bin cleaned the men's barracks and some hooches. A rural peasant woman, Bin was old by Vietnamese standards, and coarse as a lava rock. Her teeth were blackened from her habit of chewing betel nut all day, and she was often tipsy as a result of her great fondness for beer. Bin had seen many round eyes come and go, and although some treated her poorly, she got along well with most of them. When Bin was drinking she often became amorous and would seek the attention of any GI who appreciated her favors. She would rub on the men like an animal until they succumbed to her coarse, yet desirable charms. Montrell was one of those men, and on occasion . . . so was Crucianelli.

"No one's seen that damn mutt, huh?" Hardy added, not willing to let the subject go...

"I haven't seen him," Cru told him.

"Me either," Montrell added.

"Fuckin' gooks probably ate him," Flash blurted angrily.

"Damn, Flash," Montrell said.

"What the fuck, Monty, you know damn well they'd eat the little fucker in a minute!" Flash shot back.

"You don't know that," Crucianelli commented.

"I don't know Ho Chi Minh's got a prick, but I'm willin' to bet on it," Flash pointed out.

"Fuck you, Flash!" Hardy said as he walked away.

Flash didn't understand the fuss, "All I did was point out the fuckin' obvious. What's the big fuckin deal?"

"Nuthin', Flash, don't worry about it," Montrell replied sarcastically.

Chapter 8

"I labored hard to avoid trouble and bloodshed."

Chief Joseph

Montrell and Crucianelli were worried. The change in command in the Kansas NCO's operation was causing them problems. Denton didn't like them, or Redmond and Hardy either for that matter. "Bunch of smug goddamn Yankees," Denton complained. "They tell that alky Prentice where to shit and how fucking high. They'll be sorry if they ever try to cross my ass."

One day Denton came to see them in the back of the Tool Issue Center. "You fuckers can stop pretending to work. I don't buy your bullshit," he snarled.

"What can we do for you, Denton?" Montrell asked him firmly.

"I need the jeep washed. We got some VIPs coming in tomorrow and everything needs to be presentable . . . including you fuckers. You need to get regulation haircuts and keep your fatigue shirts on at all times while on duty."

Hardy, who could never stand the sight of Denton, laid into him. "What's with the chicken shit, Denton?" he said. "Doesn't Richards have any boots for you to polish today?"

Denton turned his attention to the young airman from Michigan. "Listen here, cream puff," he said. "If I want any shit out of you I'll scrape it off your teeth."

"Very original, Denton, I bet you got that right off the wall of the latrine at the NCO club," Hardy shot back.

Now Denton was pissed. His eyes narrowed and he moved up face to face with Hardy. "You have your fun today, cheesedick, but you're gonna pay for this little performance you put on here today. I promise you, you're gonna pay." Turning to Montrell and Crucianelli, he ordered, "You guys get your fuckin' haircut, get them goddamn jeeps washed, and get this fuckin' place swept out and straightened up. Or I swear to God, I'll see you young punks on perimeter guard every day 'til your DEROS, you keep fuckin' with me." With that he turned around and left, Hardy and Cru sent him along with a long low catcall for good measure. All but an uneasy Montrell, who stood there quietly, broke out laughing after Denton left the area.

"What's wrong, Monty, you ain't afraid of that prick are ya?" Hardy asked.

Montrell turned toward him and replied, "Right down to my fuckin' bones, Hardy, and if you two had any brains you would be, too. You don't get it, do you? Vodka Charley can't protect us anymore. He's been demoted. Denton hates our guts and is just lookin' for an opportunity to fuck us over. You just gave it to him."

Crucianelli, trying to rationalize it, threw out the standard wiseass response when one got in trouble in Vietnam, "What the fuck can he do to us, send us to Vietnam?"

"Make fuckin' jokes," Montrell told them. "But this asshole's out to get us and he's in a good position to fuck us every way but right. You wanna keep feedin' him ammunition, just keep it up."

∗   ∗   ∗

"Well that sure as fuck didn't take long," Crucianelli remarked. Prentice had called Cru, Montrell and Hardy up to the office. Denton had a night delivery set up for the next day. The route required passing through the volatile village of Binh Dinh both ways.

"You know it's 'cause he's pissed," Cru added.

"Cru, we don't know that; more than likely just a normal detail for Richards," Prentice responded.

"Who's providing security?" Montrell asked.

Looking down Prentice said, "Webber and Schneider."

"Fuckin' A . . . no fuckin' way. Set-up for sure!" Crucianelli jumped in. They had gone out on several details with Spec 4 Andrew Webber and

Spec 5 Richard Schneider. Both men were two of the worst drug heads the 173rd Airborne encampment had to offer. They showed up for most details stoned and smoked dope and snorted other drugs the whole trip, and if Ho Chi Minh himself had popped out of the bush at any time during the detail, he would have found both men slumped over their weapons out cold in the back of the truck. The other men were protesting loudly as well.

"Okay, who the fuck do you three guys want back there? Probably a couple whores and your buddy Flash, I suppose," Prentice said.

"How 'bout Becker and Childs?" Hardy replied. "They smoke dope and bitch all the time but at least they're fucking coherent."

Montrell wasn't too impressed with those two either. It seemed like the dregs of the 173rd were always used to provide security for these missions. "We'd just as soon have Red and yeah, even Flash, along. Red can handle the weapons and Flash can boost the economy by hitting every whorehouse between here and Qui Nhon."

Prentice was getting pissed. He'd only had one small drink this morning and was getting edgy and impatient. "When you guys make general and are put in charge, you will be allowed to plan every fuckin mission in the goddamn air force. Until then just shut the fuck up and do what you're told!" He stormed back up to the front of the building. The men could hear the door slam behind him.

"Charley's gotta get another slug of Smirnoff's before he goes and reports to his daddy," Cru grunted.

About one half hour before dark, the men assembled near the outside supply storage area where the cargo had been readied for shipment. Three large wooden crates with no markings were loaded onto the ton-and-a-half stake truck. Becker and Childs from the 173rd Airborne detachment were in the back setting up a .30 caliber machine gun. Cru, Hardy, Montrell, Red and Flash were there with M-16s and .38 pistols.

Denton had inspected the crated material and was now giving the men their last minute instructions. "You will deliver this load to Gunnery Sergeant Hyram Black, 2nd Battalion, 9th Marine Division. Sergeant Black is down from Phu Bai with the purpose of obtaining much needed materials for their effort up there. He will meet you in Binh Khe where you will unload and immediately return to Phu Cat."

Hardy muttered just loud enough for everyone to hear, "Probably a load of stereos and Scotch liquor."

"You got something to say, airman?" Denton growled, glaring at Hardy.

"Not me, Sarge," Hardy replied.

"Good, cause anything a half-ass farmer from Michigan's got to say, ain't worth hearin," Hardy turned red and glared back at Denton. "You men report back to me as soon as you're back on base," Denton growled before stomping off.

Chapter 9

"Keep your fears to yourself but share your courage with others."

Robert Louis Stevenson

Hardy's remarks to Denton were in part false bravado. Ever since the convoy when they were attacked with boulders, Hardy lived in terror of again going on the road. He kept his normally cheerful demeanor up and spoke with no one regarding his fear. As the truck left the main gate at Phu Cat, Hardy, sitting in the back of the truck, gripped his M-16 with both hands until his knuckles were white and stared straight out behind the truck, speaking to no one. Now he was thinking he was a fool for not begging off of the assignment. He desperately wanted to avoid the road, but a combination of fear of hazing from the other men, as well as possible retribution from Richards kept him from speaking up. At this time Airman First Class Terrance Hardy was in such a state of fear that he considered leaping from the truck and running back to the base . . . but soon it was too late, as they moved through and out of the village of Phu Cat and into the deep darkness of the Vietnamese night.

"Hardy seem okay to you?" Montrell, driving this trip, asked Cru who was riding shotgun.

Cru replied, "He does seem on edge lately. Something goin' on?"

"I'm not sure, but I think he's scared," Montrell said.

"Fuck, I'm scared to!" Cru remarked.

"No, I mean something different. I don't think he really wants to be on this convoy," Monty said.

"Well, he was pretty upset about Noah," Cru noted.

"No, I think this started before that," Monty said. "I think it goes back to the convoy when they tried to smash us with those boulders."

Thinking about it, Cru responded, "Why doesn't he just beg off?"

"Think he'd like to, but doesn't wanna get in trouble," Montrell told him.

Turning his head and looking through the back window, Cru observed Hardy for a minute. "He looks petrified," he said. "Hope we don't run into any shit tonight."

"Well, Red, Childs and Becker are back there with him, so we should be okay," Montrell replied.

The truck moved slowly through the dark countryside, and within about two hours they reached Binh Khe. As soon as they hit the outskirts of the village they were flagged down by a Marine patrol on the side of the road. Montrell saw Black's nametag on one of them as they pulled up. The men in the back of the truck kept their hands on their weapons and remained quiet.

"You all from Phu Cat, right?" the Marine asked.

"That's right, we have a shipment for Sergeant Black, that being you, I take it?" Montrell questioned.

"Well, whoever said air force people were dumb fucks were goddamn liars," Black remarked. The other men in the small patrol laughed and snickered at his comment.

"Course they were liars, Black, cause if we were dumb fucks we'd be humpin' through the bush and you'd be ridin' in the truck, right now," Montrell replied. Now the men in the truck were laughing.

The smile disappeared from Sergeant Black's face and turned into an ugly frown. "Okay, let's get her unloaded," he barked to his men.

It took the Marines, airmen, and soldiers about an hour to unload the truck. Without the benefit of a forklift, they had to muscle each of the three large containers off of the truck very carefully. By the time it was unloaded all the men were covered in sweat and a few had crushed fingers and hands. Addressing the men who delivered the material Black told them "Sorry about givin' you all that shit earlier. You air force boys are all right. You army grunts are okay, too."

"No sweat, Sarge," Montrell told him. "We can dish it out as good as we take it."

"Yeah, I can see that," Black replied, laughing.

"If you don't mind my asking, what are you gonna do with these crates on the side of the road?" Montrell asked. It was a legitimate question, as without a vehicle there was no way the Marines were going far with the large containers.

"We expect a convoy from our unit to be here within the next three to four hours," Black told the men. "They will have a deuce and a half, and enough men to help us load up.

"You gonna sit here and guard this stuff all night, Sarge?" Cru asked.

Smiling, Black looked at Cru's nametag and replied, "Well, Sergeant Crucianell, is it?"

"Crucianelli," Cru told him, "but don't worry about it."

Black went on, "Well, Crucianelli, believe it or not, for us . . . this is gravy duty. Kind of like an in-country R & R." Cru and Montrell looked at each other.

Montrell then said, "Sarge . . . I know you guys are tough and have balls, but you could be badly outmanned if a large VC or NVA unit comes along. We do have that .30 cal. We can stay here and help you watch it 'til your unit comes along."

Sergeant Black stood thoughtfully. Montrell spoke up again, "We also have three cases of Black Label beer, warm though it is, and two bottles of Seagram's to help keep the chill off." The other Marines were all moving in now, with hopeful faces while Black was thinking it over.

"You know, we could use some extra firepower in case those little bastards wanna start fucking with us; appreciate the company, men!"

"Guess all we need is the navy and we'd have all of fuckin' MACV covered," Childs remarked.

"The navy's here also, soldier . . . meet our medic . . . Ensign Dewey R. Wellman, US Navy," Black told them.

All the men became acquainted as the night wore on. One of the Marines was an Ojibwa from a tribe in Wisconsin. He and Redmond had a long friendly conversation, as did all the others as they took turns standing

39

watch and indulging in the beer and liquor. The three cases of Black Label beer and two bottles of Seagram's were gradually emptied during the next couple hours. Some of the men quietly moved off into the bush and the pungent smell of burning Thai stick wafted back to the road. Sergeant Black ignored or pretended not to notice it and no hostiles disturbed the friendly gathering throughout the night. At around 03:00 a large convoy of Marines arrived and the containers were promptly loaded and secured. The newfound friends, drunk and somewhat rowdy, had a raucous goodbye, as both parties went off in different directions into the blackened night.

In the back of the truck again, Hardy was now riding with his spirits lifted. One of the Marines was from the upper peninsula of Michigan and actually knew some of Hardy's relatives who lived there. Hardy had spent many fall days deer hunting and fishing for muskies and walleyes with his cousins, mostly iron mine workers who lived off the land in the wild country the Youpers inhabited. The Marine had been wounded twice so far in Vietnam, yet exhibited no fear or trepidation about his future. At first, Hardy felt ashamed, realizing how this man faced grave danger every day, yet did his duty stoically. Then, as if feeling his spirit awakened, Hardy for the first time realized he could not affect many of the events in his life. He could only affect his reaction to them.

As Hardy was leaning against the side of the truck thinking about the conversation, he noticed movement just ahead and off the side of the road.

"Movement!" he yelled as he raised his M-16 and focused on the area where the movement had come from. The other men reacted quickly and also focused on the area where Hardy was looking. But they were a split second late. AK-47 fire suddenly raked the side of the truck. Montrell, reacting as soon as he heard the fire, gave the truck full throttle. Crucianelli took out his pistol and desperately searched for a target in the black vegetation beyond the road. Red, focused as always, brought out a star scope and concentrated it on the area where the fire had come from. Hardy, meanwhile, had pinpointed the shooter's position and at the same time observed the man next to him setting up a mortar. Hardy had never been this focused before; his mind was crystal clear and his reaction was almost instantaneous. Everything he had learned from his days of hunting, and the training he received on the firing line in basic training, came back in an instant. Putting the weapon on full auto he swept the area back and forth until his magazine was empty and then immediately slammed another into the weapon and fired again.

"You got 'em" Red yelled, "Good shooting, you got 'em both Hardy!"

Montrell kept the truck barreling along for the next twenty minutes before stopping just outside the village of Binh Dinh. "Everyone okay?" he asked.

"Everyone okay back here, thanks to Dead-Eye Hardy," Childs replied. Finally relaxing a bit, Becker, Childs and Red all slapped Hardy on the back.

"Good reaction and damn good shooting, Terry. They'd have nailed us for sure," Red told him.

Becker added, "Damn straight. How 'bout you transferring to the 173rd, Hardy? Most of our cheesedicks can't get a clip off that fast."

The remainder of the trip back was uneventful. As ordered, Montrell contacted Denton to confirm the delivery had been made. When Denton heard about Hardy's actions he was ambivalent. He acknowledged little gratitude to the men for carrying out the detail so efficiently and risking their lives, greatly angering Montrell and Crucianelli.

Chapter 10

"The fool who persists in his folly will become wise."

Blake

"Is Hardy on drugs?" Prentice, having heard by now about Terry Hardy's heroics out on the road was suspicious. He walked to the back of the Tool Issue Center with a wild-eyed stare and questioned Montrell and Crucianelli.

"Goddammit, Charley, instead of congratulating Hardy for what he did, you come back here and wanna hang the guy," Crucianelli didn't have much patience with Prentice. Although he was his non-commissioned officer in charge, Cru felt Prentice did little to perform his duties or earn respect from the men. "Goddamn ubriaco," he added. The Italian slang for drunk wasn't wasted on Montrell who had heard it plenty in the working-class neighborhood of Toledo where he was from.

"You gotta cut him some slack," Montrell told him. "When he's knock-down drunk, he ain't fuckin' with us, so what the hell . . . just be happy we don't have an NCOIC like that prick Jones who Childs and Becker report to."

But today Montrell was pissed as well. "Damn, Charley, couldn't you at least wait to hear the story from us before you send the guy to Long Binh?" Prentice stood mute. It was apparent he misjudged the situation and overreacted. Now he felt bad; these guys were really the only friends he had over here. Denton was out to get him. McKay appeared only interested in enriching himself and Richards had thrown him under the bus.

Frowning, he apologized, "I overreacted. You're right . . . I should have talked to you men first. Now, if I may . . . what in the hell got into Hardy that night?"

Crucianelli looked at Montrell. "You're better at this shit than I am, Monty," he said.

Montrell thought it over and then said, "I believe Terry came upon his worst fear and somehow found a way to deal with it. One of the Marines we hooked up with that night was from his neck of the woods; even knew some of his relatives. This guy had been through every kind of shit the 'Nam has to offer, yet there he was, carrying out his duty . . . and his life as if he was back home working second shift at the iron mine. Something about him, something in his demeanor got to Terry. Maybe Terry had what's called an epiphany."

Cru and Prentice who had both been looking down while listening to Monty's explanation; now looked up sharply at Montrell.

"Yeah, I know, its sounds strange," Montrell continued. "But I'm telling you something came over him while we were sitting out there drinking beer with the Marines in that long, jungle night. I ain't no kind of psychologist but something happened and that's all there is to it."

Prentice was happy for Hardy. He wished he'd have expressed himself better; he had previously been worried about Hardy making it through his tour okay. Cru and Montrell jumping on him forced him into his familiar defensive posture. He had some suspicions regarding the turn of events with Denton usurping his position in the hierarchy and he feared for the welfare of the men who went out on these road trips. He had tried to discuss it with Richards but his response was vague and somewhat curious.

"Don't get yourself worked up over nothing, Charley. They know the risks of going out on the road. Anyone wants out, all they have to do is let me know," Richards told him. "Is the shipment for An Khe ready?"

Prentice had forgotten about that. Two weeks ago Richards had talked to him about getting several hundred flight kits and one hundred helicopter maintenance tool boxes ready to ship to An Khe via truck convoy. He was meaning to ask Richards if the toolboxes for the choppers needed to include the repair kits for the new Apaches that were coming in, but never got around to it. Now he was behind the eight ball and would incur Richard's wrath again. Prentice gave himself away scratching his head and grimacing.

"Goddammit, Charley, I told you two fucking weeks ago to get that shit ready. What the fuck goes on in that head of yours? Maybe Denton's right, maybe the booze has gotten to your ability to perform. If I have to turn the job over to him, he's just gonna be on your ass even more," Richards scolded.

Turning red, Prentice countered, "You don't need to turn it over to that fucking asshole. I'll get the job done. I wanted to find out if the boxes needed to be equipped to handle the new Apaches that have been coming in."

Frowning Richards replied, "Why the fuck did you wait two weeks to ask?" Then, in a frustrated tone of voice, he said, "Why the hell wouldn't they need the Apache tools? The bills of material were permanently revised to include them."

Prentice hadn't been aware of that. He had gotten into the habit of letting Montrell take care of the paperwork end of the detail. It had worked out well, as it gave Prentice time to manage all the operations better; but not seeing the incoming changes, obviously had drawbacks. If Richards knew about the changes, he should have as well and now he was pissed at himself.

"My mistake Richards, I'll get it taken care of. When do you want the convoy to go out?"

Looking at Prentice with a frown Richards told him, "First light" and left the building.

Chapter 11

"I agree to, or rather aspire, to my doom."

Corneille

"**W**hat the fuck, we got hit again?"

Flash and Salas were working the 04:30 to 14:00 shift on the flight line, cleaning up the FOB. Foreign object damage was a significant problem in Vietnam, particularly for jet aircraft. The worst offenders were the large rice beetles that the Vietnamese prized for their flavor. The beetles liked to sun themselves on the open spaces of concrete and asphalt during the day, and often remained in the evening hours to catch smaller insects that hovered over the flat surface of the landing strip. Quite often local villagers would be found on the runways collecting the large bugs, which they ate raw, stewed, or toasted. Airman would be required to chase after them in jeeps or set security dogs out to chase them, in order to keep them off of the airstrips. They would often leave their sandals as they fled through the concertina wire surrounding the base. Flash, who often squeezed through the wire on his trips to the village whorehouse, was envious of the lithe Vietnamese, who slipped through the wire much easier than he ever could. "How them gooks can squeeze through that wire is something else," he'd say in near admiration.

Salas was used to hearing Flash complain, and only answered out of boredom. "Yeah, and we're gonna get hit a lot more, now that Tricky Dickey's pulled most of the 173rd and the Big Red One out." Nixon had pulled many combat units out, believing the Vietnamese army would quickly take up the slack. When that didn't happen the men received additional small arms and infantry training as they were now more or less in charge of their own defense.

As the war moved along in 1970, it was apparent that the situation in Vietnam was getting worse, and patience in America for the war was running out. As American combat units were sent home, supposedly replaced by Vietnamese combat units, the remaining bases came under attack more frequently and more violently. Perhaps the training was incomplete, or the sympathy in South Vietnam ran higher for the Viet Cong, than for the U.S. supported corrupt government. Cru, Redmond, Flash and the others knew things were getting worse. Mortar and rocket attacks grew in frequency on the big bases, as did sapper attacks and perimeter encroachments.

In addition to a decrease in security, control and oversight of all operations and functions deteriorated. Organization became weaker, lawlessness increased. Many units, both in the field as well as on the larger bases, often found themselves acting independent of other units that they had previously reported to, or coordinated operations with. As a result, people often improvised, conducting their operation as they saw fit, contradicting the previous regimentation of military standard. Naturally this opened the door further for malfeasance and corruption in a theatre where malfeasance and corruption were already rampant.

＊　＊　＊

"Something big's coming down the pike," Montrell said. He, Crucianelli, and Hardy had just gotten off duty. They were walking down the dirt road towards the mailroom.

"What's up, Monty?" Cru asked with a look of concern.

Making sure no one else was within earshot Montrell said, "Denton's toady, Taggs, came in to see Charley this afternoon. I was up in the office to get a spec on a couple orders for the Red Horse toolboxes." The Red Horse was an air force rapid deployment civil engineering unit that was at Phu Cat on TDY, temporary duty assignment. They needed all kinds of tools and equipment, as they had to be ready to build or repair anything on a moment's notice. Montrell wanted to make sure they had everything they needed and had decided to check on back orders.

"Taggs tried to bully Charley around, like that asshole Denton, but Charley got in his face and told him to go fuck himself and to get the hell out. Taggs backed down faster than an ARVN night patrol. It was pretty damn funny. Finally Taggs got up the nerve to take care of what he was sent to do and told Charley that he needed to prepare us for a long road trip, possibly for a couple weeks. Prentice got real concerned and asked Taggs where the fuck we'd be going, then he spotted me behind the cabinet and dummied up."

Stopping in his tracks Crucianelli said, "Damn, where the fuck they sendin' us?"

With an intense look of concern, Hardy asked Montrell, "When's this gonna happen?"

Gesturing with his hands out and palms up Montrell told them he didn't have any more information than that, but he was going to find "Ski" and do some digging.

Sergeant Bob Skelenski worked in the first sergeant's office and always kept his ear to the ground regarding anything that may affect him and his buddies. Bob was from Pittsburgh and as such a rabid Pittsburgh Steelers fan. Cru and Red were rabid Green Bay Packer fans, while Montrell and Hardy supported the Detroit Lions. They were always going back and forth, dishing on the other's team and talking up their own. They also had pick-up scrimmages on Saturdays when they usually only worked a half day, providing they had no other duty conflicts such as perimeter guard or convoy duty. Bob had worked for Sergeant McKay long enough to know to keep his mouth shut all the time, and his eyes and ears shut most of the time. McKay let Ski more or less run the day-to-day operations, as he was usually occupied with illicit activities involving the black market.

"I can't figure this shit out," Ski was telling Montrell. "Normally on a special detail like this there's a Procedure and Instructions pamphlet sent along by the originating authority. It describes the purpose of the mission, along with the timetable, and resources required. And . . ."

Montrell asked, "And what?"

Pursing his lips, Ski said, "Well, normally these Spec Dets come from Pleiku because that's where the IG in II Corps is. All of these special details have to be run by and signed by the IG. This one comes from An Khe and is signed by an army colonel I never heard of."

Now Montrell was frowning. "Thanks, Ski." Then, he set off to find Crucianelli and Hardy.

Chapter 12

"Life — the way it really is — is a battle not between bad and good but between bad and worse."

Joseph Brodsky

On the long flight over to Vietnam, Cru sat next to an Army master sergeant, Morgan Shell, who was going on to LZ English, a landing zone and small artillery base just north of Phu Cat. Their paths crossed again when Cru saw him wandering around the air base at Phu Cat one day. Cru was surprised and glad to see him again. But he was absolutely bedraggled. Most men lost quite a bit of weight in the 'Nam. Between the heat, the stress, and the workload, the pounds fell off pretty quickly. But Shell had absolutely become gaunt. Apparently he had taken over a couple of infantry platoons that were always short of materials and equipment. He had basically come to Phu Cat to beg for goods, with which to carry out his mission. Turned down going through proper channels, Cru solicited the help of the Kansas NCO, who quietly stocked him up on most everything he needed. No charge.

"Don't worry, we'll fix you up, Sarge," Cru told his friend. "You stay here and take a break. There's some C-rations in that locker, have a bite to eat."

"Thanks Cru. I'll take you up on the chance to put my feet up, and I'll sure as hell grab one of those C-rations. I haven't eaten all day," Shell said. "You tell your friend who fixed us up with all this, we owe him one."

Cru was grateful and also proud of the Kansas NCO that day. From that point on, when his friend came to Phu Cat every couple of months for supplies, the Kansas NCO never failed to fill the requirements that he could supply.

The local province chief solicited his help as well. Cru wasn't sure who ran for this position as the province of Bin Dinh went through eight of them during his thirteen-month tour of duty there. None of them died of "natural causes," and some of them flipped loyalty from one side to the other, but the Kansas NCO helped out when he could. He often supplied food, in the form of C-rations, as well as bulk powdered milk and other staples to the local villages. Occasionally he delivered medical supplies, which were always in need by the locals. He even supplied them with some "luxury" items such as the prized aviator sunglasses, cigarettes, and even liquor. Quite often the food and medical supplies were gratis, but everything else required compensation, MPC, piaster, or of course, the preferred greenbacks.

The province chief took his cut on most of the goods he sent along. After all a high-risk job like his had to have some substantial incentives for these guys to take the position in the first place. The White Mice often got their cut also, as did some of the local tribal chiefs. The Kansas NCO had no problem with this; he understood business. But if one of them got a little greedy, or skimmed too much off the top, he found a way around them. More than a few tribal elders were on his payroll, and they gave him the needed information if questions arose.

The barter system was used quite extensively in his dealings with not only the locals, but other American units and operatives and allies as well. Money was not a readily available commodity to many Vietnamese, as well as many American or allied forces in the field. But often they had access to other items of value, which could then be exchanged at some point up the supply line for some form of printed money. Souvenirs were always valued. People in the field brought back belt buckles, helmets, rifles, ears, and any number of items that the rear echelon troops or other grunts who hadn't grabbed enough souvs might want. In 1970 an ear cost five bucks, a belt buckle ten. Only the NVA (North Vietnamese Army) wore uniforms, so the belt buckles and anything with insignias on them came off dead soldiers from the north. The VC contributed black pajamas, crossbows, and homemade weapons such as punji sticks and other crude but lethal instruments of war. The grunts out in the field often wanted aviator sunglasses, Kool Aid, and always socks. It was possible to trade just about anything for any other thing in Vietnam.

Besides goodies from the small BXs (base exchange) and PXs (post exchange), people on the larger bases also had access to parts from incoming Chinese or Russian mortars, along with the Russian 122 rockets that rained on the bases from time to time. Of course these were used heavily in the field, but on the bases they could be methodically disassembled for the treasured identification plates, with points of origin, etc. In the field troops had to worry about their pack load . . . whatever they picked up had to be humped back, and it might encumber them in the event of another firefight.

49

Animals and animal parts were also on many shopping lists. Live monkeys made interesting, and sometimes edible if not entirely safe, pets as did wild cats, snakes, rats, pigs, and mongooses. Birds were always in demand, both for food and pets. Larger animals such as elephants, tigers, leopards, bears and rhinos were typically dissected prior to transport. The transported parts could be sold as souvenirs, food, or for medicinal properties, to any number of western or eastern people. Some of the unfortunate creatures found themselves fighting in pits, for money.

The Kansas NCO had people in the bush that would bring him animals of value from time to time. He was specific about which animals he wanted and where to take delivery. Getting live animals through the main gate of the air base could be problematic, even for him. Towards the end of the fiasco in Vietnam as discipline became lax many individuals would happily look the other way for a five-spot or more.

The occasional zealots that came along could be quieted, but the problem was usually the FANGS. It sometimes took a while for them to figure out the score, and until seasoned they would often tear off running to some higher echelon person with wild eyes and tales of illegal contraband, etc. Of course, the higher echelon person knew the score, and whether they approved of the Kansas NCO and his operation or not, they normally just placated the messenger and sent him on his way. The Kansas NCO certainly had his detractors, but few people turned down any money that happened to fall their way from his operation, and there was also the very real possibility of retribution for snitching, interfering, or obstructing any of his enterprises. There were enough natural enemies, both on and off base, without getting on the bad side of one of the most powerful men in the Central Highlands.

The barracks closest to the main gate at the Phu Cat airbase housed, among others, most of the men who worked in supply. This may, or may not have been a coincidence. A large number of the Kansas NCO's employees were enlisted men, working in supply. The fact that these men had access to tens of thousands of dollars' worth of goods was not wasted on him. Since a fair number of people passing through the main gate had contraband, he always had one of his contacts from the supply barracks around to direct them and communicate their presence to the operation. If a load was too large to discreetly move through the base, additional vehicles with enclosed cargo areas were sent to assist with the transit.

This arrangement also accommodated loads going off base. As vehicles left the base, men in the supply barracks could slip in fairly unnoticed.

The men riding in the back along with the load carried M16s. The men in the cab had M16s and the driver usually had a pistol as well. The men were picked for their skills with equipment and/or firepower. Cru grew up hunting, was comfortable with weapons, and had received additional weapons training at an Army facility for two weeks prior to shipping to Nam. Of course, you had to have a set of balls along with all that. Not everyone wanted to drive out into the Vietnam countryside, where various hazards lay all along the way. So, the escort and drivers were usually allowed to visit the whorehouses that were available, and do any trading they could on their own, as long as it didn't interfere with the mission.

The Kansas NCO had a rudimentary training program for prospective associates who may not have had the needed skills to perform their assigned duties. Weapons training provided help to those who lacked skill in the handling and care of firearms. The training addressed the numerous hazards that frequently occurred along the treacherous roadways. These lessons did not come in the form of classroom lectures; rather they were barked at the men while they received the orders and details of the trips. The military rule of "need to know" applied to the Kansas NCO's operations as well. They were given no more information than they needed, and of course, discussing any of this business with anyone else, especially someone not in the "operation" was absolutely forbidden. The navy motto "loose lips sink ships" was roughly translated into the Kansas NCO's operation in the form of "loose lips end up in the bottom of a swamp."

Chapter 13

"We aren't in Kansas anymore."

Dorothy, upon entering the ⟨Emerald Forest⟩ in The Wizard of Oz

SCREENWRITER JOHN LEE MAHIN

?
.

As they stood around waiting to receive the details of their assignment, a myriad of people were coming and going. Cases of weapons, munitions, food and medical supplies were marshaled into several points of the compound. High-ranking, important-looking men were conferring with the Kansas NCO and the upper echelon of his entourage. Several maps were pinned on the walls. Glancing over them gave the three a preview of their future. All were maps of Cambodia, with the adjacent border area of South Vietnam included.

Vodka Charley stood by subserviently, waiting to let the Kansas NCO know the three were there. An army colonel, the Kansas NCO, and what could only be a CIA operative were in discussion. Although outranked by the colonel and no doubt the CIA operative as well, there was no doubt the Kansas NCO was in charge. The two were giving their thoughts and advice to him, which he quietly mulled, while taking drags on his cigarette. Cru could overhear part of the conversation.

"It can be done if the intel is right and the army does their part," the CIA agent remarked.

The army colonel replied irritably, "I will see to it that we do our part . . . if your information is accurate this time, we'll have no problems." The Kansas NCO listened attentively, glancing at the two through the small slits of his dark eyes. He had the confident look of a Roman general, planning a campaign in some foreign land . . . or a corporate CEO, preparing a hostile takeover. The plan and execution would ultimately fall on his shoulders, to succeed or to fail. Success or failure might not have been as important to him, as was his destiny to carry it out. What happened happened . . . he was in command.

The Kansas NCO nodded and told them to get ready to put the plan into action; he would tell them when to pull the trigger on it. He glanced over at Cru, Hardy, and Montrell, put out his cigarette and motioned them over.

"You guys have been chuggin' my beer and enjoying gravy duty long enough. Now it's time for you to earn all those bennies you've been suckin' up. Next week we're going into Cambodia, in logistics support of the 1st Cav, and the special ops that in turn have gone in supporting the ARVN in an effort to clear the area of NVA and their sanctuary there.

"Our mission will be to bring in any and all needed supplies via fixed wing aircraft and ground transport, as applicable. You three know how I work, and you know the way of the road. We will be accompanied by elements of the 173rd Airborne, who will provide security for the ground transport and aircraft missions after landing. The NVA has been supplying the area for years, and after we off-load our cargo, we will load a select group of the NVA stores available, for return. Denton will direct that effort."

The three weren't expressly shocked, but were surprised that they would be playing such an integral role in the operation. The Kansas NCO and Vodka Charley went on to explain that they were chosen because the goods would be coming in and out of the air bases at Phu Cat and Pleiku, and Air Force personnel needed to spearhead the plan. The 173rd security detail would consist of men they had bumped into before in the Kansas NCO's operations. They would be good to have along, because the 1st Cav was a top-rated fighting machine. If they were going to be slipping material in and out under their noses, they'd need backing . . . heavy weight backing. While they might question what the 173rd was doing way over in that neck of the woods, they would have serious reservations about letting a bunch of air force enlisted men waltz in and out of a forward area transporting a whole bunch of valuable war booty. The 173rd provided credibility, along with security.

Later that day Vodka Charley and Denton gave them the details of the plan. The three of them would take a deuce and a half truck and a jeep loaded to half capacity with supplies and equipment out of Phu Cat. From Phu Cat they would proceed to Pleiku where they would hook up with a contact. There the vehicles would be loaded to capacity, and they would make their way along the treacherous roads west of Pleiku, and on to a makeshift landing zone, where their goods would be picked up by air force cargo planes and taken to their final destination in Cambodia. As always, each driver would carry a .38 caliber revolver, but with 100 extra rounds for this trip. Each of them would have a grunt from the 173rd in the cab, carrying a .38 and an M-16. There would also be a grunt in the cargo box with a .30 caliber machine gun, and a grenade launcher along with his M-16. They were issued detailed maps of the road to Pleiku, and sketched maps from there forward. They would be issued two-way radios, and one of the grunts would also have a military operational radio to call for help if they got in any kind of trouble. They received 500 U.S. dollars to bribe the White Mice, and anyone else who tried to impede their way. The cargo would be sealed in unmarked wooden boxes, and they weren't told what it was. But since they had already seen the materials marshaled in a holding area, it was no big secret and no big deal to them what they were hauling. They didn't give a shit.

Along with a long list of questions and concerns, they had some conditions. Cru wanted Redmond riding shotgun in his truck, and Montrell wanted Salas riding shotgun in his truck. They had no quarrel with the qualifications of the soldiers from the 173rd, they had proved their mettle many times in the 'Nam. But Cru wanted people they were used to. Redmond was as good with weapons as any grunt, he was an excellent tracker, and had the instincts of a wolf. Salas was solid all the way around as well, good with weapons and good to have around in any fight or crisis. Denton backed up their assessment of these two and the Kansas NCO okayed them for the mission. They still had a man from the 173rd with all the weaponry riding back with the load.

One by one their questions and concerns were addressed. One of their biggest concerns was how the hell did they expect two blue air force vehicles to get around inconspicuously in the area along the Cambodian border. They were advised that once they reached Pleiku they would off-load to two army vehicles, which traveled the area more frequently and wouldn't draw any more attention than usual. They would be given time to get familiar with the vehicle prior to their departure from Pleiku. However, there were still a couple of real issues that they had to get through. The maps showed the major incursion into Cambodia to be considerably south of the area they would be in. How the hell were they supposed to get to those areas in a deuce and a half? The answer made them suspicious of how valuable they were, to the Kansas NCO, and the U.S Air Force. Going over the map on the wall, Denton explained the plan.

"The Ho Chi Minh trail widens out from the point just above Pleiku, in Cambodia, all the way down to almost Saigon. They have gotten the shit bombed out of them for the past several months, and what they get in the next two weeks will send most of them to hell. It isn't paved, but it is flattened out from carrying the weaponry and supplies so much. There should be no problem getting the deuce and a half through. The NVA and the VC will be thrown back on their haunches, and resistance will be casual."

Casual . . . what the hell was casual? The three wondered as they stood there, silent and numb. They never had a high opinion of Denton. They knew he didn't give a flying fuck if they were sacrificed at any point on this mission, so long as the goods got through. The whole thing smelled. Why would the Kansas NCO risk a very lucrative opportunity on the assumption that some moderately experienced air force personnel could possibly sneak from an extremely hazardous part of Vietnam, into Cambodia, bringing much needed materials, and then return with war booty worth a fortune? Cru didn't like it; he had good instincts about shit like this and smelled a set up.

Cru glanced over at Vodka Charley gauging his reaction to all of this. Vodka Charley and the three of them had bonded closely these past few months and Cru thought if Vodka Charley was okay with it; they'd probably be okay. But he didn't look okay . . . he appeared to be drunker than usual, and sat silently with his head lowered, avoiding Cru's stare. Cru was sure he was wishing he could have a drink right now. Cru watched him carefully, attempting to read their fate through his demeanor. He wouldn't look up; Montrell, Hardy and Cru glanced at each other, and back again at Vodka Charley. What really pissed Cru off was the fact that Vodka Charley only seemed upset about the plan. Once he realized the three knew the score . . . when they figured out they were being thrown to the wolves . . . .

Cru felt like a trapped animal. He knew they couldn't get out of this detail, but he also knew that one or all of them would likely become casualties as a result of it. He suddenly felt guilty dragging Redmond and Salas into this. Knowing both as Cru did, he was sure they wouldn't be concerned about their personal safety, but had he known it was a setup he wouldn't have asked to include them. Both Redmond and Salas had seen enough hardship in their lives already.

Redmond grew up dirt poor on a Minnesota Indian reservation. His father was an alcoholic who beat his wife and children on a regular basis. As the oldest child, Redmond helped raise and support the family any way he could. When the old man went too far one night, Redmond whacked him over the head with a hammer, putting him in a coma for a week. Redmond was sent to a tribal detention center. There he was beaten and abused by the older inmates and staff. He joined the Marines when he was seventeen, lying about his age. After some time he left the Marines for the air force.

In addition to having balls of steel, he turned out to be a good organizer, and when temporarily assigned to help clean up the equipment mess at Phu Cat, the supply OIC snatched him away for permanent assignment. Redmond would only agree to the transfer as long as he could go out on the road, on the "ass and trash" details the supply squadron conducted on a regular basis. This relieved him of the tedium of duty on base and the danger of the road gave him his adrenaline rushes. He also voluntarily pulled perimeter guard at least once or twice a week, even though it meant going without sleep for long periods of time; again providing him with the adrenaline rushes he apparently required on a regular basis.

Salas was almost a mirror image of Redmond. Of Philippine and Chinese ancestry, his mother raised him and his five brothers and sisters in a poor village in Hawaii. His father only returned home to scrounge money, and do his part to add another mouth to feed. Salas's mother worked as a housekeeper for various tourist hotels and depended on tips and left over food from banquets to support her large family. Bill helped out with earned money from his prized fighting cocks. He proudly wore the small, sharp blades that he fastened on the cock's legs before a fight on a necklace along with his dog tags. His cousin had been killed in Vietnam when the chopper he was on was shot down, and Bill joined the air force, hoping to become a para-rescue specialist. Bill washed out when he struck an instructor who kept giving him a bad time about his Asian ancestry. Bill tried to ignore him, but when the instructor wouldn't let up, Bill caught him with a karate kick to the side of the head. The instructor went down like a sack of flour. Bill spent a night in the brig and got an article 15, the military equivalent of a misdemeanor. They stuck him in base supply where he kept his mouth shut, did his job, and volunteered for Vietnam. Like Redmond, Salas needed his regular adrenaline rushes.

Montrell, Hardy and Cru walked back to their compound. The walk was silent as the each one contemplated his future, which appeared to be a world of shit. When they got to their compound they agreed to get together later, to go over their options. They went to their bunks to gather their thoughts. Cru was sure each of them was having the same feeling: how did they get to this point? What had started out hustling beers and seating arrangements for porn shows had somehow morphed into a life-threatening mission with apparently no way out.

56

In his mind's eye Cru was obediently performing all his duties in base supply. He was just a casual observer of the Kansas NCO's operation; quietly, wisely avoiding him and his associates as much as possible Cru would complete his tour, hopefully, in twelve months and di di mau . . . get the fuck out of Vietnam and leave it all behind.

But reality, as always, was unavoidable. Cru was in up to his eyeballs and he had to accept it. The Kansas NCO was right . . . all the soft bennies and easy duty had lulled him into a state of unreality. He forgot whom he was dealing with and where he was; a big mistake, and now he was going to pay for that error. When they got together later, it was apparent that Montrell and Hardy were having the same thoughts as he was. They were depressed and uneasy regarding the prospects of their future.

"Maybe we can talk to Prentice," Hardy offered. Hardy didn't get along with Vodka Charley as well as Crucianelli and Montrell, and unlike the others who were closer, always referred to him as Prentice; never Sgt. Prentice, or Vodka Charley. Montrell and Cru looked at each other knowingly.

Montrell looked at Hardy and replied, "Vodka Charley isn't in favor of this shit, and you can tell he's fully aware of the implication and dangers of it. But he ain't going to buck Richards, no way, no how. Richards butters Vodka Charley's bread and tells him when to eat it."

"There it is," Cru offered. "Vodka Charley is our buddy, but he can't stand up to the Kansas NCO, and never could. Remember the beer dousing incident?" Some weeks earlier, during one of the Kansas NCO's porn showings, he and Vodka Charley were standing on the upper deck of their NCO barracks, drinking. Standing directly underneath them was a very large black senior NCO watching the show. While Vodka Charley wasn't looking, the Kansas NCO poured his beer on the black NCO, then tossed his can aside and stood there looking innocent. Vodka Charley looking down and holding his beer, didn't know what was going on.

The black NCO, enraged, ran up the stairs and grabbed Vodka Charley by the throat and shook him like a terrier shaking a rat. Several guys peeled the man off Charley, but not until he absorbed a fairly good thrashing. The Kansas NCO never intervened, just watched distractedly, revealing some of his inner nature as a cold, calculating individual who would sometimes amuse himself, even at the expense of his friends. Vodka Charley was pissed off about it, but he never confronted the Kansas NCO about it. No, Cru, Montrell and Hardy could not expect any help out of Prentice.

It was funny when you thought about it, Cru mused. Prentice and Richards were both master sergeants in the air force, around the same age, and had a similar background. However they were as different as night and day. To Richards, the six stripes on his sleeves meant little in regards to his actual station in life. He commanded a multimillion-dollar empire, though it be of an illicit nature. Richards happened to be an NCO in the U.S. Air Force . . . could have been the CEO of any Forbes 500 company but history and fate put him in the Central Highlands of Vietnam, in the middle of a very nasty war. Richard's predatory nature was not to be denied . . . he carved out an empire of profit for himself, and those who could manage to keep up with him.

Prentice, on the other hand, fell pretty much in line, his fate more often than not determined by others. Growing up farming in rural Georgia, he was off to the air force as soon as he came of age. Work hard, study hard, keep your nose clean, and get another stripe every few years. He had no complaints, although the dissolution of his marriage as a result of the stress of military life set him back for a bit.

The air force had been good to him, three hots and a cot almost every day, a chance at an education if he wanted it, interesting travel. (Along with ample opportunity to satisfy the hefty drinking habit he had acquired, courtesy of Uncle Sam.) Not bad for a peanut farmer's skinny son, he made it a career. He had seven years in when he pulled his first tour in 'Nam. Back then when the war, GIs, and the women were still fresh, morale wasn't bad. He was stationed in Ben Hoa, just outside Saigon, and the nightlife of Saigon made up for those occasional nights of terror, when the VC would pound the base with Chinese-made mortars. He sewed on two stripes during that first tour, got an Air Force Commendation Medal for performance, and all without a scratch, physically. His return to the U.S. and Malstrom Air Force Base in Montana proved a disappointment. He found the duty boring and the climate inhospitable. And although he didn't see all that much action during that first tour, he discovered the war had followed him home as he repeatedly awoke around 01:30 with the sounds, smells, and image of his buddy, Lanard, dying as a result of an incoming Viet Cong mortar round.

He and Lanard had bunked together during their whole tour. Lanard was a quiet non-drinker who pulled his tour without complaint, wrote his wife dutifully every day, and didn't seem to mind the raucous drinking habits of Prentice and most of the other men he was stationed with. When the mortar hit their barracks, Lanard, a Southern Baptist, had been standing saying his nightly prayers. Prentice often teased him about it, but the two got on well, looking after each other as people do in such conditions.

The chunks of shrapnel that killed Lanard missed Prentice by several feet, as he was passed out and lay completely prone underneath the bunk. Abruptly sobering up during the attack, the last vision he saw before passing out in shock was that of Lanard's severed head, dangling from his body. That gristly scene would repeat itself almost nightly in Prentice's head, only ceasing after the consumption of enough vodka to render him senseless.

Chapter 14

"On the road again,
Like a band of gypsies we're goin down the highway,
We're the best of friends,
Insisting that the world keep turning our way."

Willie Nelson

The men had never left Phu Cat with such misgivings and apprehension, as they did on this journey. Their previous road trips were mostly details lasting only one day, with a few seeing them gone for two days at most. This mission, even if everything went perfectly, would see them out on road for possibly a month. Along with their cargo, they left with enough munitions and supplies to see them to Pleiku, an air base in the western part of the Central Highlands of Vietnam.

Their first stop was An Khe. The army had a good size base there, which included an artillery contingent. "The Golf Course," as An Khe was referred to, was a welcome sight for the little convoy. The base was on top of a plateau that afforded a commanding view of the nearby countryside. Choppers flew in from all points of the Central Highlands, bringing in and carrying out men, supplies, and medical evacuees. The plan was for them to stay here long enough to refuel and rest. They had picked up the accompanying men from the 173rd Airborne unit just down the road from Phu Cat; the only cargo they carried was weapons, ammo, and enough C-rations to get them through about a week. They also brought enough hooch and dope along to keep them along with Flash, too stoned to do anything if any trouble came up and also too stoned to give a shit.

The last thing Cru and his men needed on this trip was a couple of stoned, trigger-happy ground pounders. These guys gave two shits about the mission. It was gravy duty as far as they were concerned; babysitting an air force convoy on some obscure mission. All they knew was it got them out of the bush for a while and they were going to suck up on what they thought would be some in country R & R. Spc 4 Horace Childs was a product of the Detroit slums. Coming from a fatherless family of five, he and his four siblings kept their mother busy, trying to feed them and keep them from being killed or incarcerated. As far as Childs was concerned, 'Nam wasn't that much worse than any Friday or Saturday night in the hood. Survival was the name of the game, and he intended to survive his twelve months of duty here, go back to Detroit, and with a little luck get a job in an auto factory where he could earn enough to live like a human being, something he had little experience at, thus far in life. If he did make it back, and if he could get that good job, he intended to marry Brenda, the girl who bore his child.

Spc 5 Karl Becker had lived like a human being. He knew what it was like to live a "normal" life, not having to fear getting killed just for walking down the road, or sitting on your bunk for that matter. Becker grew up in a middle class neighborhood in Milwaukee with options upon graduating from high school. He had a football scholarship from the University of Wisconsin Madison, or a good paying factory job at any one of the large manufacturing industries in the area. He chose college. His plummeting grades, however, earned him a 1A classification from the local draft board. Childs and Becker had slept most of the way to An Khe, and only woke up when the vehicle stopped and the engine shut down.

"Damn; where the fuck we at?" Childs wondered.

Becker responded, "Who fuckin' cares? We're not dead, we ain't wet, or dog-beat tired. I'm likin' this detail just fine. If it lasts 'til I DEROS, that'd be okay with me."

"You're bullshittin', man. You know you'd rather be out humpin', with your buddy, Jones," Childs countered.

Jones was their NCOIC and sworn enemy. Whenever there was a shit detail of any kind, Childs and Becker seemed to land on it. They also seemed to walk point and pull ambush more than anyone else in their company. They bitched to the OIC, Lieutenant Brauner, until he told them to just shut the fuck up and put in their time. Jones ran the company, and that was fine with him. Brauner was a ninety-day wonder who had no intention of making the army a career, or getting killed because that dumb bastard LBJ saw a commie behind every bush. All he wanted to do was finish his tour, get the fuck out of the army, get a law degree, and get paid for winning personal injury lawsuits for the rest of his life. Brauner patronized Jones; he saw him as a lifer and a loser. He felt the lifers should take the risks . . . they signed on for the security and unchallenging day-to-day military life. So when it was time to get your ass shot off, their asses should be the first ones to go.

Master Sergeant Hiram Jones had been in the army for twelve years. This was his second tour of Vietnam and hopefully his last. The first tour saw him wounded twice; he picked up a Bronze Star, Silver Star, and two stripes. He was hoping to pick up a couple more stripes this tour, only without the Purple Hearts. His attitude was: Let the young dudes take the risks; he pulled his time in the meat grinder. If his CO wasn't such a useless college punk, he wouldn't have to carry the load, and feel the responsibility of carrying the whole company on his shoulders. Since that asshole Brauner was as useless as teats on a boar, Jones was forced to take up the slack. Fuck it, he thought. I've got two months to go, could take my R & R, fiddle a week away in transit, a couple weeks in base camp, and before you know it I'd be back to the states in one goddamn piece.

He got rid of two major sources of irritation by sending Childs and Becker off on that air force mission. He had played coy with the two, regarding the actual nature of the mission. Jones was an occasional "business associate" of the Kansas NCO, and he was involved in the planning of the mission from the early stages. He knew it was a setup and a decoy for the real mission, which was being carried out about a hundred miles to the south. With any luck, Jones felt Childs and Becker would be killed and out of his hair permanently. They never liked him, and he never liked them. A damn Yankee nigger from Detroit, and a damn Yankee kraut from Milwaukee, they had given him nothing but grief through his whole tour.

He smiled to himself as he visualized them lying alongside their truck, blown up and smoldering. They wouldn't go running to that asshole lieutenant anymore, that's for sure. So he gave them a few shit details, and they had to spend a little extra time out in the bush. The other guys in the company didn't complain all the fucking time, and some of them got some extra shit duty also. To himself, Jones admitted he leaned on them a little. Never liked Yankees and got even with them any chance he got. Seems like all the new officers were Goddamn Yankees, and they ordered him around like he was a damn nigger. Fuck 'em.

Chapter 15

"Treachery returns."

Irish saying

The Kansas NCO had been developing the plan for a while. He was making enough money on the day-to-day operations to insure he would be a wealthy man for the rest of his life. The currency exchange operation alone had made him a wealthy man. The porn shows, sales of materials, souvenir sales, and entertainment operations were icing on the cake. He didn't need to take any more risks. He would enjoy a comfortable life . . . once he got out of Vietnam and clear of the military.

However the Kansas NCO was, deep down, the consummate gambler. Much of the satisfaction he received came from the sheer enjoyment he got out of getting away with things. He outsmarted the U.S. military, the South Vietnamese military, South Vietnamese civilians, and even the Viet Cong and the NVA. Most of his contacts among the people he dealt with were complicit in his operation, so it wasn't as if he was taking advantage of any specific person or organization.

Besides, he spread the spoils around. Everyone involved in any of his many dealings got something in return; whether it be money, equipment, supplies, food, or any other desired commodity. He never solicited. Those in need came to him. Of course, it was known that the Kansas NCO was the man who could get things. Not only could he get them, he could get them when you wanted them and where you needed them. All aspects of people from every corner of the Central Highlands of Vietnam sought him out for his goods and services.

Had the members of the Kansas NCO's Cambodian mission, as it came to be known, known of the plan they would have understood the deep morass which Vodka Charley had been steeped in these past couple of weeks. Normally a happy drunk, Vodka Charley had become brooding and quiet, and kept to himself unless duty required otherwise.

Campolo

Although he bitched and groused at the men all the time, Prentice had bonded with them. He had become depressed upon learning their role in this latest mission for the Kansas NCO. Although only middle aged, Prentice felt his best years were behind him. The collapse of his family life, his increasing dependence on alcohol, the edge of duty in Vietnam and his position as a subservient accomplice in the Kansas NCO's illicit operation weighed upon him like a huge stone which he was tethered to and forced to drag along.

It hadn't always been like this. There was a time he had a promising future in the air force and a wonderful young family. As time went on, and the residue of military life collected on every aspect of his being, things unraveled. If he could have gotten control of his drinking . . . things would have been okay, he thought. He went to the meetings, and usually got through all the required steps and processes to stop. Inevitably during a long night of duty, or a gathering of comrades at the NCO club, or some off base honky tonk, he forgot all those steps and the reasons he took them and the demon slipped back in. Long ago he quit trying. Somehow he learned to carry out his duties as a senior NCO while drinking enough vodka to carry him through the day in a condition of numb satisfaction.

The Cambodian mission called for the two air force vehicles leaving Phu Cat to be used as decoys. They would have loads of the standard military equipment used by remote operations, and an itinerary taking them to the off-load point and back within three weeks or less. The truth was they were being used as sacrificial lambs—decoys for the real load and return of goods traveling farther south.

The real load returning would be full of opium, the value of which would be in the high six figures. These trucks would be standard army deuce and halfs, and would be in a convoy of around ten vehicles. The purported mission of the two air force trucks would be leaked to known Vietcong sources, making them a high profile target . . . and sealing their doom.

Prentice, try as he might, could not talk the Kansas NCO into altering the plans. He felt the Kansas NCO knew that the decoy mission was doomed, but felt the cost was worth the reward in the huge payoff once the high value opium from the Iron Triangle was sold on the streets of the U.S. and Europe. The Kansas NCO had, up until this mission, avoided dealing in drugs of any kind. It was strictly a business standard. He wouldn't knowingly buy or sell from any drug users. It wasn't a moral issue, he just felt that people who used drugs were unstable, and that greatly increased the chance of compromising his operation. What

64

lured him into this sordid affair was information from a CIA agent he occasionally did business with. The operative told Richards of his plan convinced him that it was foolproof and would be foolish to turn down because someone else would jump on it if he didn't.

Richards didn't like the potential loss of life, or the nature of the cargo, but he couldn't resist the challenge — or the money. He knew Prentice would object, but with a little pressure go along with anything he asked.

The plan they worked out called for the real convoy to fly down to Ban Me Thout on an air force C-130. From there, they'd load into the army trucks, and head into Cambodia. At the rendezvous site, they'd unload the materials they brought, hook up with the CIA agent's partner, and receive the opium. They would then head back to Ban Me Thuot, only this time they would take a CIA aircraft, probably a C-123 and fly all the way back to Phu Cat.

At Phu Cat, Richards and the CIA agent would meet the aircraft on the ground, and arrange for repackaging and shipment back to Tyndall Air Force Base in Florida where contacts would receive the shipment, get it off base and to people who had connections with multi-national drug dealers.

This was another source of grief for Vodka Charley. His favorite nephew, while home on leave after a tour in the killing fields around Hue, had succumbed to an overdose of heroin. Jeffrey Prentice Mechar was an All-American linebacker as well as a scholastic high achiever at the University of Georgia prior to enlisting in the U.S. Army. Prentice was depressed about being involved with the same illicit substance which had led to the death of his sister's oldest son, but if he stayed drunk enough, he didn't have to think about it.

Normally, Prentice readily forgot any problems after the first few slugs of vodka. But the upcoming mission, risking the lives of Crucianelli and the others bothered him immensely. After a while, he made up his mind. It was too late for him to save his nephew, and probably too late to save himself . . . but he was going to do whatever he could to save Montrell and the others.

Chapter 16

"Dem thit nop mieng hum."
(The meat has been brought to the tiger.)

Vietnamese saying

The grunts hoped to hang around An Khe as long as they could. This was gravy duty as far as they were concerned. Three hots and a cot every day and all the cold beer you could steal. Crucianelli was having no part of that; he had been on the receiving end of the wrath of Msgt. William Richards, when he screwed up his part in an operation and his memory of that incident was vivid in his mind.

For a short time the grunts thought they could push their air force associates around. Crucianelli put a quick end to that. If his icy glare and harsh response weren't enough, Red and Salas would have been more than happy to bring these two clowns in line. Veterans of many road trips, Redmond and Salas had vivid memories of their small air force convoys getting bullied on the road by the larger army convoys they frequently encountered. Sometimes the encounters were a nuisance, but other times they turned dangerous. Redmond and Salas mounted a .30 caliber machine gun on the truck they used most often. The weapon was intended for use on VC, greedy Vietnamese police, and any menacing army convoys they encountered. To date, it had been used on VC three times, brandished at the White Mice about a dozen times, and at surprised army convoys dozens of times.

The small convoy left An Khe and proceeded to Pleiku on Highway 19. Highway 19 wasn't as well traveled as the infamous Highway 1 or "Highway of Death" as it was known, but there was enough traffic to keep everyone's finger close to the trigger. Any bicycle, motorbike, or pedestrian could easily toss a grenade or satchel charge into anyone of the vehicles as they passed by. The narrow road could also have been booby-trapped to detonate only under the heavier weight of one of the large American vehicles. As the miles sped by and routines settled in, each of the men drifted into his own divergent thoughts. None had previously been on this route. Many steep inclines and twisting curves added to the tension as they motored to their destination.

As they proceeded toward the settlement known as Le Trung, the convoy suddenly came under intense small arms fire while coming out of a sharp curve. The ambush was well planned as the trucks could neither increase speed nor turn back. Breaching protocol, the vehicles stopped and the men in the cabs jumped out, desperately searching for the direction and source of the shooting.

Redmond found it first and returned fire with his M-16, spraying the area with clip after clip, and was soon joined by Crucianelli and Salas as well. For some reason the .30 caliber was silent. After being certain the attackers had been dispersed, Redmond angrily moved to the back of the truck where Becker and Childs, along with the silent .30 caliber, were positioned. He yelled for the others, who then came running to the back.

Childs was withering in pain. An AK-47 round had entered one side of his lower jaw, and exited out the other. Skin and flesh were hanging onto the side of his face he was clutching. Next to him, Becker lay dead. One round had pierced his flak jacket just under the heart, and two others had passed through his neck, just above the Kevlar vest.

The joint he was smoking was still in his hand, smoldering. Redmond and Crucianelli jumped in the truck and felt for a pulse but Becker was gone. Redmond grabbed a rag and put it to the bleeding side of Childs face, applying pressure. Childs was going into shock and they didn't have much time to deal with him before he became completely immobile.

Shit, what the fuck were we gonna do now? Crucianelli wondered. Out on the road and both their machine gun operators were out of commission. Moreover, they were out of radio range from their last outpost. Redmond and Flash put Becker in the body bag that was in the storage box on the big truck. Crucianelli absentmindedly wondered why there was only one body bag in the store. There was also a first-aid kit, but it had been used before and only a small piece of gauze, some hydrogen peroxide, and a couple of ace bandages were left.

They had nothing to give Childs for the pain, and he was in plenty of it. He moaned and groaned so pathetically they thought he might have been dying. Finally, Flash pulled out a small plastic wrapper with some white powder in it. They knew Flash hit the dope pretty hard, and they all took speed the dispensary dished out, but no one figured Flash to be a heroin whore, but there he was with it.

"Yeah, I brought this shit along," Flash said. "Who the fuck else has anything to kill his pain?"

"Give it to him," Redmond said. "No one's bustin' your ass about it."

Flash poured a little on his finger and rubbed Childs' lips with it several times. Childs started moaning less and soon he fell into a drugged stupor.

"I don't know how long it will last," Flash remarked. "So we'd better figure out what the fuck we're gonna do with him."

They were too far along to turn back to An Khe, and too far away from Pleiku to get there in time to get Childs the medical treatment he needed. The trip was turning to shit in a hurry.

Crucianelli and Redmond discussed the options. Le Trung wasn't far ahead, but chances were that's where the VC who ambushed them came from. Even if they didn't the villagers weren't likely to help the men out, knowing the VC would be visiting soon to square up with them. And what were the chances Le Trung had a radio or anyway for them to call for help?

Shit, Crucianelli thought, I can't believe this is happening to me. I should have kept my old job in base supply. Yeah, the incoming mortars and rockets were bad news, and the constant racial battles were a pain in the ass, but at least I had a pretty good chance of making it back to the world. Now I'm out here like a fucking grunt, fighting for my life, with one guy dead, and another seriously wounded. Realizing that sitting around feeling sorry for himself wasn't going to help, Cru shook it off and he and Redmond pounded out a plan.

They were going to ask for a meeting with the village chief at Le Trung. Back in the world Crucianelli had shirt-tail relations who were in the mafia. It wasn't a secret in his family, and he never judged the family members who did or didn't get involved. He chose not to. It wasn't for him but he learned to appreciate some of the tactics they employed. When things got really bad, you could always ask for a "sit down" with the boss and those involved. The face-to-face meeting would often be enough to diffuse the situation, whatever it may be.

Redmond's background taught him the value of a face-to-face meeting. When problems arose, a gathering with the tribal council would usually come up with a solution for a difficult problem.

A face-to-face meeting with the village chief would involve negotiation. If they expected to receive help, in the form of first aid for Childs, communications assistance, and cover from the local VC, they needed something of value to negotiate. That required something of sufficient value that the village needed. The materials they were hauling to Cambodia were of little value to the Americans . . . but of great value to the Vietnamese.

Of course, the value of the contents handed out to save the life of this mission, and possibly Childs' life, could prove a problem at the other end of the road, when the intended goods were to be exchanged. Crucianelli didn't care. He was scared . . . scared for Childs and scared for himself. He wanted out of the immediate area and didn't care what happened in two or three weeks back at Phu Cat.

If the Kansas NCO had any problems with the detail dipping into the stores to save their skins, he could go fuck himself. Crucianelli had no idea he was just an expendable decoy for the actual plan being carried out further to the south. He had always thought the Kansas NCO deep down, was a good guy who happened to be shrewd enough to make some money in this shithole. He didn't realize the Kansas NCO was not only shrewd, but ruthless as well. In time, this would all be revealed to him.

As it turned out the village chief of Le Trung was accommodating and ready to negotiate. The trucks had two cases of medical supplies, which included twelve quarts of iodine. The Vietnamese used iodine for everything from malaria to snake bites, and Le Trung was badly in need of some. They also had several midwives who were capable, if not educated, surgeons. They staunched the flow of blood from Childs' wounds, and sutured him up as good as any flight surgeon could manage. They applied iodine and sulfur to his wounds, which made him cry like a baby until they gave him some buds of a plant to chew on, whereupon he immediately fell into a deep sleep.

Upon observing the effect on Childs, Redmond and some of the others grabbed up as much of the bark as they could. Redmond grew up chewing on peyote buds and his spirits lit up considerably at the thought of easing his spirit with the Vietnamese counterpart. Flash and Crucianelli thought it would be neat shit to crash on.

69

The village also had several vats of beer that they brewed from the kava plant. It was somewhat bitter, but heavy and satisfying. The alcohol content was more comparable to liquor than beer, and Flash was soon wandering around the village in an intoxicated state. The villagers were amused by this, and had some fun at his expense. They tricked him into eating stale rice cakes, which had fermented. This made Flash even drunker. Soon he passed out and lay in a drunken stupor in the far end of the village.

Later, when he came around Flash, always horny and ready to go, had his eye on a couple of lovely young village girls. They flirted with him, until an old mama san intervened and sent them scampering away. Not to be put off, Flash kept right on, flirting with the old mama san. She found Flash's antics to be quite humorous and laughed and teased him along, deftly avoiding his clumsy attempts to corner her. When she had enough, she gave him a sharp elbow in the sternum and walked away. Flash, now bent over trying to catch his breath, cussed up a storm.

Redmond and Crucianelli, concerned about how the village elders might react to Flash's antics, gathered him up and threw him on the back of one of the trucks, instructing him to knock off the bullshit and shut the fuck up, till they were out of the village. They didn't need a war with the local villagers added to their other problems. Feeling it was too dangerous to move out at night the men spent the night in the village, taking turns keeping watch.

The next morning found Flash hung over and lethargic. Crucianelli had to push him to get cleaned up and ready to go. He wanted to hit Pleiku by the end of the day. The body bag containing Becker was beginning to smell, and the villagers thought it foolish not to bury the dead man right away. His spirit would go wherever it needed to, be that to his home ten thousand miles away, or any other place that drew it. The body needed to be put back to nourish the earth. After years of foreign influence, the villagers spiritual practice blended Buddhist, Christian, and pagan beliefs. They offered to cremate, or bury Becker. Even though they were viewed as invaders, the villagers felt they had to do right by the dead to sustain their own spiritual future.

Flash and a few of the other men were all for that as they were getting nauseated by at the smell. Imagining the trouble he would find himself in for abandoning the body, Cru insisted they take it along. They wrapped it in some burlap along with some aromatic local plants, that somewhat dulled the odor.

They left Le Trung around 09:00, keeping a slow pace through the narrow winding roads. They pressed on until around 15:00, when they started to see aircraft, which were no doubt from the air force base at Pleiku. One, a C-47, flew down close for a look at the convoy. The pilot tipped its wing as a sign of recognition. Cru hoped it was a Spooky, which was a C-47 transport aircraft converted into a heavily armed gun ship. The Vietnamese feared these, along with Puff, a C-130 cargo aircraft turned into a gunship, more than any other American weapon of war, with the possible exception of the B-52 bomber. They might leave the scraggily convoy alone, if they felt the gunship was protecting it. Cru was also deeply regretting having Flash along on the mission.

Redmond was thinking the same thing. Red was uncomfortable on this trip. He had to depend on too many other people, and Redmond was basically a loner. Five years earlier, with few prospects on the reservation, Redmond had joined the Marines. He made it through basic training without a hitch. He made it to special guerilla warfare training at Camp Lejeune where he found himself impatient and butting heads with the NCOs for not being a "team player." Finally, his CO called him in and squared with him. He told Redmond he was one of the finest Marine recruits he ever had. Redmond would excel as a sniper, or maybe even one of the special ops guys in one of the other services. These guys often went alone on missions and had only themselves to depend and worry about.

The Marines needed team players, for day-to-day patrol operations in Vietnam. So Redmond, discouraged and bitter, washed out. He joined the air force and breezed through their basic training, hardly breaking a sweat. He asked for training and duty with an Air Force Combat Control Team, an elite group that often conducted insurgent missions.

The air force didn't need combat controllers at the time. The bases in Vietnam that they were used on had been secured, more or less, and the security for them was now in the hands of the Army Airborne divisions, or the very capable Republic of Korea (ROK) Tiger and Capital divisions. With Richard Nixon's Vietnamization in full swing, the Air Force needed people to tear down billets, Quonset huts, warehouses, hangars, and pack up material and equipment. So Redmond was assigned to warehousing supply, and sent to Phu Cat Air Base, Republic of Vietnam, to be a part of that mission.

Redmond was somewhat amused at many of the other airman who bitched constantly about the heat and long hours of duty in 'Nam. Some of the white boys, and blacks as well, were out of shape and fat when they came over. They had a hard time dealing with the climate and the workload. Combine that with the occasional mortar and rocket barrages from the local VC, the on-going racial problems on the bases, and you ended up with significant discontent.

Redmond sneered at them and didn't mingle much. He volunteered for perimeter guard as often as he could, and frequently went on truck convoys transporting materials and equipment to some of the other American installations in the Central Highlands. These convoys were dangerous. One in five would encounter an ambush or attack of some kind but none of them were as dangerous as this mission. Although the adrenaline rush he encountered during the attack was exactly the kind of action he was looking for, he felt somewhat anchored by the other men.

He felt Becker and Childs were poor examples of army fighting men. All they did was bitch, drink, and do drugs thus far on the mission. Then, as soon as the convoy was attacked, they were out of position and managed to get themselves shot up.

Crucianelli was okay, Redmond thought. Back in Wisconsin, Cru grew up hunting and fishing, and at least knew how to handle a weapon. Physically he was in as good as shape as any grunt, and had a keen mind to go with it. Even though Crucianelli and Redmond busted each other's balls about their respective ancestry, neither one took it seriously. They understood each other and thought alike. Cru told Redmond that as a Wapahoo he was a "Native American" just like Redmond and as such, should get a special entitlement. Redmond would reply that if it wasn't for that dago Columbus, the Indians could still call America theirs. Many of the convoys Redmond had gone on were also accompanied by Cru . . . and that was fine with him.

Flash was a good guy, a helluva fighter, but somewhat unreliable, a druggy and not the sharpest arrow in the quiver. Redmond liked Flash and as the three of them should have been on this trip together, so they were . . . on a mission which might well be there last; but together as always. Redmond respected Salas; the big Hawaiian was a good hand at most details and a tough fighter. Redmond and Salas had butted heads from time to time. Although he respected Salas, Redmond didn't entirely trust him.

They coasted into Pleiku about 19:00. Although not as large as Phu Cat, the base had a chow hall, small BX, and small airman's club. Crucianelli had orders to meet with an associate of the Kansas NCO prior to making contact with anybody else. He was anxious to hook up with the guy so he could dispose of Becker's body as quickly as he could. He took Childs to the base hospital immediately. Shortly after dropping off Childs, he made contact with Sergeant Leonard R. Pruitt, the Kansas NCO's counterpart at Pleiku.

Pruitt then took them to the mortuary where they off loaded Becker's body. He also helped Crucianelli fill out a report about the attack at base operations. Through the demeanor of the men they encountered, it was obvious that Pruitt held the same status at Pleiku as the Kansas NCO did at Phu Cat. Pruitt took them to the NCO's billet area where they were given a Quonset hut of their own to bunk in. After showering and napping, the men gathered around the Quonset hut, waiting for Pruitt.

Pruitt came back and called for a muster. One by one, Montrell, Hardy, Salas, Flash, Redmond, and Crucianelli raised their hands. He was confirming the roster the Kansas NCO had sent him, and appraising each one as they went along. He didn't want any fuck-ups to ruin his cushy station in the Kansas NCO's operation. The incident on the road had demoralized Hardy, and to some degree Montrell. Only at Pleiku a short time, Montrell was already drunk. Hardy was somber and sat by himself staring at his hands in his lap. They hadn't signed on for this. Buyer's remorse, Hardy thought. I should have gutted it out in the stinking tool issue center instead of going after the soft duty . . . now I'm paying for it.

After his review, Pruitt conferred with Crucianelli. "Montrell and Hardy are gonna have to be replaced," Pruitt observed. Crucianelli agreed and was fine with that. Montrell, Cru, and Hardy had become as close as brothers in Vietnam and Cru didn't want them to get harmed. They both had girls, who they talked about all the time, waiting for them back in the World, as everyone in Vietnam called the States. Montrell was already way over the top with his drinking and he didn't need any more baggage to bring back with him. Hardy was too sensitive for duty in the 'Nam, and no doubt, would be affected by it for the rest of his life.

Let 'em go, Crucianelli thought. Maybe they'll get an early DEROS date, an early out from the air force, and will then get on with their lives again. He wondered who their replacements would be. That information would soon be revealed to him with shocking results.

While waiting for the personnel information from Pruitt, the detail was ushered to the airman's club at Pleiku. Placed in the section normally reserved for NCOs, E-5 and above, no one raised an eyebrow when Pruitt brought them in and sat them down. He instructed the bartender on duty to let them drink for free, but not to let them get too hammered.

He wanted them on the road early the next morning, and if they got too comfortable hanging around the club, or too smashed, an early departure was unlikely.

The club that day was featuring a Philippine band, which like many USO contracted bands went around to the various installations in Vietnam, performing several shows a day, usually for three or four days in a row. They sang most of the current favorites, including the typically humorous oriental rendition of "Plowed Mary." No one minded though, as two of the band members were pretty young girls, scantily clad. The crowd soon warmed up to them, whistling, jeering, and shouting lewd comments.

A number of troops were infantry units in from the field. They were in heaven, sipping cold beer and ogling young flesh. So long as the beer and shots kept coming and the girls kept shaking, thoughts of the horrors that awaited them out in the field were held at bay. Security police normally kept a close watch on these clubs, as fights frequently erupted. Any number of things could start trouble, but more often than not it involved race, friction between the upper and lower ranks, or brawls between members of different military units or services. Today was quiet, as most of the men seemed content to drink, yell, and whistle at the girls, as they worked up a sweat dancing to the music. After an hour or so, Pruitt came back to retrieve Crucianelli. Once outside they got into a jeep and drove to the supply warehouse.

Following Pruitt into the large metal structure, they proceeded to the back of the building where there was a small office area, with several desks, filing cabinets and chairs. Several men were casually sitting around drinking coffee and smoking cigarettes. Crucianelli balked when he saw the group, for sitting in one of the chairs was none other than Vodka Charley.

"Sergeant Prentice!" Crucianelli half yelled. Prentice got up and they shook hands. It was obvious they were happy to see each other. "What the hell are you doin here?" Crucianelli asked. "Did the Phu Cat NCO club burn down?"

"No, no, the NCO club's still there, and I wish I was in it!" Prentice replied. The two moved off and in a solemn voice, Prentice revealed the whole story — the details of the mission, and how Cru and his team were nothing more than expendable decoys, "compromised" to insure that the real mission succeeded. Cru sat there, with his head lowered, listening. When Prentice was finished he put his arm around Crucianelli's shoulders and asked him if he was all right. Cru sat there, motionless for several minutes before speaking.

"This is Richard's idea?" he asked, somewhat incredulously.

"It was his," Prentice replied. "Look, I know how you feel, but it's nothing personal. You know how Richards is; everything is always about business with him."

"Doesn't help," Cru responded. "So what the fuck, you came all the way out here to tell me that shit?"

"No . . . no . . . that's not why I'm here", Prentice responded.

Chapter 17

"There are no hopeless situations; there are only men who have grown hopeless about them."

Clare Boothe Luce

"I'm going with you", Prentice stated.

Now Crucianelli was flabbergasted. "Are you fuckin crazy? You knowingly come out here to join up with a suicide mission?"

"It doesn't have to be a suicide mission", Prentice softly replied, "I've been doing some planning of my own."

He went on to explain that since Denton had blamed him for the problems the guys on the real pick up were having, the Kansas NCO forced him into a corner. He had been up days and nights trying to figure out how to rectify the situation and save himself, and he finally developed what he thought to be the best and only way to get out from under the mess. For the next fifteen minutes, he talked and Cru listened, occasionally interjecting an objection or a question. But after the discussion Cru felt better than he had before, the plan was sound and if it worked, would save the whole team from certain death, although it was still fraught with risk.

The rest of the working day involved the unloading and reloading of the trucks. The .30 caliber was cleaned and re-loaded by Pruitt's men, something that made Crucianelli slightly suspicious. Much to the relief of Montrell and Hardy, they were excused from the mission. After receiving the news of their dismissal, they went back to the club and drank themselves unconscious.

It's funny, Cru thought. *We always referred to Prentice as Vodka Charley and not by his real name of Prentice.*

Cru had gained new respect for him, and now felt good that Master Sergeant Charles Prentice would be on this mission with them. He wasn't sure what kind of hand he was with a weapon, but he was a quick thinker, even while drunk, and Redmond and Salas could handle most of the defense issues, as long as they had one or two other halfway decent hands along. They needed two more men. Not surprisingly no one from Pruitt's operation stepped up to volunteer — or anyone else for that matter. They were only moving on with only a pick-up and a deuce and a half truck. The .30 caliber was remounted on the pick-up truck. They were provisioned and debriefed on the route by an army master sergeant who had been involved in operations in the area west of Pleiku all the way into Cambodia. He was both helpful and empathetic with their concerns about reaching their destination and getting back; the lines and contours of his weathered face spoke volumes about the possible success of the detail.

The next morning, Cru, Salas, and Redmond were closely checking their weapons and going over the day's route. Heading west from Pleiku the road curved south before turning west again on the way to Le Thanh, the last major Vietnamese outpost before hitting Cambodia. Out there were a myriad of challenges along the roads. Ambushes, booby traps, rockslides, and wash outs could occur at any time and every point, at any given time.

Cru was looking at the map, and pondering whether a half dozen or so GIs with a .30 cal could negotiate each and every hazard they might encounter. Once they got close to the Cambodian border they had to factor the Ho Chi Minh Trail into the hazards; which might be the single biggest problem they had to face. The trail, though targeted often by B-52 bombers, jet and prop gunships, choppers and artillery fire was an active and vibrant artery for the flow of weapons and supplies for the NVA and VC south of the DMZ.

The trail wound through the jungle like a python; moving from side to side as conditions warranted. Underground bunkers, including hospitals, food stores, weapons and ammo dumps dotted the trail all along its path from North Vietnam to South Vietnam and into the Mekong Delta. Elements of the NVA and VC protected the trail, patrolling it and monitoring it like soldier ants along a feeding trail, eliminating any activity deemed threatening.

The eye of the tiger, Cru thought, as he checked over the trucks. As he looked up he was surprised to see Hardy and Montrell approaching the convoy, with their gear in hand.

"When we were at the club yesterday, we both realized it should be all three of us, or none," Montrell said. "We knew you couldn't back out of this, and we won't either," Hardy added.

"Are you fucking stupid or still drunk?" Cru replied. "This mission sucks and you know it. It's a set-up for that prick the Kansas NCO, a decoy to deflect attention from the convoy on the real mission, which is goin' down about a hundred miles south. Vodka Charley and I have been trying to figure how to get out of it, and save our asses . . . you guys better rethink this shit."

Hardy and Montrell looked at each other. They hadn't figured on that kind of answer. After a moment Montrell replied, "Well, whatever the deal is, we're in. We can load, watch, or ride shotgun if we have to. We ain't no kind of Green Berets, but we'll carry our load. We're in . . . that's it."

Pruitt had been keeping an eye on the progress, he wanted them loaded and gone. Once they were on the road west, his part was over, and he could report the information back to Phu Cat. He wasn't too concerned about Montrell and Hardy re-joining the mission. If they had gone back to Phu Cat, they might have started talking to the wrong people and questions might have come up. Pruitt thought it was unlikely any of these men could survive the trip they were embarking on . . . and if they did; he could take care of that detail as well.

Chapter 18

"Luck is a very thin wire between survival and disaster, and not many people can keep their balance on it."

Hunter Thompson

The smell of raw diesel fuel was strong as the men were fueling the vehicles prior to heading out on the road. Deuce and a half trucks, APCs and other vehicles were fueling up alongside them, preparing for another day delivering supplies, and patrolling the roads. Curiously, Cru noticed Pruitt, back in the small motor pool office speaking with the man on duty, and glancing in their direction.

"What the fuck is he pulling?" Crucianelli thought to himself. After fueling they proceeded to the gate and stopped. He asked Redmond if he was satisfied with the .30 cal and the weapons the other men were equipped with.

Red said he was okay with the weapons. Each driver had a Smith and Wesson .38 caliber revolver with a 6-inch barrel on a waist holster full of shells. They also had an M-16 behind the bench seat, within reach, along with five extra clips. The men in the back of the dump truck had thirty ammunition belts for the .30 caliber, along with their M-16s.

Slowly they pulled out and headed west. The weather was threatening, the skies were low and heavy as only skies in Vietnam could get, so they ran with the headlights on and at about half normal speed. The pick-up took the lead, with Crucianelli driving and Prentice riding shotgun. Hardy rode in back. Flash drove the dump truck with Montrell riding as shotgun. Salas and Redmond rode in the back, close to the .30 cal. As they moved along, Prentice and Crucianelli got caught up again. Prentice knew Crucianelli had an ailing mother back home and asked about her.

"She's having a hard time," Cru replied. "She's had these abdominal problems for a long time, and of course she's worried about me bein' over here..." His mother had to deal with two sons in the military, one already in Vietnam, and the other probably soon to be on the way. The stress had been hard and Cru's father wasn't much help, telling his wife, "Dammit, it's the boys' duty and they're doin' it." He had served in World War II, along with four of his brothers, one who had been killed. Cru's brother was in the army in the Big Red One and Cru worried about him coming over as well. He felt as long as he was here, they might not send his brother, and planned on extending his tour before it ended.

Maybe by then, that asshole Nixon would have the war ended, like he promised. Cru had only had a casual girlfriend back home, and as soon as she found out he had orders to Vietnam, she dumped him like a bad penny. "Fuckin' bitch," Cru often thought. "She liked me well enough when I was stateside and sent her ass money every month."

Prentice went on to discuss his plan, which would get them free and clear of the Kansas NCO if it worked . . . when they got back. *If it worked . . . when they got back.* The discussion lingered on and off... until bone-numbing explosions rocked them out of their lull.

Crucianelli and Flash both veered to the left instinctively as the rounds, coming in from the west, came closer and closer. The VC were finding their range and walking rounds in toward the convoy. Prentice and the other men yelled and flailed about for their weapons, hoping to seek out and silence the source of the attack. Crucianelli realized they couldn't outrun the incoming mortars, yet they couldn't stop either.

Reacting on instinct, Crucianelli turned down a narrow mud path that pitched down an embankment. Flash, driving the dump truck, followed and as a result of its heavier weight, soon caught up to the pick-up and pushed it down the embankment and into the flowing river at the bottom of the ravine.

Hardy, in the back of the pick-up, was now riveted with terror. Between the mortar rounds and the site of the huge bumper of the dump truck pushing them down the ravine, he thought for sure he was a dead man.

Mired in muck, at the bottom of the ravine, Flash, Montrell, and Redmond looked on helplessly as the pick-up carrying Cru, Vodka Charley and Hardy, was washed down the river by the strong current.

Redmond yelled that Salas was wounded and Flash and Montrell quickly jumped out and climbed into the back of the truck. The three of them saw the gaping holes in the metal sides of the box, where a huge chunk of shrapnel from a mortar shell had passed completely through. Salas lay motionless facedown in a pool of blood. When they turned him over they saw that the shrapnel had passed through his neck; his head dangled awkwardly, nearly severed.

Flash could barely contain his panic. Salas was dead, Cru, Prentice, and Hardy were washing down the river to God knows where, and their truck was buried in at least four feet of mud at the bottom of a ravine. Redmond, however, had assessed their situation quickly and knew what to do. Although the mortars hadn't followed them down the ravine, he knew it would only be a short time before VC or NVA troops stormed down upon them. He popped the .30 cal off its mount and grabbed as many ammo bandoliers as he could carry. He yelled for Montrell and Flash to grab their weapons and as much ammo as well. Montrell complied immediately, but Redmond had to grab Flash and yell in his face to snap him out of his stupor, which he did.

"Follow me and don't stop, whatever happens," ordered Redmond. They scrambled as fast as they could through the thick jungle, stumbling, and grunting in pain from cuts by the sharp vegetation. Redmond knew they had to get as much distance between them and the truck as they could in a short amount of time. He was hoping they'd soon find a cave, or even an abandoned VC bunker, where they could take cover. He didn't figure Montrell, and especially Flash, could last too long at the pace they were going, but if they stopped before they found a hide, they'd be found and killed, or tortured and then killed.

*   *   *

Soon after entering the river, the cab of the truck filled with rushing water. Crucianelli and Prentice climbed out the windows and got into the back with Hardy. Hardy was petrified, still gripping the side of the bed with all his strength. Cru and Prentice had their M-16s and Cru noticed Hardy's was nowhere to be seen. They were travelling down the river at a pretty good clip, so the chance of any attackers on foot keeping up with them was remote. But sooner or later the vehicle would get hung up on rocks, or branches, or mired in mud. Prentice started opening the ammo boxes and filling his fatigue pockets with ammo clips; Crucianelli soon did the same.

"It may be better if we jump out We're pretty conspicuous in this truck," Prentice yelled. "We might have to wait for an open stretch to see what's ahead. Are you gonna be okay, Hardy?"

Hardy looked at him with wild eyes, "Yeah, yeah I'm okay. What the fuck we gonna do?"

"We'll be all right!" Prentice shouted. "Just keep cool." He really didn't believe it. He wasn't in any kind of physical shape for a running battle in unknown territory with the VC and he knew it. Neither was Hardy for that matter. Cru was the only one of them who might be in physical condition to get through the kind of ordeal they might be facing, and even he would need a lot of luck to survive.

Goddamn that fucking Richards, Prentice thought. *We're all gonna be killed so he can get richer. I should have fragged that bastard back at Phu Cat.*

* * *

Redmond, Montrell, and Flash were still running. Redmond, in the lead, spotted a deep depression in an embankment just up ahead and to the left. He signaled the men and they followed, slowing so they could crouch down and crowd into the semi-shelter of the hollow, which had a roof of fallen branches and deadfall. They were breathing so hard they feared anyone following would hear, so they covered their mouths until they settled down.

"Well we're fucked now," Flash said.

Montrell looked at Redmond for a sign that the situation might not be as hopeless as it seemed. Redmond glanced back, but his look provided no relief.

"Any ideas?" Montrell asked, somewhat pleadingly.

Redmond paused, and then said, "It seems there aren't any foot soldiers after us, or they'd have caught up by now. Could have been some local VC trying to make a quick score, or the local White Mice for that matter. Who the fuck knows? We can wait 'til night, then follow the river downstream and try and hook up with Crucianelli and the others, if they haven't been killed by then."

"What if they have?" said Flash. "Maybe we should walk the road and take a chance we might run into some grunts. I don't wanna spend any goddamn night out here with the fuckin' VC!"

"Who the fuck does?" Redmond replied. "We ain't back in Bin Dinh. We can't just hitch a ride back to the base. There have been no other Americans on this road all day, and there ain't much chance of us runnin' into any the rest of the day. We go boppin' down that road like we're on base walkin' to the club, we'll get our asses blown off in a fucking minute! We have to be cool and hope they send a chopper to look for us when we don't reach the next check point at Le Thanh."

"Fuck, that might not happen for two or three days, if at all!" Flash responded. "What do you think, Montrell?" Flash was hoping Montrell would back him and maybe Redmond would concede to taking the easy way on the road.

Mired in his own thoughts, Montrell was only half listening. *What the fuck did I get myself into?* he thought. *That fucking Richards — that bastard got me into this mess, and I may not get out of it.* He felt like a damn fool. Now he fully understood what Richards really was . . . a ruthless criminal who would step over or on top of anybody to achieve his goals.

"Probably best follow the river," Montrell muttered. "We should at least try and find out what happened to Cru and the others."

"That's what we're gonna do," replied Redmond, glaring at Flash. "And I ain't gonna listen to any bitchin' and whinin'. Anyone don't like the view, they can go their own way."

∗   ∗   ∗

Several miles downstream, the pick-up carrying Crucianelli, Prentice, and Hardy hit a tree branch hanging from the bank, and got hung up. No longer moving with the current, the flowing water started breaching the box of the pick-up, forcing the men to stand up with whatever equipment they could hold.

"This is gonna go under. We're gonna have to get off," Crucianelli yelled. One by one, they climbed onto the deadfall and crawled onto the bank.

Prentice yelled at Hardy, "Where the fuck is your weapon?" He had given him Childs' M-16 to replace the one he lost floating downstream earlier.

"I couldn't hang onto the goddam weapon and the fuckin' tree at the same time. It fell off." Hardy yelled back.

"Fucking great," Crucianelli exclaimed.

Calmer now, Prentice spoke up, "Okay, let's get somewhere where we can dry off, and get an idea what the fuck we're gonna do." Prentice was thinking about the irony of the situation. The Kansas NCO had set them up for a suicide mission, to deflect heat off the real mission. He figured they'd get killed and no one would come back and tell any stories. As inept as this bunch was, the Kansas NCO probably could have put them out in the bush, two miles from the Phu Cat Airbase and the same thing would have happened. But as they were walking through the thick, hilly terrain, for the first time in many years, Prentice felt inspired. He started thinking how he was being challenged for the first time in a long time. Maybe it was damn time he started acting like a senior NCO in the United States military, instead of a bumbling, drunken slacker, biding his time to the end of his hitch. Maybe he could save himself after all.

Chapter 19

"They wrote in the old days that it is sweet and fitting to die for one's country. But in modern war, there is nothing sweet nor fitting in your dying. You will die like a dog for no good reason."

Hemmingway

Redmond, Montrell, and Flash spent most of the rest of the day working down river. The going was slow; the brush was thick and required a macheté that they didn't have to cut through it. As a result, each step met with resistance, from thorn branches that tore at their clothing and flesh. Leeches, ticks, ants, and spiders crawled on them, sucking and biting; tormenting them mercilessly. Montrell had a canteen, which they filled frequently in the river, and drained just as frequently struggling through the steamy jungle. Every twenty minutes or so, Flash stopped to rest. Redmond was impatient to keep moving, but it was clear Montrell and particularly Flash could not keep the pace they needed in order to have any chance at catching up with Cru and the others. Darkness was setting in, and they had to find another shelter. No doubt it would rain all night, and to endure that without shelter would mean a sleepless miserable night, jeopardizing their ability to move on in the morning.

"Hold up," Redmond whispered. Up ahead, and to the left there appeared to be a bunker. They all froze, their eyes riveted on the structure, which based upon the lack of vegetation around the entrance, appeared to be intact and possibly active. After waiting a bit, Redmond moved toward the entrance, eyes focused, weapon ready. Flash and Montrell followed as quietly as they could.

Once near the entrance they could hear activity inside. Flash and Montrell wanted to run, but Redmond signaled for them to remain still and keep quiet. He slowly inched into the entrance, and then rushed in before Flash and Montrell could even react. There was a commotion in the bunker, Vietnamese voices; female, crying out in terror. Soon, all was silent. Montrell and Flash, looking at each other in terror, started backing away just as Redmond reappeared at the entrance. "Get in, follow me," he ordered. A dead woman was lying just inside the entrance, her throat cut and still gushing blood; she had the bayonet from an AK-47 in her right hand.

"Fuck!" Flash gasped.

"Shut the fuck up!" Redmond ordered. Near the dead woman, who looked to be in her thirties, was a young Vietnamese girl, possibly sixteen or seventeen, squatting, and in a state of shock.

The bunker was small, divided into two sections. It had another entrance on the opposite side, which was secured from the inside. There was medicine and bandages on crude shelving, along with two cots, which were caked with dried blood. Flies covered the blood and the smell of death permeated the compound. Flash ordered the Vietnamese girl to stand, but she remained squatting, her eyes full of terror.

Redmond spoke up, "Leave her be, the mama san I killed was probably her mother."

"Damn," Montrell whispered.

"She came at me with that bayonet. Didn't leave me any choice," Redmond went on. "It was her or me. She knew how to handle that bayonet. Went at my abdomen with it. I barely was able to dodge the bitch. Keep your eye on this one, she'll probably try to get even when she comes around."

"Maybe we should just kill her, too," Flash suggested.

"No, Goddamit!" Montrell yelled. "We ain't killin' anybody. You fucking kill her and I'll shoot you myself, you bastard!" Montrell glared at Flash, then at Redmond. It was apparent by the look on Redmond's face that he too entertained the idea of killing the young girl. They were in no position to take hostages, and if they left her she would put any VC or NVA right on their trail. The decision to keep her alive was tentative and temporary at best.

* * *

Downstream things were going somewhat better. Prentice quickly realized that Hardy was going to be a problem. He just didn't have the training, or temperament for the situation they were in.

"Hardy, you stay between me and Cru," Prentice told him. "I want you to keep your eyes alert for anything up ahead that looks out of place." Prentice knew that Hardy was a photo bug. No matter what the situation, he was snapping pictures every which way he could. He would use Hardy's eye for detail to possibly identify variances in the jungle, which could either possibly mean shelter, or trouble in the form of an ambush.

Hardy seemed happy with this assignment. "Okay, Sarge, I'll keep my eyes open," he replied somewhat enthusiastically.

Crucianelli caught on to Prentice's reasoning, and thought it a good idea and excellent way to keep Hardy alert and involved. *We may not get out of this goddamn mess, but we ain't gonna roll over and die either,* Cru thought.

They kept moving downstream, moving away from the ambush site, and hopefully closer to an area occupied by friendly forces. Cru had his doubts, however, as the maps he studied prior to departure showed no permanent U.S. or ARVN posts in this region. They might stumble upon a unit conducting operations, which could be good or bad. They would have to take care not to get killed by "friendly fire," as any unit on patrol would likely shoot first and ask questions later. True to his word, Hardy alerted them to suspicious objects along the way. He forewarned them of several abandoned bunkers that had been overgrown with vegetation, and even spotted a downed chopper hung up in the triple canopy treetops and was dangling by one of the rotor blades.

As evening approached, Hardy spotted an abandoned bunker. They decided to spend the night there and resume their trek in the morning.

"We'll have to come up with a plan, in case we don't run into any friendlies tomorrow," Cru stated.

Prentice agreed, "Yeah, we'll have to come up with something."

✳ ✳ ✳

The next morning Redmond, Flash, Montrell, and their Vietnamese hostage left the bunker and headed downstream. Depressed about their situation and the death of Salas, Montrell was having uneasy thoughts. He wished he were with Cru, Hardy, and Vodka Charley instead of these two guys. He always felt both Redmond and Flash had the capability of becoming cold-blooded killers, and he feared not only for the young Vietnamese girl but for his own life as well. They might decide to knock

Campolo

off the girl for expedience sake. And having done that, they might be compelled to kill him, too, to avoid any possible repercussions later on.

The girl was tethered to Redmond with a short rope and initially she resisted, pulling and pushing Redmond. Redmond put up with it at first, and then finally backhanded her so hard she collapsed in semi-consciousness. When she got up he snarled at her, "Keep it up, bitch, and I'll beat your ass to death right here in the fucking jungle!"

"Yeah, you got it, Chief, let's waste the little bitch right now," Flash pitched in. Montrell looked on apprehensively. What would he do, or could he do for that matter, if these two decided to kill her?

Redmond glared at Montrell and resumed the trek downstream, dragging the girl along as he went. He was as angry with himself as he was with the young girl. He had lost his temper and let things get out of hand. He didn't want to kill the girl, or even harm her for that matter. But he couldn't take a chance on letting his guard down and having her stick a knife between his ribs, or possibly breaking free and getting away. He also had to make sure Flash knew he was in control, or Flash may take it upon himself to unburden them of the girl.

He didn't want Montrell to think he was a ruthless killer, like half the other assholes in this fucked-up war, but someone had to assume leadership or their already slim chances of getting out of this were nil. He felt he was the only one qualified to do that. Montrell was smart, but didn't have the temperament to assume the role. Flash wasn't smart enough, and neither one of them was in good enough physical condition to fulfill the job.

Redmond felt bad about Salas also. They had butted heads on occasion, but he always thought Salas was a solid dude and a straight shooter. He silently wished it had been Flash who had gotten killed. Flash was a loose cannon; he took a lot of drugs, and indulged himself in any way he could. Big, strong, drugged and unpredictable; Flash was dangerous.

* * *

Cru and Prentice, meanwhile had worked out a plan. They felt the road probably paralleled the river all the way down to the village of Plei Me, which was considerably south of their destination of Le Thanh, but a reasonable destination for them to shoot for, since it had the best chance of containing any friendlies. They would attempt to access the road every

88

hour on the hour, in order to look for any sign of friendly or unfriendly travelers. Prentice gave Hardy his .38 revolver.

"Don't take it out unless you have to; keep the leather tied across the grip while it's holstered, so it won't fall out while you're humpin' through the bush," Prentice instructed Hardy. "And don't lose it, goddamit!"

Then he added, "You stay between me and Cru; Cru will bring up the rear."

Cru wished they had 12-gauge shotguns instead of the M-16s. In the kind of action they were likely to get into a 12-gauge with double aught would do a lot more good than an M-16. Blow away anything within thirty yards, and clear a path for 'em to boot. Well the M-16 would have to make do but at least, Cru thought, he had enough ammo for whatever they may run into. That is what he thought.

Chapter 20

"Fear cannot be without some hope, nor hope without some fear."

Baruch Spinoza

The river that the men were following flowed between the villages of Le Thanh and Plei Me. But it wasn't close enough to either so as to be visible from either the road or the villages; as a matter of fact, it was quite far. The river itself flowed on into Cambodia until it merged with the Mekong, which eventually blended into the fertile delta in the very southern part of Vietnam. All along the river, local villagers trapped fish in nets, washed their clothes, and used the waterway to move back and forth as needed. The VC and NVA scoured the river frequently for American and ARVN patrols, which crossed it regularly in the course of their operations. Since the river frequently ran shallow, the American brown water navy avoided it, as it would not readily accommodate their large powered craft. Americans traveling downstream in the adjacent jungle were rare.

"What the fuck happened to our two-way radios?" Redmond asked to no one in particular. It occurred to him that they had packed two, one in each vehicle, in the event they got separated or just needed to communicate to each other. They only had a working range of about four miles, but it would have been nice to have them.

"Fuck, yeah!" Flash exclaimed, while reaching into the rucksack he was toting. Before they abandoned the vehicle Redmond had hurriedly stuffed the sack with extra ammo clips and a first aid kit. Noticing the two-way radio lying on the floorboard, Flash grabbed it and stuffed it in as they got out.

He pulled the radio out of the rucksack and before Redmond could stop him, he keyed it. Immediately a hail of small arms fire cut through them like a sharpened scythe hacking through wheat. Flash and the girl were both dead before they hit the ground.

Huynh and three others had been trailing the Americans since they left the bunker with the makeshift hospital. The Vietnamese woman who had been killed was his mother, the abducted girl his younger sister. He was seething in anger and grief as they followed the signs of the fleeing Americans. His mother had been the survivor of countless helicopter and B-52 raids. She had nursed many wounded patriots back to health, all the while raising her family in the austere surroundings of poverty and war. Both of his brothers had been lost to the war, one killed by an ARVN patrol, the other captured by Americans and turned over to the ARVN. He had not been heard from since.

Huynh's sister, Bin, was learning how to heal from her mother, who in turn had been taught by her mother, who had treated wounds of Japanese and then French invaders. The animosity Huynh felt for the Americans was almost as high as the animosity he felt for the corrupt ARVN and White Mice, who constantly bullied the local Vietnamese and cheated them out of what meager provisions they had.

In Huynh's youth he had been taught that America was the home of the free and the brave. When they first came to Vietnam, the people rejoiced. They believed the Americans would help them achieve independence from France, and their corrupt Vietnamese lackeys. But instead of imparting freedom and hope, the Americans supported the French bastards, who along with their Moroccan soldiers slaughtered and tortured thousands of Vietnamese to death. Huynh was out for revenge.

When Huynh and his party had found the abandoned truck they took a radio that the men had left behind. They monitored traffic on the radio in hopes of catching to the Americans. Close behind the Americans when Flash keyed the radio, they opened fire to prevent further communication going out.

* * *

"You hear anything?' Prentice asked Crucianelli and Hardy. Though the jungle was thick and steaming and the river nearby, Prentice had faintly heard what he thought to be gunfire.

"I can't hear shit, anyway," Crucianelli replied. During his second month at Phu Cat, an incoming 122 rocket had exploded near him, killing one of his good friends along with four others, wounding over a dozen, and wrecking his hearing. Crucianelli had been in a state of shock for several days. Eventually the hearing in his left ear pretty much returned. However, he still had some problems with the right ear.

"How bout you, Hardy?" Prentice asked.

"I didn't hear nuthin' either," he said. "You gotta bottle of vodka we don't know about, Charley?" They all laughed.

"No, wish I did, though," Prentice remarked. Then he shrugged, "Probably nuthin'."

"Well, let's keep movin'," Cru advised. "It's about time for someone to crawl up to the road and take a look around. You guys sit tight, I'll be back soon as I can." That was all right with Hardy who was having a difficult time keeping up.

Back at Phu Cat, he mostly handled the paperwork involved in the base supply function. He usually bribed his way out of perimeter guard and seldom pulled any other hard labor details of any kind. He wondered how Prentice could hold up so well. Although only in his late thirties, Prentice was dissipated from years of drinking and stress. Judging by the looks of him, he must have been pretty physically fit at one time. He was lean, and his body was taut and muscled, despite the constant abuse he piled onto it. *Well,* Hardy thought, *good genes, I guess.*

Before Hardy could get comfortable, Crucianelli jumped into the small hide they were in. He was breathing hard. "VC!" he panted. "Three of 'em up on the road, about two miles behind us."

"Were you seen?" Prentice asked, alarmed.

"No . . . .no, I don't think so. But they were heading this way. It looked like they might have had prisoners, I couldn't make them out very well, but it looked like two with their hands behind their backs, like maybe they were tied or something."

"Did it look like Montrell, or Salas, or the others?" Hardy asked.

"I couldn't see that clearly, but I think there were only two of 'em," Cru responded.

* * *

When Redmond, Flash, Montrell, and the girl were attacked, they had actually gotten within two miles from Cru, Prentice, and Hardy's position. Sharp woodsman that he was, Redmond's path was a short cut, walking due south, as opposed to following the winding river. When Flash keyed the radio, the VC immediately picked up their signal, and from experience knew exactly where their enemy was. Before Huynh could voice a protest the other two had cut loose with their AK-47s. When Huynh and his party reached the Americans, they jumped Redmond and Montrell.

After the two Americans were bound, Huynh saw the body of his sister and let out a loud shriek. Furious in his grief, he beat both the Americans with the butt of his weapon, knocking them semi-conscious. He then screamed at his men, cursing them for being so careless as to kill his last remaining relative.

"Let's kill these two squashed penises," one of Huynh's men shouted.

"No!" Huynh said. "These bastards are going to take a very long time to die. We'll get them back to the cadre who will squeeze information out of them, and then I will get my turn."

Still in shock, Redmond's and Montrell's hands were bound behind their backs with lengths of rope. They were then pushed up the hill until they came to the road, where they stumbled and fell onto their faces. The VC kicked and screamed at them until they managed to get back on their feet. They then were tethered together and pulled along the road, heading in the same direction they originally were going. Redmond's head hurt badly, and blood was trickling down his ear and neck, which was soon covered with flies. Montrell fared no better, stumbling along in pain, feeling the need to stop and vomit. The group pushed on in the steaming heat until Montrell could walk no further. He stumbled and fell. No amount of kicking or screaming could get him up.

"You want to keep this piece of dog shit, you carry him," one of the VC said to Huynh. "Otherwise we cut his dick off, shove it down his throat and push him down the hill where the tigers and boar can fight over his carcass."

This enraged Huynh. "You kill him you bastard, and you join him!" he promised. "These pigs killed my mother and my sister and they will suffer greatly before they enter the next world." The tone of his voice, and look in his eyes convinced the other two to drop it.

"Ok, but we won't make camp for days dragging these two oxen. They might even die before we make camp."

"Then they fucking die", Huynh replied, "but their deaths will not come easy."

Chapter 21

"And what does anyone know about traitors, or why Judas did what he did?"

Jean Rhys

Back at Phu Cat Master Sergeant Howard McKay had been monitoring the progress of the Cambodia Operation. He and Denton were going over the latest reports. "Looks like the pickup's been made, the trucks are heading to the load point, should be here by tomorrow," Denton remarked.

"Yeah, not a hitch so far," replied McKay. "And it looks like our little problem with the other group may already have been taken care of."

"If they haven't checked in at Le Thanh by now, they're not likely going to," Denton cheerfully added. "But if they do happen to make it that far, we have assets in place to make sure things we'll be taken care of."

"Is our crew ready to handle the incoming shipment tomorrow?" McKay quizzed Denton. "Do they have all the paperwork they need?" This was a concern. Cloaking a large shipment of heroin was a delicate affair. The illicit traffic of Southeast Asian heroin back to the States had gotten so out of hand; the U.S. government was attempting several new strategies in an effort to thwart the process. One of these included the use of drug sniffing dogs trained at Lackland Air Force Base in San Antonio, Texas. Fortunately for McKay, he had an associate at Lackland who just happened to be on TDY, temporary duty assignment, at Phu Cat. That associate was a fellow master sergeant, working for the canine squad in base security.

"I brought my own dogs this trip," Master Sergeant Willford Tulley happily explained to McKay. "They couldn't smell a hundred pounds of smack if you packed it in hamburger." His associates laughed.

"Good, that's great Tulley," said McKay. "I knew I could count on you. The shipment is going to be on a C-130, aircraft number C37504. The aircraft will have some other goods coming back along with our shipment . . . as well as some two dozen body bags. Those body bags will be ours. After Tulley's dogs go through, our men unload the body bags and take them to the morgue where they will be validated. Our man at the morgue will take care of those bags, making sure no one else gets a look at them; and tag them with the appropriate paperwork to move them on to Cam Rahn Bay, then on to the States. Denton will bird-dog the shipment clear through Cam Rahn. I don't want to lose this bird, which is in our hand right now. If we all take care of our end, nothing will happen."

Branch McNeil spoke up, "What about Prentice and the others? What if they do make it back?" McNeil had been in the air force seven years and before that the army and he had served two tours in 'Nam.

"If they make it back and start talking we'll all be in a world of shit," McKay replied. "Our plan to take them out before they get to Le Thanh is the best scenario. If they do make it to Le Thanh, as you said, our assets there take over. If they should get past them, we have a situation. Now, we need to go give Richards our report."

*   *   *

Prentice, Crucianelli, and Hardy had been watching the VC approaching. Although they couldn't yet see their features, it was clear to the three the prisoners were American; they were much bigger than their captors.

When the group came within recognition range, Prentice said, "It's Redmond and Montrell." Hardy had a difficult time maintaining his composure. He and Montrell were best buds in the 'Nam.

"Let's get 'em the fuck away from those bastards!" he whispered harshly to the others.

"Just be cool, Hardy, we have to be careful. We shoot these guys up on the road, and a hundred more VC will pop up in a few minutes," Crucianelli told him.

"He's right", Prentice agreed. "We can trail them until we're sure they're no other VC nearby, then we can sneak behind them with our K-bars and take care of them."

"What fucking K-bars?" Hardy asked. The U.S. Air Force officer survival kit included a knife called a K-bar, the choice for hand-to-hand fighting by the U.S. Marines. As a result, there were usually plenty around, to be scarfed up by enlisted personnel who wanted a souvenir, or something to sell or trade. Others, like Crucianelli and Redmond who spent time out on the road, came to depend on them as a last line of defense.

"Just because you don't think to bring nothing but your fat ass out in the bush, don't mean we are just as fucking stupid," Crucianelli snapped.

"No one told me we were gonna be fighting hand-to-hand, like a bunch of fucking grunts," Hardy whined. Prentice saw where this was going and cut it off.

"Okay, let's keep our cool. Cru and I will handle the knives, you will put up a diversion," he said to Hardy.

"What kind of fucking diversion? You gonna stake me out like a goat?" Hardy whined.

"Not a bad idea," remarked Crucianelli.

* * *

Redmond, meanwhile, had been weighing their options. With his hands tied as they were, even a quick dash in the bush would leave him helpless. He had to free his hands somehow. Then he'd have a chance.

Montrell was despondent. He thought about his mother, and how hard she would take the news that he had been killed. Widowed for some time, Doug and his older sister was all the family she had left. Doug had convinced her that his air force duty in base supply, although not completely safe, was about as safe as any duty you could get in Vietnam. She accepted that, with trepidation, and now Doug felt he betrayed her. His involvement with the Kansas NCO had not only put his air force career and future in jeopardy, but now his life as well. The two were dragged and pushed along for about two miles before their captors abruptly halted, shouting and pointing down the road.

About 100 yards down the road, Hardy had emerged from the jungle with his hands in the air. He was repeatedly shouting for the VC not to shoot him. After a short pause, the VC caught up to him and forced him on the ground, holding his neck and arm down with their sandaled feet. As he coughed and sputtered the VC carefully scanned the area for others.

"I surrender, I surrender," Hardy kept yelling. One of the VC apparently knew some English as he translated for the others. Huynh barked at him in Vietnamese to get his hands behind his back, while forcing him to do so. Hardy struggled and resisted prompting a good kicking from Huynh. When he continued resisting, the other three VC joined in.

With their backs turned, and engrossed in issuing Hardy a beating, they never saw Prentice and Crucianelli come up behind them. Prentice knifed one under the armpit and another through the neck before the other two had a chance to react. As soon as they brought their weapons up Cru, using the butt of the knife as a club, crushed the skull of one and badly wounded the other. Seamlessly, Prentice inserted his K-bar into the throat of each, then went back and did the same to the first two.

Hardy, still stunned by the beating he had taken, wretched and groaned. Cru cut his bindings and gave him one of the VC's canteens. Prentice did the same for Redmond. The four of them sat there, drinking water and taking stock of their situation before speaking.

"Where's Flash?" Crucianelli asked. Redmond told him what had happened to Flash. He and Prentice looked down, saddened by the news.

"We better look over Hardy and see if he's okay," Prentice directed to Crucianelli.

"I'm okay," Hardy groaned.

"Can you take a look at him, Red?" Prentice asked, remembering that Redmond was a healer back on his reservation.

"Just lay still," Redmond instructed Hardy. With his hand he probed Hardy's back and abdomen, already turning black and blue from the beating. When he finished Redmond instructed Hardy to rest for a while. Redmond then motioned Cru and Prentice off to the side.

"He's bruised but not too badly," he told them.

"You sure?" Crucianelli asked.

"He'll stiffen up if we don't start moving, so we better get going," Red replied.

"Can he travel?" wondered Prentice doubtfully.

"Be the best thing for him right now," Redmond stated.

"Well, let's get these goddamn gooks off the road and let's get the fuck out of here before more show up," Crucianelli said in frustration. They dragged the bodies down the embankment, cleaned up as much of the blood as possible, got Hardy on his feet, and headed down the road. They had about three hours of daylight left.

Chapter 22

"It is a characteristic of wisdom not to do desperate things."

Thoreau

After only two hours, Hardy had slowed to a near crawl. Crucianelli and Prentice were concerned. At least when Becker and Childs were shot up they had motor transport to haul them with. No way could they carry Hardy any great distance and it was apparent he wouldn't be traveling on his own much further.

"We'd better find a hide for the night," Redmond stated.

"Yeah, we'll get into some chow and rest for the night. We can also kick around some ideas for tomorrow," Prentice offered, but he was not hopeful. With all of them banged up somewhat, deep in enemy territory, few provisions and no backup of any kind, things looked bleak. Moreover the fact that no matter what happened to them, they still had to deal with Richards if they made it out nagged at him.

Richards had made it clear this crew was expendable; clear enough for Prentice to almost lose hope. His plan, if it worked, only dealt with getting clear and free of the Kansas NCO. His immediate problem was to get back alive.

Redmond went ahead to scout, while Crucianelli, Prentice, and Montrell hobbled along with Hardy. Redmond was looking for something far enough off the road to be inconspicuous, yet not too far, as they would probably have to carry Hardy most of the way down to it. He was also scanning the area for any sights or sounds of any human activity in the area. If they bumped into any Vietnamese it would be trouble, as any out here would more than likely be VC or VC sympathizers. Best to avoid them altogether, he felt.

The best he could hope for would be to run into an American patrol. He knew the 1st Cav operated in the area, probably some Special Forces as well. He was about a quarter of a mile ahead of the others when he heard shooting behind him. He jumped into the bush and spun around to see what the hell was going on. He heard what he thought to be unfamiliar American voices yelling. He crept through the jungle and peered over a small berm.

There, along with Cru, Prentice, Montrell and Hardy were two Americans. They wore jungle fatigues with no insignias or identification of any kind. They also carried short automatic burp type weapons favored by the Special Forces. He could see the relief on the faces of Prentice and Crucianelli, who had lowered their weapons upon recognizing them as friendlies. Montrell used the pause to tend to Hardy.

Redmond was about to get up and join them when one of the Special Forces men suddenly lowered his weapon and fired a burst into Hardy, killing him instantly. Screaming, Prentice and Crucianelli turned and lunged at the killer but it was too late, the other man with him hit Crucianelli squarely between the eyes with the butt of his gun, sending him down like a bag of bricks. Prentice was immediately tackled and taken down hard as well. Montrell just sat there stunned.

"Damn!" Redmond thought. "What the fuck!"

The two Special Forces operatives, if that's really what they were, started to lower their weapons on Prentice and Crucianelli. Quickly Redmond put the M-16 on full auto, trained it on the two, and swept them repeatedly, emptying his clip before they could get off another shot. They slumped down on top of Prentice, dead before they hit the ground.

When Redmond arrived on the scene, Montrell was sobbing uncontrollably. Crucianelli was holding his face with both hands, moaning softly. Prentice had not regained himself. Redmond scanned the area, making sure there were no others to back up these two murderers.

Satisfied they were alone; he put his weapon down and gently rolled Prentice on his back. Prentice's eyes opened slightly and his breathing became regular. Redmond splashed some water from his canteen on Prentice's face and massaged it in a little. He could see no other signs of injury. He then turned to Crucianelli who had one eye completely shut and some bleeding from the bridge of his nose. He gently washed Cru's face with water, although Cru resisted and cried in pain at the touch.

"I'll be okay, just give me some time to shake off the cobwebs," he moaned.

Montrell, though not physically injured, was in the worst condition of the three. His best friend lay dead in his hands. Redmond let him be. At this point he knew they were all very much at risk to survive, and he needed time to think.

Those guys didn't just wander out of the bush at random. They were sent to kill them. As these thoughts ran through his mind, Redmond stared at the two dead men. *Nice shooting,* he thought. *Caught both in the chest and torso with multiple rounds.*

He turned each one on their backs and went through their pockets. Their pockets revealed nothing. Each had several extra magazines, and some Military Payment Certificates, U.S. greenbacks, and Vietnamese piasters. Standard fare for Special Ops types, no letters from home, chits from an NCO or officer's club, ration card, or lucky charms. Further inspection revealed a K-bar strapped to each ankle. Neither wore the traditional GI dog tag necklace or anything that would reveal the origin or background of either man.

Prentice had almost completely recovered, and came over to take a look at the two assailants.

"Anything?" he asked Redmond.

"No . . . nothin' at all, no ID, no pictures, documents, tags or anything," Redmond replied. Prentice looked at one of them thoughtfully.

"Help me pull off his shirt," he said.

Redmond looked at Prentice curiously. "No, I'm not fucking drunk," said Prentice. "I think I've seen this guy before and want to verify it."

As soon as they pulled off the man's shirt, Prentice examined his upper arm and found what he was looking for. Inches below the man's shoulder was a tattoo of a white eaglehead with a spiked ball underneath.

"You recognize that tat?" Redmond asked.

"That's the symbol of the CIA," Prentice answered. "I've seen this guy a couple times at Phu Cat. He attended some of Richard's porn shows, and was also involved with some dealings in his operation, the fucking rat."

"Well that confirms it," Redmond added. "We are in big fucking trouble. They won't quit at this. Fuck, we got problems. How's Cru?"

Crucianelli was alert and engrossed in their conversation. "I'm okay, got a big time headache, but I'm okay. What the fuck are we gonna do? I'm guessing these birds came down from Le Thanh. If we show up there, no doubt there will be more goons ready to finish the job. We can't go back to Pleiku; that bastard Pruitt will finish us off there. We can't stay out in the fuckin' boonies. The VC or NVA will be fighting over our carcasses before the week is up. We gotta come up with a plan."

"We will, we will," Prentice said firmly. "We're not gonna lay down and die for these bastards. No doubt they are already spending the money they think they're gonna make off that H . . . but if it's the last thing I ever do, I'll see to it they never see a dime, and they'll do time as well."

Redmond looked at Prentice soberly. Prentice, looking back added, "Yeah, I've been involved and any time they do, I'll do as well. But I don't give a shit. Maybe I'm getting soft, maybe my brain is addled, but the air force has been good to me all these years, and it's time I started bein' good back. It's time I did my duty for the good of the service and my country. Guys like Richards have been fucking the air force, the taxpayer, and honest GIs for too long in this Godforsaken country. If I go down with 'em so be it . . . but I'm gonna stop the bastard."

"We better keep moving in case these assholes had anyone at some kind of base camp waiting for them," Redmond said. "Before I turned back I saw a place that looked like a good stand for the night. Let's get there. If it's okay we'll settle down and come up with some ideas."

"Montrell's gonna have to pull himself together. We can't carry Hardy's body under these circumstances. I'll stay back to bury it best I can. If you guys can take Montrell along with you, I'll catch up," Crucianelli stated.

Prentice thought for a moment. "Don't waste too much time trying to bury Hardy. Take his tags and any other personal affects, so no one else gets them. Better tell him about where we'll be," he directed at Redmond. "We can't afford to spend time lookin' for anybody. Now let's get Montrell and get moving."

Montrell now spoke up, "I'm staying with Hardy until he's buried, won't go until it's done." Prentice gave Montrell a long, irritated look.

Crucianelli interjected, "We ain't got time for this shit. We can't be held up."

"You can leave me, but I ain't leaving till Hardy is in the ground," Montrell replied.

"Whoever stays behind to take care of Hardy will have to hustle their asses to catch up when they're done," Prentice stated, giving Montrell a hard stare.

"Well, let's get it done," Crucianelli said to Montrell.

Redmond told them where about they'd be and he and Prentice started down the road. "When we get settled, we'll have to check all our weapons and ammo," Redmond said. "We don't know how long we're gonna be out here, and we may need to conserve our supplies best we can."

Prentice agreed and added, "We'll have to check our food as well. Bein' close to the river, we don't have to worry about water, but we may need to rustle up some food somehow. Most of our C-rats went down with the truck. I got a couple candy bars and maybe one can of ham and motherfuckers, but that's about it."

The motherfuckers Prentice referred to were the beans that accompanied many of the mystery meats in a variety of K-rations. Much of the food had been canned and in storage since World War II. Although many of the old stocks had been consumed during the Korean War, tons remained from the WWII stockpile and were still a staple in the Vietnam War. Once in a while a bad can was found, and the results could sicken a whole unit, if they didn't smell it first. For the most part the C-rats were still good, and a few even quite tasty. Redmond and many others particularly liked the minced ham and eggs.

The Vietnamese, always on the brink of starvation, relied heavily on these K-rations, which the U.S. dispersed heavily throughout the country. The K-rations and C-rations were a part of every GI's diet in Vietnam, even on the large bases that had regular chow halls on them.

The chow halls often served subpar food, which was not fresh and often tasteless. At least the canned rations had plenty of salt for flavor and many GIs carried their own bottle of hot sauce in their rucksacks or jungle fatigue pockets. The hot sauce often made poor tasting food palatable, and was also handy for making various concoctions of Bloody Marys from the prodigious amount of vodka available most everywhere in the 'Nam.

Cru and Montrell did the best they could with Hardy. A shallow grave, a moment of silence, and they were off following the road about twenty-five minutes behind Redmond and Prentice.

By this time Redmond had found the earlier hide they were looking for, an old Buddhist temple about the size of a large outdoor fireplace back in the States. Its interior was big enough for the four of them and should keep them suitably dry during a rainstorm.

"I'm gonna go see if those two are coming," Redmond stated.

"Okay, I'll be here," Prentice replied.

Redmond made his way back up the road, using a slightly different route. Creating a worn path would signal anyone of their presence. Soon he observed Cru and Montrell heading his way. He sat in the bush, keeping an eye out for any sign of trouble. Then Redmond went out and met them. He led them to the temple where they'd be spending the night.

Prentice had all their provisions laid out on the surface of what appeared to be an altar in the temple. "You guys get out all your stuff and lay it out as well. We need an inventory of our ammo and provisions, so we have an idea of how long we can survive if we have to stay out in the bush for a while," he said.

Montrell looked uncomfortable. "How fucking long might that be?" he asked.

"Long as it takes to come up with a plan, to get our asses back somewhere where we won't get wasted," Redmond responded. "Unless you got a plan hidden up your ass, we have to come up with one."

"Ok men, let's just cool down and deal with the shit we got in front of us," Prentice injected. "Buttin' heads with each other will do no good. We are in a big fuckin' jam, and will need a plan, with fallback options and a lot of luck to get out of it. We each need to concentrate on developing and then executing our end of that plan. Now let's get to it."

They all nodded in agreement and began kicking around ideas and thoughts on the dilemma facing them. After a couple of hours they hadn't come up with any solid plan. Prentice suggested they might need to get a better understanding of the surrounding area. They needed to know what other population centers, large or small, besides LeThanh were in the reachable area. Since LeThanh was their known destination and more likely a trap, they needed to avoid it completely.

"We'll need to know where the vills are, and any other military units, friendly or otherwise," Prentice added.

Redmond stated he thought there was a 1st Cav unit close by, and the 1st Cav was a Class A fighting unit, and very unlikely to be tangled up in Richard's web of graft, corruption and murder.

"How can we find 'em, Red?" Cru asked.

Redmond reached back to some of his earlier learning experiences; the ways of the stealthy hunter he learned in his youth, to find game on the reservation, and the tactical unit training he acquired in his days as a U.S. Marine. "We are going to do some area recon," Redmond told them.

"Hey, I'm an airman working in base supply," Montrell kicked in. "What the fuck do I know about 'area recon'?"

Redmond went on, "It's not tough. Basically we are going to divide a workable area into smaller zones. We will each take a tactical point in that zone and make observations in a given timeframe. Each of us will note any and all movement or activity along with a description of the activity in our segment of the zone, or area. After the timeframe has passed, we should have a good idea of the activity in the zone we are working on. We hook up, go over our observations, and analyze. If we don't like what we've seen . . . we move out and onto another area. If we luck out and find the friendly forces we are looking for, we make contact."

Prentice was proud of Redmond. He applied thought and training to solve a problem. You have a situation; you work towards a solution. You have a mission; you work to achieve the goal until it is accomplished.

"That's a good plan, Red, and we will all do our best to execute it," stated Prentice.

Crucianelli thought so as well, "That makes sense. We can handle that."

Even Montrell looked more hopeful, upon hearing a rational, organized plan to get them out of this mess. "I'll do the best I can," he added with a tone of resolve.

Red went over specifics. "Okay," he said. "We'll take a quadrant about a quarter mile square. We'll each take a corner and observe 360 degrees for two hours. If anyone sees anything, sit tight. If you get in trouble, signal. We'll do our best to get you back."

"Okay, but how do we signal? We fire off a round and half the VC and NVA in II Corps will be down our throats," Cru said.

"Those assholes who tried to kill us had a satchel full of shit stashed out in the bush about fifty yards from their ambush. I found it on the way in and threw it in our rucksack. There are about a dozen smoke grenades, among other things in there. We'll each carry a couple, and signal if we are in trouble. That's only if you are in big trouble!" Redmond emphasized.

Chapter 23

"The Buddhas do but tell the way;
it is for you to swelter at the task."

Prince Siddharta

Redmond and Cru took opposite points of the quadrant. They had estimated the distance from point to point, and selected a good observation point near each corner. Before they moved, they realized they would need another way to communicate, besides smoke flares and radios which could easily be picked up by the enemy.

"We can use the talk of the Ojibwa," Redmond suggested. Back on the reservation, the Ojibwa used the sound of their land, for communicating during times of war, hunting, or reconnaissance type activities. Redmond went on to explain, "When my tribe needs to go unheard, they use the voice of nature." The men looked at him puzzled.

"Can you give us some examples, Red?" Prentice asked.

Redmond thought about it, and then with his tongue made a kind of cracking sound, often heard in Vietnam. The sound was actually from a small tree dwelling lizard, and could be heard throughout the countryside, day and night.

"That's pretty cool, you sound just like one of those damn lizards," Crucianelli said.

"That's the idea," Redmond responded. "You all try it."

One by one Crucianelli, Montrell, and Prentice attempted to duplicate the sound of the little insect-eating lizard that made so much noise. Eventually, they all mastered it well enough to be mistaken for one.

"We sound like a bunch of damn chameleons!" Montrell remarked. They all laughed and relaxed a little.

Prentice spoke up "Okay, now we need to use a system. How bout one chirp there's movement. That will alert each of us that something's goin' on. Two chirps is a friendly . . . three chirps is a bad guy."

"How the fuck we know who's a good guy and who's a bad guy?" Montrell asked, thinking about the two American sons of bitches that killed Hardy.

"Good point," Prentice replied. "We have to assume any Vietnamese out in the bush is a bad guy. Up on the road, you will get mostly poor villagers, but if they're sneakin' through the bush, that's not good. NVA will be wearing their uniforms and should be fairly apparent, on the road or in the bush. Now when it comes to Americans, we have to assume anyone without any insignias, chevrons, or in plain jungle fatigues are more bad guys. Again, the 1st Cav operates around here and we all know what their insignia looks like, right?"

All the men nodded in agreement. They made sure their canteens and clips were full and then moved into their positions.

Crucianelli sat alertly scanning his area, and keeping an eye out on the four corners of the quadrant. He wasn't worried about Redmond. No doubt Redmond could traverse North and South Vietnam and survive, remaining unheard and unseen. His people had been living a lifestyle of such stealth up until only a few generations ago. And they still practiced their skills, although many had succumbed to liquor, tobacco, and drugs; all of which they seemed to take to like a baby to milk. It was a shame how such a noble people could succumb to such garbage, Cru thought.

Prentice was an old trooper, and Crucianelli was just learning that he was tough and also wise. He had succumbed to the vice of alcohol and greed, but here he was out in the bush for many days without a drop, and didn't seem to miss the bottle a bit. He also seemed to be a far better NCO than the drunken slacker they all made jokes about back at Phu Cat. *Transformation,* he thought. When the shit hit the fan, Prentice and Redmond had become invaluable. If someone had told him that a couple of months ago, Crucianelli would have laughed in his face. With Redmond it wasn't so hard to believe, he just needed a challenge but Prentice had done a complete 180.

On the other hand, Crucianelli was concerned about Montrell. He was probably the smartest one of this bunch and he knew it, but Montrell had never been inspired enough to do anything with that great intelligence of his. He hit the bottle pretty hard, and also used some of the myriad of drugs available in the 'Nam. He just kind of floated along, taking things as they came. Things had already gotten pretty rough, and could get rougher before their ordeal ended, whichever way it did end. If they were to have a chance, they would need the strict attention and effort of each of them. These thoughts kept Crucianelli preoccupied until the distinct sound of a chirp echoed in the little valley they were occupying.

Damn, Cru thought. *Where'd that come from?* After scanning the area, he pinpointed the noise as coming from Prentice's corner of the quadrant.

Redmond had heard it also, tracked it to Prentice, and was anxiously awaiting the next chirp sound, which would tell them if the visitors were the good guys or the bad guys.

Montrell heard it as well, and tried to focus his eyes in the direction from where the sound came. He couldn't remember who was where, but was confident that he knew the corner it came from. *I think they're supposed to chirp again,* he thought. Then he went over their discussion and remembered, two chirps is a friendly, and three chirps a bad guy. *Come on two chirps,* he repeated. *C'mon two chirps!*

Prentice had seen the brush moving before he saw the human figures. He followed the movement for about three or four minutes, before two figures briefly walked through a clearing before re-entering the thick jungle. He swallowed a couple times and let out one chirp. The problem was, he knew there were two people walking toward Montrell's position, but he couldn't identify them. The quick glance he had was not enough to reveal them as Vietnamese, Americans, VC, or whatever.

Damn, he thought. *I gotta do something.* He lowered his rifle, double-checked the clip, and moved quickly in the direction of the two intruders. He intercepted what he thought to be their path and stealthily, but quickly, moved toward them.

Before he got too far, Redmond appeared alongside him. "What's up?" he whispered.

"Two people. Didn't get a good enough look to ID them," Prentice whispered.

"Okay," Redmond said. "I know they're going this way, you keep moving up behind them, I'm gonna try and outflank 'em..."

Prentice nodded, and Redmond disappeared into the bush. *Damn, that fuckin' Indian could sneak up on a snake,* he thought.

Crucianelli had also been following the action. From his vantage point he saw Prentice leave his post, and also saw Redmond moving toward Prentice. He determined to hold his post until he got more definitive signals from either of the two. He intended to watch the whole area to make sure no others came sneaking in.

Montrell was still waiting for the other signal as well, but saw none of the activity that was going on. He checked his clip and put the weapon on full auto. He had no idea that two intruders, followed by Prentice with Redmond flanking were rapidly approaching his position.

From the corner of his eye, Montrell saw movement. He instinctively turned toward the movement, preparing to fire. The first figure in view was that of a young Vietnamese male, wearing the traditional black pajamas that adorned most Viet Cong men, and carrying a well-worn AK-47. Without hesitation, Montrell fired half a clip at the man, who screamed in pain and went down. His companion took off through the bush like a scalded cat.

"Hold your fire!" screamed Redmond. "Hold your fire"!

"I got one Red!" Montrell shouted.

"You hit fucking Prentice!" Redmond yelled back.

Montrell froze. *God no,* he thought. *God please no!*

But unfortunately he had shot Prentice, who was trailing the VC by only about fifteen yards. When Montrell shot, Prentice yelped and Redmond, realizing what happened, immediately moved over, where he found Prentice on the ground writhing in pain.

Soon Montrell reached his two companions. He saw the pain Prentice was in and grimaced. One of his rounds had passed through the Viet Cong then hit Prentice in the calf, finally entering the ground a short distance behind him. Prentice's wound, although not life threatening, was painful and bled profusely.

"Damn, I'm sorry Charley!" Montrell started.

"Who the fuck else did you hit?" Redmond asked.

"I hit a fucking VC. There were two of them, and I got one," Montrell replied.

"What about that other one?" Redmond asked. Before Montrell could say another word an AK-47 opened up on their position. Within a split-second an M-16 answered. The withering AK rounds missed all three men, but not by much. They took cover immediately, Redmond dragging Prentice behind some thick cover.

"I got him . . . hold your fire. I'm coming in," Crucianelli shouted from the direction of the shooting.

After the shooting started, Cru had worked his way cautiously toward the area of the quadrant where the shooting originated. Just as he was approaching the area where Montrell, Prentice, and Redmond were positioned he saw the second Viet Cong, who had circled back, preparing to fire on the three. The VC got off a short burst before Crucianelli brought him down with his M-16. He made sure the VC was dead before approaching his companions' position.

"C'mon in," Redmond yelled back.

"Who the fuck was that?" Montrell asked.

"A VC with a damn AK," Cru responded.

Redmond realized what happened. "There were two. Montrell got the one, and this one must have circled back. Prentice took a stray shell in the leg, but he'll be okay."

"Fuckin' hurts like hell, though," Prentice groaned.

Redmond cut away his pant leg and cleaned out the wound. The bleeding clotted on its own so he applied some hydrogen peroxide and a heavy wrap. "What do you want for the pain?" he asked Prentice.

"A bottle of Smirnoff's would be nice, but since we don't have that, how 'bout some of that fuckin' powder Flash had back at Pleiku?" Prentice said.

"We could all use a shot of Smirnoff's right now," Cru laughed. "Did anybody think to take that H off Flash?"

Quietly Redmond pulled a little plastic bag out of one of his pant leg pockets.

"Good deal, good thinking, Red," Crucianelli stated.

"How much do you take?" Prentice asked.

Pot, speed, heroin and all that other crap floating around the last few years were thought of as garbage by Master Sergeant Charles Prentice. Especially after his favorite nephew had died from a drug overdose. He felt anyone who used the stuff was weak, and untrustworthy. It never crossed his mind that his own dependence on alcohol was not much different than someone else's dependence on any of the stuff he deemed as intolerable. He was from a different generation and background than the new recruits coming in over the past couple of years. He didn't understand their music, their drugs, or their way of thinking. Blacks and other minorities were becoming equal, young GIs coming in didn't accept the notion of "Theirs not to reason why, theirs but to do and die."

This new generation questioned everything, the war, the system of rank, everything. Prentice and many of his kind felt threatened by the new thinking, not just going on in new recruits, but all across the United States. Right now he didn't give a flying fuck about any military standards, norms, morals, or any of that shit. He was in fucking pain and wanted it to stop.

"Just rub some on your lips," Redmond offered. "You should start noticing a difference right away. Not too much though; we can't carry you and don't need you to pass out."

"Yeah," Crucianelli remarked. "And we wouldn't want you getting hooked on that shit and stopping at every fuckin' vil to try and make a score."

"No problem with that shit," Prentice replied. "You young fuckers probably got enough to fuck up the whole NVA army, anyway!" All the men chuckled a little.

Then Redmond spoke up, "We better go find this fucker Montrell shot and see if he's still there, or what the fuck."

"Damn, yeah, the little gook might be crawlin, back here looking to get even," Montrell contributed.

"How bad was he hit?" Redmond asked.

"He was hit bad, he might still be alive, but he ain't runnin' no fuckin' marathon or anything," Montrell responded somewhat proudly.

"Let's go find out," Redmond stated.

"I better stay here with Prentice," Crucianelli added. "If that fucker is coming back he ain't in no shape to fight him off."

"Okay, let's go, Montrell," Redmond replied.

Redmond and Montrell stealthily retraced Montrell's path back to where he had shot the VC. There was a pool of blood and a blood trail where the VC had dragged himself away. Redmond signaled Montrell to remain quiet and follow him. After only about ten yards, they came upon the VC, still holding his AK, but barely conscious.

"He's hit in the abdomen and the leg," Redmond said. The abdomen shot was actually just a flesh wound, passing through the lower left side. The leg wound, though, had passed through the muscle in his upper thigh. Although it missed major bones and arteries it would no doubt be creating substantial pain.

"That's gotta hurt," Montrell remarked. Redmond eased the rifle out of the VC's arms and double-checked for any other weapons in his pockets or under his black clothing. He pulled out three banana clips and a dagger-type knife.

"What do we do with him?" Montrell asked.

Redmond eyed the young Vietnamese. He noted the yellowish skin, high cheekbones and slight frame. He couldn't help think about the similarity to his own people, not just in ancestry, but also in circumstance. Indigenous people trying to eject heavily armed foreigners from their native land. The thought saddened him. *Maybe I should be on* his *side,* he thought for a split second.

Forcing himself back to reality, Redmond directed Montrell, "You take the weapons, and I'll carry the gook. Maybe the little fucker will die soon, and we can leave his sorry ass.

Chapter 24

"It is hard to fight an enemy who has outposts in your head."

Sally Kempton

"**W**hy don't we just kill the fucker?" Crucianelli wanted to know.

"We may need him. He probably knows the area, knows where his buddies are, as well as any American forces we need to find. He's useful to us," Montrell replied. He hoped his answer was convincing.

"What makes you think he'll give us any information?" Cru went on.

"He'll fucking talk. He'll fucking talk or we'll release his bladder into the atmosphere," Red told him, glaring at the prone Vietnamese.

"Well, he won't do any good dead, so let's see if we can bring him around," Montrell stated. He finished cutting the pants off the Vietnamese.

"Hey," Crucianelli said. "He's got one good leg, Sergeant Prentice has one good leg, and maybe we can make one good one out of the two."

"Shut the fuck up, Cru. If I want the opinion of a goddamn Eyetalian, I'll kick you in the ass!" Everyone laughed.

"Okay, Charley, don't get in a tizzy, we'll hang onto both your legs."

"Fuckin' A", Prentice responded.

Soon the young VC started groaning. Redmond had put a splint on his leg, and also a poultice from mud and wet vegetation. This mud contained bentonite, a natural occurring mineral found in the soil of the American Midwest and Vietnam, amongst other places. From experience Red knew the natural composition of bentonite drew toxins from wounds and was an ancient healing tool. Red put the same poultice on both sides of Prentice's wound. Prentice was feeling no pain at all, and was higher than a kite.

"Give the gook some H," Redmond told Crucianelli.

"What the fuck for?" Crucianelli protested. "We may need all of that shit for ourselves!"

Redmond looked at him and quietly responded, "If this fucker starts moaning or yelling in his condition, we'll see a hundred of his little buddies in no time at all. We dope him up and gag him. Keep him quiet until we want him to talk."

Crucianelli realized Redmond was right. "Yeah, that makes sense," he replied. "I just gotta think smarter; I'll get my shit together. How long before he can move? We probably shouldn't stay in anyone place too long."

"It won't be too long," Redmond responded. "But he'll have to be carried for the first couple of days. Prentice won't be able to move too fast, either, so we'll just have to bide our time and move along as best we can."

"If he has to be carried, we damn sure can't move too fast," Cru replied. "This would be a damn good time to run into the 1st Cav."

"Yes, it would," Redmond agreed. "Yes, it would."

Crucianelli, Redmond, and Montrell took turns carrying the Vietcong. Someone also had to walk beside Prentice and hold him up as well. After trudging for three hours through the bush, they barely made a mile.

"We'll stop here for a while," Redmond said. After getting Prentice and the VC down, Cru and Montrell all but collapsed. Redmond and Cru looked at each other. Redmond was tired as well. Hacking through the thick jungle, while carrying these two, was exhausting even for him.

"What do you think?" Cru asked him. "Maybe we should go the road?"

Redmond looked at him, half frowning. "I don't know, that could be suicide," he said. "Maybe we should travel at night. There'd be less chance of running into anyone."

Cru protested, "Cut through the jungle at night, carrying these two? I don't see that as much better than what we're doin' now."

Redmond knew he was probably right. Probably end up on the goddamn road, and getting their asses shot off.

"Well, maybe we'll have to take the road. But one of us will have to travel ahead and scout, otherwise it's too dangerous."

"Sounds good to me," Cru replied, relieved.

Listening in on the conversation, Montrell added, "Sounds good to me, too. At this rate we'll be old men before we get out of here."

"You move like an old man already," Redmond jibed.

"Well, at least I'm a live old man, and dammit, wanna stay that way!" Montrell replied.

"We all do, Monty, let's kick it around some more," Red advised.

"My fuckin' head is killin' me!" Prentice complained. "No, my head and my leg are fuckin' killin' me." They had stopped to rest and plot out the rest of the day which would see them on the much easier traveling, but more dangerous road.

The Vietnamese had started moaning a little also.

"I'd better check those wounds," Redmond stated, inspecting Prentice's wound first, followed by the young Vietnamese.

"*Sao, thế là thế nào?*" Redmond, Cru and Prentice jumped when they heard those words. "*Làm sao mà...?, làm thế nào mà...?*" The spoken Vietnamese words were not surprising in themselves, but very surprising since they came not from the young Vietnamese man, but from Montrell.

"*Tôi nhức đầu,*" the young Vietnamese groggily responded.

"He says his head hurts bad, too," Montrell told them.

Prentice, Redmond, and Crucianelli looked at each other incredulously.

"Where the fuck did you learn Vietnamese?" Prentice asked. He would have thought Redmond might have learned some during his training in the Marine Corps, but Montrell? Though a smart young man, nothing in any of their experiences with their friend Douglas Montrell indicated he knew pig Latin, much less Vietnamese.

The three sat there in stunned silence as Montrell and the young Vietnamese continued a short conversation. They could see that although Montrell struggled for some of the words, the two understood each other well enough. After a time, Montrell provided an explanation.

"In my third year in college I was required to take two languages. I was on a scholarship from the VFW relating to my dad's service in World War II. The VFW had some funding from the U.S. government, which required that the students receiving financial aid take some classes which may ultimately benefit the government Vietnamese translators are at a premium, so that's what I took."

"Well, you sure been holdin' that one under your vest," Crucianelli commented.

"If the lifers knew I spoke the language, they'd have me working with the security police patrolling the roads every day, or some other such shit," Montrell responded. "I ain't hankerin' to be no fucking hero, or to get my ass blown off either."

"Goddamn," was all Prentice could say, shaking his head.

"Ask him what's up ahead," Redmond told Montrell.

Montrell spoke to the Vietnamese, who hesitated before answering.

"He says there's a village about five miles ahead on the west side of the road,"

"Is that his village?" Red asked.

Montrell spoke again to the man and he again spoke back. "No, he says his village was destroyed last year by American planes. He lives in the jungle with others of his kind now."

"Family?" Redmond asked.

"He said the rest of his family was killed in the bombing."

"Well, no surprise he don't fuckin' love us," Crucianelli commented.

"Don't care if he loves us or not," Red replied, "Just as long as he gives us straight answers."

"And how will we know that?" Cru asked.

"We'll just have to be careful with what he tells us. First sign he's fuckin' around, we give him a lesson he won't forget," Redmond said.

Montrell, looking at the young Vietnamese quietly remarked, "Think he's already had some of those lessons."

Though it was hot on the road, and the mosquitos tormented them unmercifully, it was still a piece of cake compared to moving through the bush. Redmond and Crucianelli took turns scouting, staying about a quarter mile ahead of the others, and scanning the area alert for any movement or sign of others. Prentice's wound had improved enough for him to hobble along.

The young Vietnamese also proved to be very tough. Redmond had made a walking splint for his legs, and cut him a heavy branch for a crutch. He kept up just fine though it was evident he was still in pain. Montrell spoke to him in Vietnamese as they walked along. The young man seemed to take to Montrell. He described how he had gone to a French Catholic school in his younger days, and learned not only French, but a little English as well. He studied about America, and American history. Like many Vietnamese, he thought the Americans would help them throw off the yoke of French imperialism, and was bitterly disappointed when the Americans supported, then took the same role as their replacements in Vietnam.

Montrell, in turn, told him about his life in the Midwestern part of the United States, and how his father, a B-17 pilot in World War II, had come back disabled. He told them how he, like many young Americans, felt ambivalent about the war, but the pressure to go and serve like their fathers had before them was difficult to resist. He had no quarrel with Ho Chi Minh, and just wanted to finish his tour and go home.

Crucianelli, moving with the group, commented on Montrell and the young VC's discussion, "You find a long lost cousin, Monty?"

Montrell laughed, "No, just talking about the way things are over here. He doesn't seem to like this war any more than we do."

"I don't doubt that at all," Cru replied. "These people've been getting fucked over for a long time. The Chinese, the French, then the Japs, then back to the French, and now us."

Montrell looked at Cru, puzzled.

"Oh, you didn't think I knew all that shit?" Cru chastised.

"Well, I never heard you express any kind of understanding of this place, or even a hint that you gave a shit," Montrell responded.

"What fuckin' good would it do to talk about it?" Cru was getting irritated. "All these fuckin' shithouse lawyers that sit around the barracks drinkin' and smoking dope are always talking, LBJ this and Nixon that. What the fuck good do they do, for themselves, the Vietnamese, or anybody else? These people gonna get fucked over forever, or at least as long as their natural resources hold out."

Montrell half smiled. That was always the problem, wasn't it? Someone had something someone else wanted. You have to fight to protect your resources, fight to protect your way of life . . . fight to survive . . . the eternal song of humanity.

Red appeared trotting back down the road and waved for them to take cover. Crucianelli hustled the VC into the bush, with Prentice and Montrell following. He put the gag, which had been removed earlier back over the VC's mouth.

Red soon appeared and was slightly out of breath. "The vil is just ahead," he said, panting. "Looks to be around thirty people, mostly women, children, and a few older ones. They don't appear to be very well armed, but no doubt will alert the local VC soon as they spot us." He looked at Montrell, "See what else this guy knows about that village."

Montrell thought about the translation then spoke to the Vietnamese. The young injured man spoke back, shaking his head. "He says he doesn't know anything about this village, except they were attacked and almost all killed by the ARVNs last year," Montrell said.

"Then they're VC for sure," Crucianelli remarked. "We better try to go around 'em, probably better to travel at night."

"VC are more active at night," Redmond responded. He continued, "We may have to go way around them, and avoid detection all together."

"Dam, I sure don't feel like whackin' through that jungle anymore. It'll *TYPO* take us about a day to work around that village at the rate we moved last time," Crucianelli stated.

119

Redmond looked at their captive, then at Montrell. "This guy should know a different route around that vil, maybe we should see what he says," Redmond stated.

Prentice looked at the captive with a concerned look. "I don't know, he might lead us into a big fuckin' trap."

Cru took the gag off of the young VC and Montrell offered him some water, which he took. "What if he wants something in return?" Montrell asked.

"Depends on what it is. We can't let him go, at least not for several days. He'll put his other buddies on us for sure," Crucianelli replied.

"We aren't one hundred percent certain he's a VC," Montrell remarked.

"Get the fuck outta here!" Crucianelli protested. "He's walkin' through the fuckin' jungle wearing black pajamas carrying an AK. If it looks like a duck and flies like a duck and quacks like a duck . . . it's a fucking duck, Montrell."

"And what about his buddy, he was locking down on us," Redmond added.

Montrell responded, "We shot his buddy, maybe that's why he was locking down on us."

Prentice interjected, "You're right, Monty, we don't know for sure he's a VC, but the evidence points to it, and we aren't in any position to take a chance. We let him go and he comes back with VC we're screwed. We let him go and he comes back with another weapon, we're screwed. We gotta hang onto him and watch him close, at least 'til we're out of the mess we're in right now. Monty, you seem to connect with the guy. Talk to him; see if you can get an alternate route out of him. We want to keep heading south and southwest until we run into the 1st Cav. He doesn't need to know that, but give him any information he asks for, that won't compromise us. If we hook up with the 1st Cav we can turn him over to them. Just as important, we have to figure out how to deal with Richards and his bunch. We can't go back to Phu Cat, or anywhere we've already been or we're goin'. We can come up with ideas while we're sloggin' through the bush."

Montrell and the VC talked back and forth, as they were moving slowly through the jungle, out of sight and earshot of the village just up ahead. Without giving him too much detail, Montrell told the man how they were under a threat from a group of corrupt Americans. He explained how they were like castaways on the road, with no place they could go to for safety. They weren't out on patrol hunting VC or anything like that they were just trying to find a refuge from their situation.

The young man believed Montrell, as these men didn't look like the usual infantrymen sent to hunt and kill his people. He recognized the uniforms as American air force, and was not used to seeing them out in the bush. He asked about Redmond and Crucianelli. Seeing them in action he suspected they might have been Special Forces of some type. He was somewhat intrigued by Redmond who looked almost more Asian than Caucasian.

Montrell explained that Redmond was an American Indian, and lived on a reservation in the northern part of America. During this conversation Montrell learned the VC was named Ngyuen Than Hoa. He also learned that he was seventeen years old and was from a family of two sisters and two brothers, before they had all been killed.

After several discussions back and forth Hoa looked at Montrell and in Vietnamese told him, "I can lead you to where you want to go."

Chapter 25

"Does the sound of the sea end at the shore, or in the hearts of those who have heard it?"

Gibran

Prentice looked at Montrell, then at Redmond, Crucianelli and then back at Montrell again. "He wants to go where?" he asked, not sure if he had heard right.

Somewhat sheepishly, Montrell replied, "The land of the big BX . . . America. He wants to go to America. He says he knows where the 1st Cav base camp is and will take us there if we promise to get him to America."

"Fuck," was all Prentice could say.

"What makes him think we have the ability to take him to America?" Crucianelli asked.

"He doesn't know any better. He sees the stripes on Prentice, knows he's a higher ranking individual, thinks he can do all kinds of shit, I guess," Montrell replied.

All four gazed at the young Vietnamese, who sat there, stone-faced. Could they trust this guy? What if he just plans on leading them into a trap? His request was preposterous enough to have them all questioning his sincerity and motives. And even if his motives were sincere, how would he react when they told him what he requested was beyond their power. Should they lie to him and go along until he led them to the 1st Cav? Where did the young man acquire such a foolish idea?

Back when Hoa had a home, a village, and a family, life was simple and good. The French had left and the Viet Minh left his village alone for the most part. They came by to shake them down about once a month; the same frequency as did the ARVN soldiers they contested. They were two predatory groups of people, who were fighting over the scraps of the poor, but when the Americans came with their monstrous weapons of war, things deteriorated rapidly. Hoa and his village had never really known true peace.

Before the Americans it was the French, before the French it was the Japanese, before the Japanese, the French again and before them waves of Chinese, Indos, Muir, and others going all the way back to the Mongols, whom the Vietnamese had repelled successfully. Vietnam was a land of beauty and rich natural resources coveted and taken by many, without asking. The shores of the ocean and the brackish inlets teamed with shrimp and other fish. Rubber grew naturally throughout the country, as did bananas, tea, and, of course, rice. However, the past decades had destroyed much of the infrastructure and culture, as the recent conquerors squabbled over the booty.

Hoa had spent part of his youth in Saigon. Hoa's father wanted him to get an education and his cousin who lived in Saigon agreed to take Hoa in while he attended schooling there at the French schools.

His father had hoped Hoa could perhaps become an engineer or even a doctor. "You must carry the family further than it has gone before," he told Hoa.

From his remote village Hoa traveled to Saigon to live with his cousins and get an education. Hoa did receive an education in Saigon, though not the one his father had in mind. Hoa quickly learned the way of success in Saigon came via servitude to the local French and American advisors and military personnel.

Attending scholastic studies ended after only a short time, and soon Hoa had worked his way into a position doing laundry on the sprawling Tan Son Nhut airbase. There he became both envious and hostile to the large, impolite, boisterous Americans. While he was in awe of their horrifying military machines and deep wealth, he noted how they tended to bully the Vietnamese men and abuse and disrespect the Vietnamese women.

Hoa came to despise the Americans, while also envying them. All the big military installations had a base exchange, known as a BX or PX. The Vietnamese who happened to see the facilities were awestruck. Though small, and Spartan by American standards, they were by far larger and more luxurious than anything the Vietnamese had ever encountered. When hearing about life in the United States, the Vietnamese could only imagine a place of such wealth and opulence. Hence, they came to refer to the United States as "the land of the big BX." Hoa was especially impressed by the facility. From his first visit he dreamed of going to America, living in peace, and becoming successful. He would send for his parents and siblings, support them and insure that they were also successful. He would drive a large American car, wear American clothing, listen to American music . . . and would even become a Christian.

Unfortunately in Vietnam dreams were often short-lived, crushed by the reality of war along with death, injury, disease, and poverty.

"Well . . .?" Montrell asked somewhat irritated.

"Well what?" Crucianelli responded.

"What the fuck do I tell him?" Montrell asked.

Prentice, looking down at Hoa expressionless, interjected, "Tell him I'll do it."

Montrell looked at him and replied, "Okay, but when he finds out your bullshittin', I'll let you do the explainin'."

"Just shut the fuck up and tell him, Montrell. This ain't the fucking U.N.," Crucianelli jumped in. "You don't like it, go fuck yourself . . . you wanna live just as much as the rest of us and if telling this little bastard we'll fly him to the moon gets us out of this shithole, then that's what we tell him."

Montrell turned to Crucianelli and without a word leveled him with a kick to the chest.

Surprised, Cru went down like a pole-axed steer. Grimacing and grasping for air, he sputtered, "I'll kill you, you fuckin' bastard."

Redmond, surprised as anybody at Montrell's karate kick, jumped between them to keep Montrell from seriously hurting Crucianelli.

"Get the fuck up and the next one'll be upside your fuckin' head," Montrell raged.

"Okay, Monty, cool down, cool down. I'll do the explainin' when the time comes. Let's not start fighting amongst ourselves, we got enough problems without that stuff, okay?" Prentice interjected.

"Okay by me, but I ain't takin' anymore shit from this asshole," Montrell said.

"I'll kill him," Crucianelli croaked.

"Just cool off, Cru, cool off," Redmond told him. "Prentice's right, we start this shit and we ain't got a chance. We pull together, or we'll all die out here."

Sitting stone-faced, Hoa watched all this with inner amusement. These big round eyes were out of their element and in trouble. He had power over them. The dumb bastards hadn't figured out that he knew enough English to understand the discussion. He knew they'd promise him anything to get out of the trouble they were in, and he also knew they did not have the ability to send him to America. But he would use them, nonetheless. They were as useful to him as he was to them.

The one they called Montrell seemed like a decent man, but Hoa recognized him as not having strong convictions. Although he might sympathize with Hoa, how far he would go to really help him was unknown. He did attack the one they referred to as Cru regarding the deception they intended on him and Hoa took note of that.

These Americans were a funny bunch; torn between the good they wanted to do, and the bad they were actually doing. During his short stint in the French school in Saigon, Hoa had studied both French and American history. He noted that the Americans seemed to stay closer to their roots of supporting liberty and freedom for themselves and others, despite their misplaced allegiance to the French and corrupt Vietnamese government in South Vietnam.

He also learned through GIs and the Vietnamese Liberation Front, which was the political arm of the Viet Cong that the war was very unpopular in America and many Americans wanted it ended. He saw some of that rebellion in Montrell, and guessed that Redmond also did not completely believe in what he was fighting for, although he did his job stoically and efficiently. Prentice, the old man, appeared to be a decent man, who led quietly and thoughtfully. The one they called Cru, however, seemed to be suspicious and abrupt. As his thoughts moved around each of the men he was now with, Hoa was prompted to think about a plan for later. He would have to be careful, especially of Cru the suspicious one, and Redmond ... the hunter.

Before Hoa returned to his village from Saigon, he learned that deception comes in many forms. Hoa had worked in the base laundry at Tan Son Nhut Airbase for several months, gradually working his way up to laundry worker supervisor. He was earning a good living, sending money back to his family and had even met a young girl who he felt might someday make a fine wife, and mother to his children. Although she was not anxious to leave Saigon for life in a peasant village, Hoa felt he would convince her over time.

Things were progressing very well for Hoa until the day he was falsely accused of theft, and summarily released from his position and banned from further work on the base. His immediate supervisor had called him into a small office, where the American enlisted NCO in charge of the laundry was also in attendance. To his surprise, his friend and work associate Ban was there as well.

"Sit down," his supervisor ordered him sharply.

Something was wrong, but Hoa didn't know what. Ban sat with his head down and his eyes focused on the floor.

The mean-looking American NCO appeared angry. "Your little band of thieves has been caught and your scheme has been uncovered," the Vietnamese supervisor told Hoa.

"Scheme?" Hoa asked. "What scheme? What band of thieves?"

"Ban has confessed to the whole thing, you need not proclaim or pretend your innocence. We have been tracking the theft of GI valuables for several weeks. The trail led us straight to the laundry detail. Ban was caught red handed and gave us your name, as well as the others involved," he said.

Hoa turned on Ban who was now fidgeting uncomfortably in his chair. "What did you tell them, what did you do, you lying piece of dung?"

Looking at his supervisor he said, "He is lying! I stole nothing and took part in no such activities."

"Then how do you explain us finding stolen merchandise in your footlocker?" the supervisor asked.

Hoa felt like he had been hit by a ton of stones. For several weeks, Ban had been bringing back merchandise he told Hoa he bought at the BX and had asked Hoa to store it, since he had no more room for it in his footlocker. Hoa thought no further of it until today.

"You bastard!" Hoa yelled, lunging at Ban.

The American NCO grabbed Hoa and slammed him to the ground. Ban was ushered out of the room by the supervisor who then returned.

"Because you had an excellent work record you will not be prosecuted and jailed. You will be fined two months' pay, terminated from your job, and banned from working at any American installation in the future," the supervisor stated.

Hoa was taken to his footlocker, given his clothing and other personal belongings, and escorted to the main gate by military police. Hoa was devastated. He went back to his quarters at his cousin's home, but his cousin's family had already heard the news and had unceremoniously thrown all of Hoa's belongings out onto the road. They told him not to return, and they were going to send news of his disgrace to his family back at their village.

Worse than all other insults, the girl Hoa had hoped to marry and take back to his village, also believed the false accusations. Hoa attempted to visit her home, but her father intercepted him and physically threw him off the premises. Devastated, Hoa had no choice but to return to his village, where he was treated like a criminal and had to live in disgrace in a hut used to house pigs on the edge of the village. Hoa soon turned to life in the jungle, intermittently associating himself with the local VC, who cared nothing about the accusations, be they true or false.

Chapter 26

"Honesty is for the most part less profitable than dishonesty."

Plato

"That way" Hoa said, pointing toward a ravine about a quarter mile ahead of them.

"First sign it's a trap, he dies," Crucianelli grumbled.

"Okay, Cru, let's just go along and give the guy a chance," Prentice replied. "How far did he say he thought it was?"

"About 15 or 20 klicks he thought," Montrell replied.

"We have provisions for about two more days," Redmond offered, "I don't think we can make more than 10 klicks a day in this terrain, so we should start rationing our provisions."

Prentice considered the situation. "No problem with water, with the river next to us, but food and medical supplies may be tight. We'll have to watch it. Keep our eyes open for bananas or other fruits we might be able to eat. A slow moving bush pig or deer wouldn't hurt either.

Crucianelli, feeling better now moving, threw in, "Yeah or if anyone sees a nice steak fry from the club, that would be nice to." They all laughed,

"Yeah and a case of Black Label, warm, of course," Redmond offered.

The little group slogged along most of the day. The wounds Prentice and Hoa suffer were healing well and not slowing them down too much. *Youth and cantankerouness*, Prentice thought.

Despite their hardships, loss of life, and dire predicament Prentice felt better than he had in years. He hadn't had a drink in two weeks and was getting physically hardened by the trip. His spirit lifted as he felt he was finally fulfilling his obligation as a senior NCO, as a leader of men. He thought about how each member of the group brought something needed. Redmond's skills in the bush and instinct were top rate. Crucianelli had an edginess that fired the whole group up a little, keeping them sharp and alert. Montrell's ability to communicate with the Vietnamese, of course, was invaluable. Yeah, they just might make it out of here, but even if they didn't they would go out with honor. They hadn't rolled over and they hadn't let their circumstances defeat them.

Prentice's plan to deal with the Kansas NCO also occupied his thoughts as they slowly moved through the jungle. Prentice knew the weak link in the operation was Master Sergeant Howard McKay, the first shirt of supply back at Phu Cat. McKay was clever and shrewd, but greedy. He had been shipping weapons from the operation back to the states, unbeknownst to Richards, or Prentice. Richards, a very calculating and careful man had taken pains to insure that no one went rogue in his operation. No doubt, he knew, that some of his underlings thought about striking out on their own, or attempting to acquire more than their fair share. So he kept the top chain of command in his operation happy by giving them what he thought was more than adequate compensation for their efforts. Many of them had earned enough to muster out after their tour of duty in Vietnam, and live a very comfortable life. But upon seeing the immense opportunity available, Howard McKay wanted more.

Master Sergeant Howard McKay was the first sergeant of the supply squadron at Phu Cat Air Force Base, Vietnam. A fourteen-year air force veteran, McKay had moved up in the ranks very nicely during his career. He had started out in the Air Police where he distinguished himself during tours in Germany and Osan, Korea. One night at Osan breaking up a bar room brawl, he tore all the ligaments in his right arm. The arm surgically repaired, required a six-month rehab. No longer able to perform his duties in security, he was allowed to retrain and transfer to an administrative position in supply.

Young and ambitious, McKay was disappointed that his career in the Air Police had been derailed. He had hoped he would receive enough training and skills to be able to muster out and get a job with a civilian police force. Now those hopes were dashed, and he found himself an armchair warrior, pushing paper around for the endless flow of materials moving in and out of Keesler Air Force Base in Mississippi. As fate would have it, McKay happened upon fellow Master Sergeant William Richards, who became a close acquaintance and business associate.

Back at Keeler, Richards honed the skills he had acquired from an old WWII vet, Melvin Holden. Holden fought in the Battle of the Bulge and the Unsan in Korea. He was battle hardened and business shrewd. He didn't figure the U.S. government would begrudge a two-war veteran a few perks and benefits. In Richards, Holden found a protégé and a quick study. Richards took care of all the penny ante card games at Keesler, along with the not so penny ante games and crap games as well. Holden got two percent, Richards got one percent.

By the time Vietnam rolled around, Holden had mustered out, but left a very entrepreneurial replacement in William E. Richards. Richards identified men like McKay and Prentice who were smart and seeking opportunity and included them in many of his business operations. He taught them the fine art of the military con, and they all made a tidy little profit out of it. Having been taught by one of the best, Richards knew that the chaos of war provided much opportunity and benefit for those who knew and understood how to obtain it. Admiring their patriotism, their squadron commander at Keeler was happy to forward the three volunteers for duty in Vietnam. But as providence behooves, patriotism had little to do with it.

In March of 1967, McKay, Prentice, and Richards arrived for duty in Vietnam. While Prentice served in Ben Hoa, McKay served in Cam Rahn Bay, and Richards pulled his first tour in Da Nang. All three men had access to hundreds of thousands of dollars' worth of equipment and supplies, and all three men were in a supervisory capacity; and of course all three men worked in concert, developing one of the largest illicit black market operations in Southeast Asia.

With Richards directing, the three established markets for all the goods flowing in from America, along with connections and networks to move the goods as needed. They could move the materials anywhere in South Vietnam, and even into Thailand and the Philippines; anywhere the U.S. had an airfield. Of course, an operation of this scope required many accomplices, and some of those needed to be high up in the chain of command. The Kansas NCO fostered relationships with many people in the process of setting up the core business. Many large army bases received the materials prior to shipment to the air bases, so Richards developed working relationships with many NCOs along the way.

Personnel from the brown water navy, as well as the large naval detachments in Da Nang, Cam Rahn, and other coastal units also fostered mutually beneficial relationships with Richard's operations, as did elements of the U.S. Marines, who were always in need of quick and easy access to a variety of goods. But the single most important player, outside of the U.S. Air Force, was the CIA, which had been involved in all aspects of the Vietnam War even prior to American military involvement.

The CIA conducted business in a clandestine fashion. The operatives working in II Corps were frequently seen in the presence of the Kansas NCO or one of his many associates. Stealth and covert activity were the preferred method of operation between both groups, so it was natural that the two organizations would gravitate towards one another. Mutually beneficial relationships developed as time went on.

Richards' access to men trained to perform difficult and delicate tasks in harsh conditions would become useful in many operations. What this meant was that Prentice, Cru, Red, and Montrell were up against hardened, ruthless killers, among other things.

Chapter 27

"By preservance the snail reached the ark."

Charles Spurgeon

"**H**old up, Hoa." said Prentice. The group had worked their way through endless jungle tangles for most of the day and was played out.

Prentice thought it best to find a place to hold up for the night. If Hoa was right they'd have another two or three days slogging through the current terrain, and Prentice knew they would have to marshal their activities and closely monitor their food supplies in order to accomplish that.

"Red, let's get a look around for a place to hold up for the night. Monty, make sure Hoa thinks we are still on the right path to hook up with the 1st Cav. Cru, why don't we see if there are any edible plants or critters nearby before we lose our light."

After Monty's discussion with Hoa, the other men took hold of their tasks. Redmond found a large depression in the side of a hill that was sheltered from rain and would suit them for a night bivouac. Montrell sat with Hoa and discussed the day's activities, listening for any signs that Hoa thought they might be off track. He found none.

Crucianelli, using the coordinates of the makeshift camp, started walking off measurable segments, while scanning for any available food. They were still close enough to the river to not have to worry about water, but at the rate they were burning up energy food was a concern. Cru found few edible plants or animals, for that matter in his effort but he did come up with a plan.

Back in Wisconsin, Crucianelli learned to fish and hunt at an early age. Teeming with rivers and lakes, it was only a matter of finding out which fish was in season in order to take advantage of the abundant natural resources. Cru and his buddies would go out at night, overturning rocks and logs. Using a flashlight they would find crayfish to use for bait on small and large mouth bass as well as perch. In spring, shoals of smelt inhabited the shores of Lake Michigan, coming close to shore in their annual spawning run. Fisherman with nets of all kinds would catch them by the thousands at night.

Spring, summer, and fall, frogs could be gigged, and fish of many species were caught from lake, river, and stream, and enjoyed fried in the pan, smoked, or thrown in the stew chowder cook pot. In the winter, large holes were chopped through the ice, and northern pike, walleye, and many types of pan fish were caught and enjoyed during the cold months as well. If nothing else, Cru knew how to find fish.

Using Hoa's mesh shirt, Cru and Hoa set up a net in a narrowing of the fast moving stream. Every couple of minutes they pulled it out, and removed the snails, small fish, and amphibians that had become ensnared. Within an hour they had enough of a catch to feed the group for a couple of days. Cru didn't trust Hoa, and Hoa didn't trust Cru. Despite the natural suspicion the two men had for each other, as it turned out they also had much in common. They were both in tune with the ways of the land; fishing, hunting, and farming were in their background and blood.

Hoa instinctively knew what Cru was trying to do in the bustling waters of the stream, and Cru could see that Hoa had learned to gleam the bounty of the waterways. After several hours they worked in tandem and for a short time, both forgot the war, their losses, and the dire outlook they shared. They were just two young men; exploring a stream, taking in the bounty of nature, and enjoying a late evening's catch. To say they bonded would probably be a stretch, but they came to an understanding of each other. They became lost in the endless quest of man, exploiting their environment to sustain themselves and their people. Both came to realize that they were not so different. They were only two people, trying to survive in a world that neither one understood, or had any control over.

As Redmond improved the depression in the side of the hill for their living quarters, events of the past several days, as well as thoughts about their future occupied his mind. The single element that most occupied his mind was the emergence of Prentice as a leader of men. In Redmond's culture, a man like Prentice was invaluable. Through his spirit, the people walked. Redmond sensed the awakening of Prentice's spirit and was himself awakened. No doubt this ability was always in Prentice's spirit, but the challenges they had come up against had brought it to life. Redmond knew the way of the Spirit and the way of man. He also thought of Hoa, Cru, and Montrell these past days. He sensed in Hoa a kindred spirit, a person who had been pushed to the edges of existence, a person who despite circumstance had pushed ahead in his journey, a person who survived.

"This stuff ain't bad," Prentice commented. They had settled into their little fort, built a small fire and cooked up some of the small fish Cru and Hoa had brought in. Prentice went on, "Monty, I think we finally found some duty that Cru can handle."

Laughing, Montrell added, "Damn, straight Sarge. When we get back to Phu Cat get him a transfer to the galley. This sure beats that slop they been servin' over there! We'll get Hoa hired in as his assistant. If Cru don't poison 'em, Hoa can place a sapper charge under their table."

Cru fired back, "Alright, you cheesedicks, don't get too fuckin' excited. I've been cleanin' and cookin' 'fish since I was a runt, but draw the line when it comes to trying to salvage food left over from World War Two."

Smiling, Montrell responded, "Yeah, and you're still a damn runt, Crucianelli!" All the men laughed. At five foot six inches, Cru wasn't much taller than Hoa. He had gotten the short jokes all his life and took them in good humor. Though he and Hoa were close in height, the similarity ended there. Like most Vietnamese, Hoa was slender and lithe. Cru, on the other hand was built like a fireplug. He had a thick torso, wide back and heavily muscled arms, which dealt out punishment to those unfortunate enough to push him too far. Usually good humored, Cru's Italian temper would show itself from time to time.

The men went on with their meal, cutting up a bit and relaxing. Red, Cru, and Montrell took shifts on watch throughout the night. In camp, Prentice noticed the short timer's ribbon on Montrell's fatigue shirt. It was customary for GIs in Vietnam to consume one bottle of Seagram's for each month of duty they had left, once they got under one hundred days remaining on their tour. The ribbon, peeled from the top of the bottle was then tied to a shirt buttonhole.

"How much time you got left, Monty?" Prentice asked.

Montrell looked at Prentice, half a grin on his face. "I had thirty-five days when I went on this shit detail," he said.

"Damn, you'll be just about ready to get on the big bird once we get back," Prentice commented.

"Yeah . . . If I get back," Montrell said quietly.

Prentice looked at him soberly, "You'll make it, Monty. We'll all make it. We've had our share of bad luck out here, but now things have changed. We'll fight back like wounded Green Berets, every minute till we get back to Phu Cat."

"Then what?" Montrell quietly wondered. "Get murdered in our sleep, or on guard duty by Richard's stooges?"

"No! No, by God! We are gonna take that bastard down and his fuckin' stooges along with him," Prentice stated, with conviction. "He won't be fuckin' no one else over, after I'm finished with him," he went on, his anger rising. Staring at Prentice, Monty said nothing.

Montrell knew that Prentice was sincere, but Montrell was a realist, and he had his doubts. He knew what they were up against. In Richards they were pitted against a supreme predator. Throughout man's history, the strong and cunning always preyed on the innocent and the weak. Men weren't much different than animals, really, Montrell felt. They were only smarter. After his earlier discussions with Prentice, as well as his own experience, he knew that Richards was the head of a large, well-trained, ruthless organization. How could Prentice and this little bunch of nobodies, floundering out here in the middle of hell, possibly believe they could defeat him? Wishful thinking . . . the power of prayer . . . what could Prentice be thinking?

Chapter 28

*"For the strength of the Pack is the Wolf, and for the
strength of the Wolf is the Pack."*

Kipling

The next day at first light the men broke camp and continued making
their way through the terrain, hacking away as best they could,
going around areas that proved too thick for them to work through.
Having eaten a decent meal, and gotten a good night's rest, the men's
spirits were up a bit. They were getting used to the tough terrain, and
long days. Their bodies were hardening to the conditions. Their hearing,
sight, and even sense of smell became more acute. They came to trust
Hoa well enough to leave him untethered. He seemed to be warming up
to them as well. Although still occupied with the dilemma of dealing
with Richards, Prentice was confident his plan of getting at Richards
through McKay, the weak link, had a good chance of succeeding.

After about an hour Redmond, who had been on point, came back to the
group and signaled for them to stop. "We are being followed," he said,
somewhat out of breath. Immediately the other men stopped and looked
around sharply, scanning the bush for any sign of trouble. Redmond
holding his hand out then told them, "Not by men."

"Red?" Prentice questioned curiously.

Red caught his breath, "A large cat has been tracking us since we left
this morning," he said. "It must have been hanging around our camp
most of the night. I'm not sure if it's a large leopard or a tiger, but it's
been trailing us and even circled us twice."

"Monty, ask Hoa about tigers in these parts. Tell him what Red found.
Find out if they attack people," Prenticed directed.

Montrell and Hoa conversed. Hoa looked around gesturing several
times during the discussion.

Montrell then addressed the others, "He says there are many tigers and leopards in this area. Usually the leopards don't interact with people at all, but occasionally an old one or a very immature male seeking territory will attack a villager. But they usually don't track humans. He believes if this animal is tracking us, it must be a tiger. Tigers, again especially old or young ones, do occasionally prey on the local people. Several local villagers are killed each year by them."

"Fucking great!" Crucianelli exclaimed. "Not bad enough we're hunted by VC and Richard's henchmen, now Tony the fucking Tiger's after us."

"Well, nothing we can do about it," Prentice stated. "Just stay close together and be alert. Cru, you and Red take point together. Let Red keep an eye on the movement of the tiger, you watch for other threats. Red, let us know if the pattern of the animal's movement changes."

"Right, Sarge," Red replied.

"The Southeast Asian tiger is smaller than the Bengal, but just as dangerous," Montrell proclaimed. "A male's range is around 200 square miles, a female's about half."

Somewhat surprised, Crucianelli spoke up, "What are you, a fucking zoologist and an interpreter, Montrell?" Prentice and Red laughed.

Somewhat defensively, Montrell replied, "When I was going to the U of Ohio I minored in natural resources of the world. We learned about flora and fauna from all regions. Some people are surprised to learn that there are also elephants and rhinoceros in Vietnam."

Listening, Cru looked at the others and replied, "Well if an elephant or a rhino starts tracking us, my ass is goin' AWOL!" Laughing and shaking their heads, the men pushed on.

* * *

As agreed, the two out men came in around 14:00.

"Anything?" Prentice asked.

"No sign of good guys or bad guys," interjected Crucianelli.

"What about the cat?" Montrell directed at Redmond.

"Still out there, but not moving in any closer," Redmond offered.

Prentice said, "Ok, we'll take a thirty minute break, anyone having any physical issues, or any problems at all?" The men responded that they had no problems or issues. They broke out some dry rations, checked to see how their stores of fish were holding up in the heat, and then rested. Montrell and Hoa meanwhile engaged in a discussion that seemed not related to the current situation.

"Still okay with Hoa's directions?" Prentice asked Montrell.

"Yeah, he says we're on course, and I believe him," Montrell responded.

"You two seem to have found some things to talk about," Prentice added.

Montrell looked at Prentice. He knew Prentice was concerned that Hoa might be sucking him in.

"We've been talking about his request to go to America," Montrell replied. "I asked him what's waiting for him there, and that kind of shit. You might be surprised at his answer."

But Prentice didn't have time to find out. Suddenly withering AK-47 fire began leveling the vegetation around them. They all dove for cover.

"Follow me!" Red yelled. He had found a crease between two large boulders, which led into another small valley. They all squeezed through it and moved through the subsequent jungle as rapidly as they could. After fifteen minutes, they stopped to catch their breath. Listening and watching closely, it appeared no one followed them into the little valley that then merged with another, larger valley.

"Everyone okay?" Prentice inquired, panting and out of breath.

Everyone was unscathed with the exception of Crucianelli. He had taken a round through the fleshy part of his upper arm, and although not a serious wound, it bled profusely and caused him a great deal of pain.

"Let's get a tourniquet on that," Prentice directed. "How bad's the pain? Can you move?"

"I'll be okay," Cru squeaked. "I can move."

Redmond put a heavy wrap on Cru's arm and not being able to take any chances, the group moved out again at a quick pace.

"You let me know if you have trouble keepin up, Cru," Prentice said.

"Right, Sarge," he groaned back.

They moved through the valley for several hours, stopping every fifteen minutes to check on Cru, and to see if they were being followed. When it got too dark to go any farther, Red found another undercut embankment they could use to sit out the night. After they were rested a bit, Prentice suggested they break out the dry rations and get another inventory of their provisions. They got away from the AK attack with their lives, but unfortunately most of their provisions were lost in the panic. It was going to be a cold night, with dry rations. And worse, they had no painkiller left for Cru. They had used the last of their heroin supply on Prentice and Hoa, and didn't even have an aspirin left.

The three Americans grilled Hoa extensively about the attack, suspecting it might be an attempt to rescue him from his captors. Hoa told them that the people who attacked them were probably just nearby villagers, scared of them as much as they were scared of the villagers. If his people had attacked, they would not have escaped with their lives.

"Well, I guess that's a comfort," Prentice snorted. "Let's get some sleep; I'll rotate watch with Red. In the morning we'll try to move on."

The little group kept moving most of the next day, but it was evident that Cru's wound was festering as he was in considerable pain. They had to stop frequently and weren't making good time.

"Thuoc," Hoa said, stopping and pointing to a plant.

"What's he talking about, Montrell?" Prentice asked impatiently.

"Thuoc . . . medicine. He's saying medicine," Montrell replied.

The men stood looking at Hoa. Before anyone could move, Hoa grabbed the K-bar knife out of Cru's sheath and hacked some of the thick plant's stems. He brought the stem up and showed them the white liquid foaming from around the gash he had made.

Looking at Cru's arm and making a rubbing motion he repeated, "Thuoc."

139

Prentice looked at Redmond and asked, "What do you think, medicine man?"

Looking at Prentice with an irritated frown and then at the plant, Red replied, "Well, it looks a lot like the thistle our old medicine woman used to apply to cuts and wounds; wouldn't be surprised if this was from the same family of plants."

"I'll take it," Cru groaned. "I won't be able to go on much further today unless someone cuts this fucking arm off."

Prentice, after looking everyone over, said, "Okay, we rest here for the time being. Red, rub some of that shit on Cru's wound and let's hope it works."

After the application to his arm, Cru fell into a deep sleep. Prentice and the others worried. An infection in the jungle often spread quickly and was difficult to heal. Minor wounds often festered for weeks.

After a time, Redmond looked at Cru's wound and said he thought the treatment seemed to be helping. The festering subsided and Cru's fever had broken.

"Sure could use a belt myself right now," Prentice said to no one in particular.

"Yeah, I bet you could," Redmond replied, "I'll have one with you."

"A shot of Jack would taste real good right about now," Montrell contributed.

"Or a hit," Red commented, glancing at Montrell.

"Yeah, or a hit," Montrell agreed.

"Well, we got no juice, and we got no fucking dope, so I guess were all screwed, lessen Hoa finds something else in the bush," Prentice interjected.

Looking at Hoa, they all began wondering. Hoa was sitting, chewing on some betel nut. The narcotic berry used by many rural Vietnamese helped get them through long days in the field, childbirth and many other stressful situations, not least of which was the constant warfare they had been subjected to for many years.

Seeming to read their minds, Hoa reached into his satchel, brought out a handful of betel nuts, and offered it to the men. Red and Montrell looked at each other and with little hesitation accepted a handful.

Startled, Prentice yelled out, "I need you fuckers sober and straight! The last thing we need is you two stumbling around, passin' out on some kind of psychedelic shit!" His remark elicited boisterous laughter from Redmond and Montrell. Even Hoa chuckled a bit, understanding enough of what the discussion was about to appreciate the humor.

Montrell responded, "Don't worry, Sarge, this shit won't get you buzzed any more than that Wisco weed Crucianelli used to smoke back on the farm."

"Yeah," Redmond agreed "I've chewed peyote buttons that could get you nice and high, and this shit ain't no fuckin' peyote."

"I don't care," Prentice interjected. "I need you fuckers awake and on alert; not trippin' over your dicks, with black shit foamin' out of your mouths!" This got them laughing harder; even Crucianelli was up and snickering.

"Don't worry, Sarge, we'll do John Wayne for you whenever needed," Montrell added.

Now Prentice grinned a little. The group was soon moving again, hoping to make several more hours before the blackness of the jungle night engulfed them completely.

Chapter 29

"We must embrace pain and burn it as fuel for our journey."

Kenji Miyazawa

"There are people up ahead," Redmond reported. He had fallen back quietly from his position on point and gestured for the others to hold up and remain quiet.

Prentice responded, "What's up, Red? Are they friendlies? Did you get a good look at 'em?"

"Couldn't tell. Could be a base camp, but could also be a small vil. I wasn't close enough to hear any voices or anything," Red replied. "Didn't want to get seen by a lookout; couldn't see one but didn't want to take the chance."

"No sweat," Prentice replied. "We'll have to go around them."

Concerned, Montrell spoke up, "That'll add at least an extra day to get to the 1st Cav camp. We're low on provisions and Cru ain't in any shape to go foraging again."

"I can do the foraging," Redmond offered.

"No . . . no we need you on point and lookout," Prentice interjected. "Montrell and I will have to manage the foraging. Hoa will have to help." All the men glanced at Hoa, wondering how far he could be trusted.

"I will gather food," Hoa stated, in accented, but understandable English, startling the four men.

"Damn!" Redmond half yelled, looking at Hoa. "Did you teach that little fucker English already, Monty?"

Montrell, gazing at Hoa, replied," No, no I didn't. He knew some before we hooked up with him. No doubt he's picked up some listening to us talk the last couple days. Or maybe he was just playing dumb."

At that Crucianelli spoke up, "Sure as hell wouldn't want my kid learning anything from a bunch of dumb fucks like you."

Laughing, Montrell shot back, "Well Cru, after listening to you speaking to us would damn sure be an improvement!" The men all laughed, even Hoa.

Hoa spoke up again, "I will help you find food, shelter, and the army unit you are looking for. You have treated me fairly, more fairly than some of my own countrymen have in the past. When I was a child my father told me of a place where men were always free, and fought for the rights of others to be free. He told me the name of the place was the U. S. In Saigon, I studied about your country, and although you support the corrupt Saigon government, I believe deep down, you mean well. I wish to live in the U. S., where my children will be born in freedom, live in freedom, and die in freedom. I will help you . . . but you must take me back with you."

Thoughtfully, the men gazed at Hoa, then at each other.

Prentice felt it was time to level with Hoa, "Hoa, we must be truthful with you," he said. "I've come to know and respect you, and it would not be right to lead you on. My position as an upper level non-commissioned officer in the military does not give me the authority to take refugees back to America, much as I appreciate your plight, and understand your desire to go there."

"I know that," Hoa replied.

He then turned and spoke in Vietnamese to Montrell. After a short back and forth discussion Montrell turned to Prentice and said, "He needs a sponsor, and a high-ranking officer to write an affidavit that he has a legitimate need to leave the country and be taken to America. He learned the requirements when he was in Saigon. He can even help you fill the paperwork out."

Prentice had concerns regarding this. "Okay, so I'm his sponsor and the paperwork gets filled out," he said. "What high-ranking officer is going to sign that affidavit and why?"

The discussion went on for a while. Hoa seemed to have given the process considerable thought. He had it mapped out, along with contingency plans along the way. He didn't have an answer as to how they would get a high-ranking officer to fill out the paperwork. By 1970 most officers in 'Nam were like everyone else, they wanted to get their ticket punched and get the fuck out. The war was going badly and everyone knew it. The sense of failure was like the smell emanating from a large dead water buffalo on the side of the road. You could go around it and go past it, but you couldn't avoid the stench made by the dead, stinking beast, fermenting in the steaming heat. It stuck in your nostrils and clung to your body. For hours you could smell it, and the memory of the odor now resided in your brain, coming back occasionally as events dictated. Nixon was talking about peace with honor, but he was really talking about what everyone else was talking about, getting the fuck out. An officer who stuck his head out just might get it cut off. Do your job, keep your mouth shut, rotate back to the States, hopefully in one piece, get a job, a wife and have a few kids. The American dream, night sweats included, compliments of Uncle Sam. No, Hoa would have a difficult time getting an officer to stick his neck out for a thief, and possible Viet Cong.

"I'll do what I can, Hoa, this much I'll promise you," Prentice advised. "Now we better get moving."

"I can take point," Montrell offered.

Redmond and Prentice looked at each other. Prentice replied, "Okay, Monty, we'll give you a shot at it, but not just yet. Right now we still need to find out what the people up ahead are, or who they are I guess. Red, take point again and see if you can ID them. If they are just villagers we'll be okay, if they look like patrolling VC or NVA we'll have to cut a wide swath. And let's hope they're not more of Richards hired killers; cause they won't give up."

"Right, Sarge," Red said and disappeared into the bush ahead of them.

Crucianelli felt better so they could travel a little faster. They didn't have much light of day left and Prentice wanted to get as much distance as they could between them and whoever it was Red was up ahead trying to ID. They made a heavy pitch to the east of their original track, Red would have no trouble finding them, but it would take much longer, and again their rations were tight. After several more hours, Redmond had still not returned, and with poor light Prentice thought they should hold up for the night.

"I can find shelter," Hoa told Montrell.

Montrell and Prentice looked at each other and said nothing.

"I will find shelter and food if necessary," Hoa added.

Prentice said, "Okay, Hoa, we'll trust you to find that shelter. If we don't see you in twenty minutes, we'll figure you changed your mind about America and we won't wait for you."

Hoa gave Prentice an angry look and replied, "Hoa will find America, with or without your help." Then he disappeared into the bush.

"Well, damn, Charley, you ran off the only two guys who can find their way around in this shit!" Montrell commented. "If neither one of them gets back, we truly are screwed."

Prentice responded, "Yeah, well, I guess we'll see if that Boy Scout training you got in 6th grade was worth a shit or not."

"Cru's a woodsman," Montrell replied. "He can find his way around in the thickest jungle Ho Chi Minh's got."

Looking at Crucianelli, Prentice observed, "I don't know if he's stoned on that beetle shit, or just with fever, but I think Cru would have a hard time finding his dick right now."

It was true; between the betel nut he had been chewing and the fever wracking his body, Cru was pretty much played out. He was keeping up, but just barely, and Montrell had to keep behind him to make sure he stayed on the trail behind Prentice.

"Yeah, Cru ain't gonna be able to travel much longer tonight. We might have to tuck ourselves in tonight if Red and Hoa don't turn up."

In less than a half hour, Hoa reappeared from the direction they were heading. "Follow," was all he said. After a short time they came upon a VC bunker complex.

"Damn," Prentice exclaimed.

Hoa, understanding his alarm replied, "No one here, Prentice, no one here for many week, it safe."

"You first," Prentice told him, holding his M-16 at the ready. "Wait here," he instructed Montrell and Crucianelli, who could barely understand anything at this point. Prentice and Hoa went through the entire complex. It appeared to have been home for at least a patrol-sized unit. Bunks, food stores, and even a small field hospital room made up the bulk of the facility, which was mostly underground.

After he'd finished his inspection, Prentice called to Cru and Montrell, "It's safe, looks like no one's been around for a long time. There are a couple of flashlights with working batteries, some medical supplies, and even a small cache of rice. Good job, Hoa, and thank you." Cru fell on the first bunk he found and went into a slumber.

Montrell did his own walk-through of the place. "We might be able to use this as our base camp," he remarked.

"Base camp"? Prentice wondered. "That sounds kinda permanent, Monty. I was hopin' we'd be the fuck out of here, and maybe back at Phu Cat in a couple more days."

"Well let's think about this," Montrell replied. "We got one man half incapacitated, we're all nicked up a little, and we don't know what the fuck will be waiting for us back at Phu Cat. We're in extremely hostile territory, and Richards may have a plant in the 1st Cav as well. This may be a good spot to get everyone well, make tentative contact with the Cav, without giving away our position, and establish communications with the right people setting the stage for a return to Phu Cat on *our* terms."

Prentice looked thoughtfully at Montrell for a couple of moments. "That's not bad thinking, Monty, not bad at all," he said. "We could use this as our safe haven, and if we do get back to Phu Cat and things don't go in our favor, we could have a plan in place to get back here."

"Get back here and do what?" Crucianelli croaked. He had been half-asleep, but the discussion caught his ear.

Prentice and Montrell both looked his way. "Get back here and survive another day," Prentice remarked soberly.

Chapter 30

"Do not stand in a place of danger, trusting in miracles."

Arab proverb

"Worried about Red, huh Sarge?" Montrell asked Prentice. The men had settled into the bunker rather well, taken inventory, and even made a meal from some of the rice stores they had found. Mixing the remaining fish and amphibians Cru and Hoa had caught gave the rice a fairly decent flavor. As always, Cru carried a small bottle of tobasco sauce that he applied to everything he ate in Vietnam. He claimed it made the stuff edible and killed whatever germs occupied the food.

Prentice kept stepping out of the bunker and scanning the area for a sign of Redmond, who had been gone for several hours now. "I don't like it," he stated. "Red should have returned long ago. Something's wrong."

"Let me go look for him" Montrell asked.

"No, we don't need two of you lost out there. No offense, Monty, but you aren't exactly a woodsman." Before Montrell could protest, Prentice continued, "I know you are a good man, and you would do your best, but Cru and Red are at home in this shit, and even they struggle here at times.

A quiet voice then sounded from the corner, "Hoa will find Red."

Prentice and Montrell hadn't thought about the possibility of sending Hoa to retrieve Redmond. No doubt he'd have the best chance of any of them. He had proven to be trustworthy, in so far as he needed them to achieve his goal of getting to the States; and if he wanted that to happen he wouldn't double cross them.

Prentice, looking at Montrell, spoke to Hoa, "What do you need to find him?" He was hoping Hoa wouldn't ask for a weapon.

147

Hoa said, "I take the knife and water."

Prentice looked away and busied himself taking inventory of their ammunition. He checked Crucianelli's supply and asked Montrell to check his own. After a bit he looked at Hoa and said, "Hoa, go and try to find Red. Take whatever you need, and also take along some medical supplies in case he's injured. We leave in the morning, whether you and Red are back or not. Good luck."

Montrell looked sharply at Prentice who returned a sidelong glance. Hoa took some medical supplies, a full canteen, a K-bar knife and left.

Feeling Montrell's sharp gaze on his back Prentice spoke up, "If they don't get back by dawn, they aren't coming back. The three of us aren't capable of finding them. Now we could stay here for days, or even longer, before an armed patrol of something finds us and finishes us off, or we can go on. If we find the 1st Cav, they will find Red . . . and Hoa, or at least they will find out what happened to them."

Montrell, listening, wasn't satisfied. "Damn, Sarge, we could at least give them one more day. I can scout around the area here, using the coordinate system we used before. I won't get lost, I assure you, and if I don't come back after a day or so, you and Cru can move on. We already lost Salas, Flash, and Hardy, not to mention Becker and Childs. At this point, I don't feel right leaving anymore of us behind."

Prentice remained quiet, thinking.

Crucianelli now weighed in, "I'm with Monty, Sarge. I'm feelin' better now, and I can hold lookout and maybe gather food if need be. I don't wanna leave Red behind . . . I just don't." After a bit he added, "Nor Hoa, either."

Now Prentice looked sharply at Crucianelli. Prentice wouldn't feel right leaving Hoa, either. There was something about him . . . about his plight. Somehow he felt obligated to help Hoa in his quest to leave this land of war and sadness. Deep down, Prentice knew Hoa was right. Although he was never into the politics of the war, it seemed to him that the war was not serving the Vietnamese people, but rather the corrupt regime in charge.

He knew that all too well, having become associated with both the peasants and the ruling party while providing both with goods and services, while conducting his role in the Kansas NCO's illicit operation.

Too often he saw valuable American goods provided to government or ARVN officials used for their own personal profit or other benefit, never trickling down to the people they supposedly represented. They took the goods as booty, and never paid for them, in return for allowing Richards to conduct his business operations unfettered. The villagers, on the other hand, were always grateful whenever they received any help from them. The villagers always insisted on repaying them in some way. Whether it was a piglet for eating, or some homemade wine or beer, they always sent something.

"Never forget favors, small or big," they would say.

"We'll stay another day," Prentice said quietly. "Go ahead and make that patrol, Montrell, but don't get out too far. We're pretty well stocked on food for now, Cru. There's enough rice in that basket to last us a couple weeks. Maybe in a day or so, we'll need you to do some foraging.

"There's a big wooden thatch locker that is woven shut in that back room area. Maybe you can cut into it and see what's in there. Be sure to check for wires and make sure it's not a booby trap. Damn, we're getting to be pretty good grunts. By the time we run into the 1st Cav, they might ask for our help."

"Yeah, okay, Sarge," both Cru and Montrell laughed.

Prentice went on, "I'm gonna go over the documents we found in that hidden wooden box. There were some drawings and what looked to be maybe maps. I'll see if they can be of any use to us." The men went about the tasks each had taken. As always the day was hot and steamy, but there hadn't been rain for a couple days.

Thank God it's not the monsoon season, Montrell thought as he moved through his coordinates and making observations.

Montrell also thought how they were now really beginning to understand the life of the "grunts." The "ground pounders" really were the salt of the earth, Montrell felt. He saw them often, while on convoy duty, when they were walking the road. Caked in red dirt, sweat, and loaded with weapons and ammunitions, they trudged along, accepting their difficult and dangerous lives. They would often come onto the airbase at Phu Cat from out in the field, marveling at the easy conditions and comparatively soft life of the airmen stationed there. But when the stand-off rocket and mortar attacks the airbases were subjected to came thundering in, they didn't find it quite as enviable, but for the most part they enjoyed their little time removed from hell as best they could.

Montrell knew Red had trained as a Marine, and Cru had been spent additional time at Hamilton Air Force Base in California, above and beyond the standard ten-day, pre-Nam weapons training, learning additional infantry technique from army NCOs. Those guys had a taste of what the army and Marine infantry training involved, and were more mentally prepared.

Now he found himself out there, in the bush, seemingly forever, his best friend dead, and his own life hanging in the balance. He sure as hell didn't sign on for this, but probably deserved whatever he got for trying to take the easy road and getting involved with the Kansas NCO in the first place. He knew Cru and Prentice felt the same way, and possibly Red as well. But Red had the stoic nature of the Native American that was more or less accepting of whatever life dealt them. Hoa's Buddhist ancestry subscribed to a similar stoicism, but Hoa had broken the mold; he had had enough and wanted out.

Chapter 31

*"Life is a shipwreck but we must not forget to
sing in the lifeboats."*

Voltaire

Hoa crept in for a viewing position, and then crouched down on one knee. He was trying to determine what he could do to possibly help Redmond. Redmond had been stripped of clothing and was tied spread-eagle by his wrists and ankles. Three young Vietnamese were taking turns, beating him with their fists. Red was conscious, but obviously groggy and in pain.

Hoa recognized the one who appeared to be the ringleader as Trang, an old acquaintance. Though dressed like Viet Cong, Hoa knew that Trang was no more than a common criminal. He had a short career as an ARVN soldier, where he perfected his cruel nature abusing his fellow villagers. Tossed out of the army for keeping too much stolen booty, Trang drifted in and out of the ranks of the Viet Cong, until they also expelled him. Although the VC raped, robbed, and pillaged whenever they felt the need or compulsion, Trang's total lack of regard for any human being was too much, even for them. Disgraced once again, Trang, more than ever, rode roughshod on his people, seeking vengeance for his own shortcomings.

"Cut his nuts off," one of the men yelled.

"One thing at a time," Trang replied. "Let's make this bastard suffer a long time before the worms take him back." Trang then picked up a long switch he had fashioned from a nearby branch. He started methodically whipping Red about his chest and torso, occasionally hitting his legs.

Hoa knew he had to act quickly. Red would be unconscious soon. He picked up a large rock with both hands and quietly moved behind Trang's two companions. Steadying himself, Hoa raised the rock over his head and when the switch next met Red's flesh, he brought the rock down hard on the head of one of the men, who collapsed, dead before he hit the ground. Startled, the other man turned and brought his weapon up to shoot. Before he could pull the trigger, Hoa smashed him in the face with the rock, knocking out several teeth and a piece of the man's gums. The man screamed once, before Hoa brought the rock crashing down on his head.

Spinning around, Trang looked at Hoa in surprised recognition and was motionless for a split second. "You bastard!" he yelled, lunging for his AK-47. But before Trang could grasp it, Hoa was on him, repeatedly plunging the K-bar knife into his neck.

"Die, you traitorous piece of dung!" Hoa yelled. "Die!" And die Trang did, with the look of surprise and anger still on his face. There was now one less parasite and thief for the local people to deal with. Breathing heavily, Hoa looked back at the other men. The second man he had attacked was still breathing. Hoa used the rock to hit him in the head again. The man soon was still. Then Hoa went over to check on Red.

The fresh welts on Red had risen to about three quarters of an inch. He had a large gash on his shoulder and bruises all over his body, but with no life threatening damage that Hoa could see. *This man is as tough as any Vietnamese,* Hoa thought as he cut Red down and lowered him to the ground. He took his canteen and poured some water on Red's lips. Red responded by licking the water with his tongue. Then Hoa allowed him a short drink, making sure not to overwhelm him.

"Ahh," Red groaned a little and took in several long slow breaths.

"How soon can travel?" Hoa asked him.

"Give me ten minutes" Red croaked, adding, "More water." Hoa allowed him some longer drinks. He also applied water on Red's shoulder, cleaning the gash.

"Your shoulder needs sewn," Hoa told him.

"Pack it with mud," Red replied, "I'll worry about stiches next time my woman is around."

Hoa grunted and commented, "By then she will only have a scar to look at . . . let's move."

Hoa wanted to get back as soon as he could. He knew Prentice meant what he said about leaving without them, and it would be difficult to catch up for a day or so until Redmond got his strength back. They moved slowly but steadily through the thick cover. Hoa kept his eyes and ears open for any sign of others, pausing often along the way. With stamina obtained from his ancestral warriors, Red moved along, never complaining or crying out in pain when his heavy breathing caused his bruised ribs to ache. Hoa figured it would take them four times as long to return as it did to get to where he had found Red. He had some rice in his satchel, and food he took off the dead men, but Red could not yet eat, so he gave him more betel nut to chew, which Red gratefully took.

* * *

By midday Prentice, who had kept up his vigil of looking for the two missing men every fifteen minutes or so, began to get impatient. "Damn, might be best if we go," he muttered. Montrell ignored him; he had already determined he wasn't going to leave, no matter what Prentice did.

Crucianelli was getting better and starting to feel his oats again. "Let's give 'em that extra day, Charley. You said you would, and I'm gonna hold you to it," Cru said.

Prentice looked at him noncommittally and once again said nothing.

Cru went on, "I'm feelin' okay and can go out and scrounge up some chow from the river."

This set Prentice off, "Goddamit, we don't need your ass getting lost, too!" he raged. "I can't be responsible for all you fuckers wanderin' around out in the fucking jungle, so stay the fuck put!"

Taken back by Prentice's sudden display of bravado, both Cru and Montrell started laughing. "Don't give me no more shit, you two fuckers, I ain't shittin' you now," Prentice continued. This caused Montrell and Cru to laugh even harder.

The only other time they had seen Prentice that angered was one day back at Phu Cat when they got drunk and found his hidden stash of dehydrated shrimp. They left the empty can, along with an empty bottle of Tabasco, as well as a couple dozen empty cans of Black Label beer up by the desk he shared with several other NCOs in base supply. He had put them each on perimeter guard for a week as punishment.

153

"You gonna put us on perimeter guard, Charley?" Montrell asked. At that, both he and Crucianelli roared with laughter again.

Prentice couldn't keep it up any longer and started laughing under his breath. "All right you two fuck-offs, don't give me a hard time," he said. "I wished we had that goddamn shrimp and Black Label right about now."

Amen to that, Sarge," Crucianelli replied. "Amen to that!"

Around one in the afternoon Montrell came hustling back. He had been working his quadrant patrols all morning, and other than a couple monkeys, deer and pigs, had seen nothing, until now.

"They're coming in, Hoa and Red are coming in!" he exclaimed. Cru and Prentice both jumped out of the bunker.

"Are they okay?" Prentice questioned anxiously.

"They're walking slow, Red looks hurt," Monty replied.

"Well, let's see if we can give 'em a hand," Prentice advised.

They went out to where Montrell had seen them. Montrell scrambled back up his lookout tree. After a quick look around he found them about one hundred yards ahead. "That way," he yelled, pointing. Prentice and Cru took off in the direction he indicated and soon met Hoa and Red. They half-carried Red back to the bunker. He was dehydrated and battered, but otherwise not in too bad of condition. He was more delirious from the betel nut than his injuries.

"Let him sleep for a while. Hoa, you okay?" Prentice asked.

"Okay," Hoa responded. "I sleep too." With that he collapsed on one of the bunks and both he and Red were soon sound asleep.

Seven hours later Red and Hoa still slept.

"I think we should wake them and make them take food and water, especially Red," Crucianelli commented.

Prentice thought a moment and replied, "Okay, see if you can wake them. Monty, what do we have left for grub?"

"Not much but rice and some hot sauce. The fish and other shit was stinkin' up the place so bad I had to chuck it." Montrell replied. Coming out of his sleep, Hoa held out his hand and motioned to his satchel. Inside there were several packages of C-rations that he had taken off the men he had killed.

"Damn, Hoa, you hit the jackpot," Crucianelli yelled.

The rations had been taken from an Air Force C-130 that had crashed in the jungle some days earlier. Trang and his men had heard about the downed aircraft from some local villagers and found it after a short search. They killed the aircraft's loadmaster who was hurt, but still alive after the crash. The pilot and navigator had died upon impact. Most of the equipment of value was sold to the local VC, while Trang had them cache anything they might be able to use. Hoa, in turn, gathered anything of use from them.

The rations were a welcome addition for the men. Each package contained a can of food, a can of fruit, a candy bar, along with condiments and cigarettes. Some of the items were somewhat crushed, but for men living on lizards and minnows, it was mighty fine cuisine.

"I vote we put Hoa in charge of our food supply from now on. Damn site better than those fucking lizards and minnows Cru's been feeding us," Montrell remarked.

"Get fucked, Monty," Cru replied. "If we had to rely on you for chow we'd have to live on betel nut and dead water buffalo bones."

Prentice laughed along with the men. They let Red sleep the rest of the day and through the night, putting salve on his welts from time to time, and changing the mudpack on his shoulder wound. Prentice was happy they had lost no more men, and his resolve to return and deal with Richards and his murderers was becoming stronger by the day. He resolved to do right by the men he was in this mess with, including Hoa.

"Thank you for saving Red from those men and bringing him back," Prentice quietly told Hoa. "And thank you for the help you've given us. I know life has been hard for you, and we Americans haven't done our best to do right by your people. You are not bitter, but focused on a goal to better yourself. Your ancestors would be proud . . . I'm proud."

Hoa's head was bowed while Prentice talked. After Prentice had finished, Hoa looked up and said, "I want to live among men like you, Cru, Monty, and Red. I want to belong with you. You are here trying to do your job in an honorable way. You are good Americans, you are good people."

Prentice put his hand on Hoa's shoulder. "You do belong with us, and you are part of us, Hoa," he said. "We are all in this together now, and we'll stay together to the end . . . and hopefully all the way to America."

Hoa could say nothing and looked down again. For the first time in his life he felt he belonged and felt good about his future, no matter what would happen or where it would take him.

The next morning Red was up and clear headed. The tough Ojibwa hardly winced as Hoa repacked his shoulder wound.

"Thank you," he said quietly to Hoa, who nodded and finished his work.

Looking at Prentice, who was checking to see what kind of shape he was in, Red said, "I'm okay. I'm good to go now. If we have to hang around here eating Cru's lizards and minnows the rest of our lives, I might as well go back out and fight with VC."

"Fuck you, Chief," Cru shot back. "You're eatin' better now than you did on that damn reservation back in bum-fucked Idaho and you know it. At least I don't serve no fucking bugs, not intentionally anyway."

Laughing, Montrell said, "Red ain't from Idaho. Besides we don't have to eat Cru's catch of the day anymore. Hoa ambushes VC and steals their rations."

"By the way, Cru," Prentice now got in on it. "How come you don't make some of that fucking liquini or past bazoo or some other good shit for us?"

With everyone laughing, Cru shot back, "Damn, Charley, you don't even know how to say it right, why the fuck would I make it for you? And I wouldn't waste good Italian cooking on a bunch of bubbas like you any fuckin' way. That would be like playing Mozart at a goddam hillbilly concert. You'd be just as happy eatin' fermented lizards and snakes."

"Well you're probably right, Cru," Prentice laughed.

Chapter 32

"Fatigue makes cowards of us all."

Vince Lombardi

Prentice gave the order, "Okay, let's move out." Prentice, Cru and Hoa were equipped with enough food and ammunition for about two days. They planned to find the 1st Cav base camp, or elements of it out on patrol, which would lead them to it.

Hoa figured the base camp to be no more than a day and a half away, if they moved quickly and didn't have to make any large diversions from their direction of travel.

Montrell would remain at the bunker complex, tending Red, who though much better was not ready to travel as of yet. He would also man an observation post in a tree that gave him a panoramic view from the bunker, and would allow him enough time to get back in a hurry if need be.

Prentice felt they would probably see or hear some choppers flying in and out of the base camp when they got within a couple of hours of it, so they could hone in on the flight paths if need be to pinpoint the base. There were concerns, however, and they needed to be vigilant when they did get closer. The 1st Cav usually had a small artillery piece at their base camps for defensive purposes, not to mention mortars, claymore mines and a full free fire zone around the base, backed up by two .50 caliber machine guns. If the Cav got company they weren't expecting, the incoming guests might quickly find themselves on the receiving end of withering friendly fire.

They also had to use caution regarding their traveling order. Although Hoa was the most qualified tracker, using him on point would be disastrous if any American patrol saw him and interpreted him as being from a patrol of Viet Cong. On the other hand, using Cru would have the same affect, if a VC patrol spotted him.

"Hoa will take point the first day," Prentice stated. "The chance of running into an American patrol before that isn't too risky. When we get to within a day in passing, or if we should find we are getting close to the 1st Cav base camp through visual and sound observation, Cru, you will take point from there on in."

"Okay, Sarge," Cru replied.

"Okay," said Hoa.

Back at the bunker, Red felt good enough to join Montrell at his lookout post.

"Hey, you up and around already?" Montrell yelled, seeing Red standing below the tree.

"Yeah, time to start earning my money again," Red replied. "Can't be goldbricking all the time unless I want to listen to Cru's bitchin and whining."

Montrell laughed, "Yeah, he'll be getting on your ass pretty soon, since he hasn't had the chance for a couple of days."

Red said, "A couple of months ago if you told me Cru and a Vietnamese would be out in the bush workin' together, I'd have called you a liar."

Montrell agreed, "You know Red, it's strange. Our old life on the base and convoy duty seems like a lifetime ago. Here I thought I'd be goin' home in a couple of weeks from now, and fuck, now I'm here worrying about just staying alive from day to day."

"Well, I never saw Charley sober for this long, so I guess that's a good thing," Red mused. "I've seen enough drunks on the res all my life to know how hard that is for him."

"He's getting attached to Hoa," Montrell commented.

"Fuck, so am I," Red replied.

"Yeah, but in a different way," Montrell went on. "It's like Prentice is going to do right by Hoa, to make up for something from his own past. And now he's really got a case of the ass for Richards. He's determined to take him down."

"Why wouldn't he?" Red asked. "The sonofabitch is tryin' his best to kill us all. We'll be damn lucky to ever see the fuckin' States again."

* * *

The first night away from the bunker found Hoa, Cru, and Prentice in a small earthen dugout near a riverbed. It had rained on and off most of the day, and the men were now wet and cold. Prentice didn't want to risk a fire, so the men sat there shivering for most of the early evening. Hoa found some heavy moss from a nearby old growth forest and the men used it to dry off and make a little pallet for each of them to sleep on. They were able to retrieve enough of it to fashion blankets by packing it in their poncho liners. Eventually, after having discussed today and tomorrow's plan, they addressed their major dilemma . . . the Kansas NCO.

"I've been thinking about it more and more," Cru remarked. "These guys are just like the fucking mafia; ruthless parasites. But they are organized, well connected, and will rollover us like a tank no matter how we attack 'em."

Prentice answered, "Well, we can't just roll over and play dead. We have to at least make them pay a price."

"That's it exactly, Sarge," Crucianelli responded, "Make them pay a price. Money is what motivates these guys. Only money and more money drive their operation. We have to convince them that by keeping us alive, they stand to make a bunch of money, or by killing us they stand to lose a bunch of money, one or the other."

Sitting on a log eating a can of C-rations, Prentice was mulling over his discussion with Cru. Cru might be on the right track, regarding the possible solution, Prentice thought. They would only be able to keep themselves alive by making it another business deal for Richards. Kill them and lose money, or keep them alive and make money.

Richard's weak partner McKay could be the focus of this. By going solo and astray, selling weapons on the open market, he opened the door for another big profit, or a potential huge loss. If McKay was on the right track and successful, millions of dollars could be made, moving the glut of weaponry from Vietnam to willing buyers, all around the globe. However, if things went wrong, the illicit sale of weapons by members of the U.S. military, in an already unpopular war, would create such a public uproar a heavy handed investigation would swiftly ensue, possibly taking down the whole Richards operation.

If taken down, many of Richard's close associates and immediate underlings would no doubt go down with him, Prentice being one of them. Prentice kept working it over and over in his mind. He didn't like the idea of seeing Richards get off the hook, and enriching his coffers on top of it, but it appeared to be the only way he and this little band of men would ever have a chance of getting back to the States alive.

* * *

"Movement!" It was about an hour after sunset. Red and Montrell were back in the bunker for the night. Montrell was on lookout.

"What is it?" Red whispered in a low voice.

"Can't tell, could be a small patrol. I saw at least two men, both Vietnamese."

Red and Cru both had their M-16s sticking out the lookout opening on the front of the bunker. The bunker had openings in the front and back, and although well concealed, it would be no problem for an armed group familiar with the bunker to wrest it from Red and Montrell.

"I'll take the other lookout so they don't sneak in the back door," Redmond said, moving quickly to the new position. "If we see movement we do the lizard croak once, if they are coming in we croak twice."

"Right" Montrell mouthed, nervously fingering the safety on his weapon. The men had about eight clips of ammunition between them, and wouldn't last long in any sustained firefight.

As the night wore on, Montrell had trouble staying awake. The tense alert state they were in fatigued them quickly, mentally and physically. Realizing Montrell was sleeping from time to time; Red had them switch positions, him taking the front, the more conspicuous and likely the path of attack. Though he also was fatigued, his experience hunting game at night, back on the reservation had better prepared him for an ordeal such as this.

Although not from Wisconsin like Cru, Redmond had often traveled to the northern part of that state for tribal gatherings at one of the large Ojibwa reservations there. As a result, he became a follower, and a fan of the Green Bay Packer football team. He read many articles about their storied coach, Vince Lombardi, and was impressed with his tough, yet fair attitude. Whenever he felt he might succumb to weakness, whether it be on an all-night hunt for coon, pig or bear, an all-night drill while training with the Marines, or a night stand as perimeter guard back at Phu Cat, he always thought about what Lombardi might say to him about weakness, and usually overcame his human frailty as a result of that thought.

The fact is had Vince Lombardi known Redmond, he might have used him as a role model for his football players.

Chapter 33

"Every day is a journey, and the journey itself is home."

Matsuo Basho

Preoccupied about their dilemma with Richards, Prentice wasn't totally alert, as they broke camp the next morning.

"You left your travel log, Sarge," Crucianelli told Prentice.

Hoa picked it up and brought it up, before they left for their journey into the heart of the area where the 1st Cav was known to operate.

Irritated at his own carelessness, Prentice took it from Hoa. "Let's move," was all he said after making sure he had made no other missteps.

Neither Hoa nor Cru paid any attention to the log Prentice had with him, which contained, among other things, a diary of their activity since leaving Pleiku, and a tentative plan for their return to Phu Cat, and then the States.

Prentice had kept such a log throughout his whole air force career. It helped him keep track of his goals, strategically, as well as tactical day-to-day operations, which he carried out as required by whatever his current assignment may be.

A former officer, who Prentice had worked for in two different commands, had once remarked that Prentice could advance to chief of staff of the air force, if he ever decided to give up the bottle. He had told Prentice that on several occasions, one of which involved a DUI at his stateside base, and another involving an incident with a senior master sergeant whose incompetence had almost caused an aircraft crash. The officer knew that Prentice had covered for the senior master, and advised Prentice that it was an honorable thing he had attempted, but to cover for incompetent personnel could put lives in danger, and if it happened again, he would place Prentice on report.

* * *

While Cru, Hoa, and Prentice made their way through the jungle tangle, Redmond and Montrell were outside of their bunker, carefully watching for any sign of the men who Montrell had observed the night before. Red found their sign, and the two men halted while Red tried to determine how many there were, and where they may have gone.

"Looks like only two," he commented. "I don't believe they were tracking us, probably just passing through on their way back to their vil, or maybe out hunting pigs."

Back in the states, Redmond had gone on many wild pig hunts. The prized meat of the young piglets was always a welcome treat and often flavored the dishes of many reservation meals. As a result Red knew that pigs were usually hunted at night as the voracious feeders moved throughout their range foraging on anything that might be edible. He mused fondly about those days sleeping late into the afternoon after an all-night pig hunt.

"Wish I had some roast pig right now," Montrell commented.

"We could catch one," Red replied. "They are smart, but greedy. You just gotta put out the right bait."

"Fine as a rack a ribs sounds right now, don't look for me out here at night sneakin' up on Porky fucking pig," Montrell remarked.

Red laughed, "No, you don't have to sneak up on 'em, we just put out the bait and set a snare. I noticed some wooden crates with wire rope in the bunker. It would be easy to make a snare with that. We just gotta figure out what to use for bait."

Montrell, thinking about it asked, "What do they like?"

"A pig will eat just about anything," Red replied. "Back home we'd use a bushel or two of corn or other grain, along with fish guts, deer carcasses, or anything that would stink like hell. The animal matter would bring 'em in, and the corn would keep 'em mulling around. Also need to find their trails. They usually follow the same trails night after night, searching for food."

"Fuck, let's get to work," Montrell said, heading back to the bunker.

163

* * *

Crucianelli saw it first; campfire smoke, or what appeared to be campfire smoke about a mile down the ravine they were traversing.

"Okay, let's hold up till we figure out who the fuck it is," Prentice advised. "We'll sit tight for a while just watching; maybe one of 'em will pop his head up."

Hoa spoke up, "No soldier," he said.

Prentice looked at Hoa, "What's that, Hoa?"

Hoa repeated, "No soldier."

Prentice looked at Crucianelli. Cru understood what Hoa was saying, and why.

"I agree, Hoa," Cru said. "I don't think they're military either." Looking at Prentice he said, "No soldier would make a fire in broad daylight where the smoke could be seen by anyone for miles around. I'm guessing it's some locals cooking or something."

Hoa nodded his head, waving his hand in the air as he spoke, "Cookee fish."

"Oh I get it, I think he's saying they're smoking some fish," Crucianelli said.

Hoa nodded, "Yes . . . smoke . . . smoke fish."

"Dang, smoked fish . . . that sounds pretty good," Prentice remarked.

Cru agreed, "Yeah, it does. Nothin' like a batch of smoked fish with a cold beer to chase it down."

"Cru, you'd chase a piece a apple pie down with a fuckin' beer," Prentice said. "Well we ain't got no fucking cold beer, and lessen we get an invitation from whoever's smoking that fish, we ain't gonna get none 'a that either, so we might just as well detour around 'em."

They moved away, veering to the east, but the extension would add at least a couple of hours onto their projected path.

"Fuck," was all Cru grunted, as they trudged away.

* * *

"What the fuck?" Montrell said loudly turning toward the commotion.

They had set their pig trap and returned to the bunker. It was just after dark and the pig they had ensnared was squealing loudly while thrashing around wildly in an attempt to free itself from the steel cable tightly gripping its neck.

"That didn't take long!" Red said. "We better get that fucker before half the VC in 'Nam hear the goddam thing."

Montrell grabbed his weapon and the spear Red had fashioned out of a branch. Red had hardened the tip in a fire to make it durable. The K-bar knife had gone along with Hoa, Cru and Prentice so he needed something to dispatch any pig they might catch without having to fire a gun.

They soon found the pig and with Montrell pulling all the slack out of the cable, Red went around the blind side of the enraged animal and plunged the spear behind and just above its shoulder four or five times, piercing the animals lungs and heart. The animal squealed harder for a short time, madly twisting and thrashing its tusks in an effort to gore him. After about thirty seconds the animal wound down like an old alarm clock, stopped breathing and lay still. Red worked the cable from around its neck and the two of them carried it back behind the bunker.

"Be nice to have that K-bar to butcher it with," Red remarked, breathing somewhat heavily.

With that, Montrell reached into the lower pocket on his fatigue pants and pulled out a medium-sized jack knife.

"Been carrying this ever since I left Ohio," he told Red.

"Damn, didn't know you city boys were allowed to carry anything but a switch blade," Red commented, smiling.

Montrell protesting, replied, "Hey, I was a fucking Boy Scout. Would have made eagle, too, if I hadn't been caught stealing a *Playboy* from Master's Drug Emporium."

"What the fuck were you gonna do with a *Playboy*?" Red asked, laughing, "Swat flies with it? C'mon, let's see how sharp that little pig sticker is."

* * *

The remaining part of the day saw Cru, Hoa, and Prentice working their way around the people smoking the fish and then eventually bearing back toward their original intended direction of travel. Around four in the afternoon they heard a chopper coming in from the east. The chopper was out of sight, but from the sound of the loud Huey it had gone past them to the west for about two miles before the engine abruptly stopped.

"Could be the 1st Cav base over there," Crucianelli stated.

"Could be," Prentice replied. "We'll make our way over in that direction. Hoa, is that about where you figured them to be?"

Hoa nodded, saying, "Yes, the base is close that way."

"Okay," Prentice went on. "By the time we get close, it will be dark. We don't want to walk in on them in low light. Let's get within a half-mile. If we don't bump into a patrol, we'll hold up for the night and go in first thing in the morning. Cru, you take point from here on out."

* * *

"Damn, that's good!" Montrell remarked.

He and Red had butchered the pig, roasted it and wrapped it in leaves and mud. They buried it behind the bunker to preserve the meat as long as they could, with the exception of one hindquarter, which they kept to eat immediately. They were able to apply a rub of salt and pepper from their C-rations on the meat prior to roasting, enhancing the flavor.

"Prentice, Cru, and Hoa are eatin' cold grub and bunking in the dirt again," he said. "And, we're livin' the high life. If we had some cold beer and a hot mama san, it'd be like fucking R & R!"

Listening and nodding, Redmond agreed, "Yeah, this ain't bad. I ain't had my R & R yet, so I don't have nothin' to miss, but from what I hear from all you perverts that took theirs already, I'm surprised you even came back."

Aside from going home, R & R was the most coveted and discussed event amongst GIs in Vietnam. After three months in country, a GI was allowed to take a seven-day rest and recuperation trip to the destination

166

of his choice from among five different destinations. Most GIs saved their R & R for the last six months of their twelve or thirteen month tour.

Montrell had taken his already, going to Thailand. There he spent a week getting drunk and engaging in sex with an attractive young Thai prostitute. R & R was heaven on earth, but for many GIs the prospect of returning to Vietnam after a week in heaven was almost more than they could bear, and AWOL R & R GIs produced a big problem for the U.S. military.

Redmond planned on taking his in Hawaii where his woman would join him. Hawaii was the destination of choice for happily married men or men with serious girlfriends. Thailand, Hong Kong, Sydney, Australia and Taipei were usually chosen by single men, or men who didn't give a fuck about their marriages. Those destinations were all known as raucous mavens of sexual delight. Men returning from these R & Rs talked about them for weeks after their return, driving those poor souls who had yet to go, insane with envy.

The evening ended with Montrell and Redmond both in deep thought over R & R; Montrell reliving the one he had, and Redmond dreaming about the one he hoped to take.

Chapter 34

"Sometimes our light goes out but is blown into flame by another human being. Each of us owes deepest thanks to those who have rekindled this light."

Albert Schweitzer

At first light Cru, Hoa, and Prentice started making their way toward what they hoped to be a base camp of the U.S. Army 1st Cavalry. The 1st Cav was one of the finest fighting units in the U.S. military. While many other units had long ago lost their espirit de corps in the huge morass that the Vietnam War had become, the 1st Cav prided itself on its dedication to fulfilling its military mission, under all conditions regardless of the circumstance.

Captain Thorton T. Glover commanded Base Camp York. Glover, an African American, originally from the Watts section of Los Angeles, was everything a 1st Cav officer aspired to be. He fulfilled each and every mission his unit was assigned, with no delays, and few missteps. Every senior officer Glover had served under spoke with high praise of the man, and more importantly every man under Glover respected and admired him. Every grunt wanted to soldier under Thornton Glover. He tolerated no slackers, whiners, or kiss-asses, yet always rewarded good soldiers with trust, respect, and made sure they each got the individual recognition they deserved.

He looked over his men like family. He refused to take unnecessary risks with his men's lives, and would not allow others to do so either. Glover was a fanatic about training, and whenever they were in base camp his men were required to continually hone their skills in weapons and small infantry technique. He also made sure the training was appropriate to whatever theatre of operation they were in.

"No sense conducting large column flanking technique, we're not facing Caesar's legions out here," he would say. He also insisted his men learn the local culture, and more importantly respect it. To understand why people fought, it was important to know what motivated them to do so. For each of his men who were killed or seriously wounded, Glover himself penned a letter to the family.

Racial conflict, although rampant in most military units during the later years of the Vietnam War, did not exist in Base Camp York. Having felt the sting of racial prejudice as a youth, and while breaking into the ranks of the officer corps, Glover would not tolerate denigration of any individual for reasons of race, ancestry, religion, or beliefs. One was judged on performance of his duty and conduct as a representative of the U.S. military. On the other hand, he tolerated none of the black militancy and confrontational posturing that many blacks routinely conducted in many other units during that time in the U.S. military.

When a black NCO had breached etiquette by donning an Afro haircut and engaging in the militant, boisterous greetings that blacks often carried out in public during that time, Glover took him aside and reminded him that as a senior NCO in the U.S. Army his behavior was unacceptable.

"If you want to pull that H. Rap Brown shit, you ain't gonna do it in this army," he said. "It comes to my attention again I'll run your ass out." The problem never reoccurred.

Captain Glover was at mess around 07:00 when his master sergeant brought him curious news from a patrol. The news was regarding another small American unit of dubious origin that was traveling through their area.

"Who?" Captain Glover said incredulously.

"An air force patrol, Sir," the master sergeant said.

"You mean a downed aircraft crew?" Glover asked.

"No Sir, apparently some kind of air force convoy unit that was on their way to Le Thanh," the master sergeant replied.

"What the fuck is an air force convoy unit doing way the fuck out here?" he asked.

"Don't know, Sir. But we're bringing them in and we intend to find out,"

* * *

Hoa, Crucianelli, and Prentice had been under observation for some time, before members of the 1st Cav out patrol intercepted them.

"Halt! You are under armed observation by out patrol Wolf, Base Camp York," the squad leader ordered. Cru stopped immediately and held his hand up. Prentice and Hoa having heard the order were already frozen in their tracks. The young 1st Cav Spec 5 went on, "Lower your weapons and identify yourselves."

Cru yelled back, "We are members of an air force convoy from Phu Cat, ambushed on the road to Le Thanh." Members of the patrol immediately circled Cru, Hoa and Prentice.

"What the fuck you doin' out here, Sarge?" the spec 5 asked Prentice.

"I've been asking myself the same damn question, soldier. You bring us into your camp and get us some hot coffee and grub, we'll tell you anything you want to know," Prentice replied.

A few minutes later, they were inside the perimeter of Base Camp York. In a meeting with Captain Glover, Prentice immediately appraised him of the other two men in his party who were still out in the bush. He was coy about the real purpose of their circumstance and gave Glover an unbelievable story regarding it. Glover had seen it and heard it all, and Prentice's tale of delivering supplies to a joint services forward observation unit near the Cambodian border didn't fool him in the least.

"Sergeant Prentice, I'm not in the U.S. Air Force, but my radar is still pretty good. You wanna spread bullshit then fine. When you're done with your chow, we'll just set you and your little troupe here outside the perimeter and you can continue on your way.

"If you are on some clandestine operation that I don't know about, I don't give a shit. In that case you will have your orders and someone to hook up with, I'll help you as far as our theater of operation encompasses. If there's more to it, and you are in some kind of trouble, which I sense is really what's going on here, I'll do my best to sort it out for you. You think about it and let me know if you want our help in anyway, and how. But don't try blowin' smoke up my ass again."

Prentice, looking directly at Glover, sheepishly replied. "Yes, Sir."

* * *

Back at the bunker, Montrell and Red were on edge.

"Goin' on three days, I know they said they'd be at least three out, maybe four or five, but feel kind of helpless hangin' around here all day," Montrell remarked.

"Yeah, nice to lie around getting fat on fresh grub, but sooner or later we'll have to move out if they don't get back. We better come up with our own plan," Redmond offered.

They had gnawed just about all the meat off the hindquarter of pig they had roasted. They wanted to hold off cutting further into the delicacy until their partners returned. They figured if they came back unsuccessful they'd be half starved and worn out.

Montrell offered, "Okay, this will be the third day. Let's say if we don't see 'em after five days, we pull out."

Looking at Montrell, Red responded, "Pull out and go where? Our choices are, go out and try to find them or try to make it back to Pleiku on our own . . . and do what, I don't know?"

Thinking it over Montrell told Red, "Maybe we get back to Pleiku, find the OIC there and tell him the whole goddam story."

Frowning, Red replied, "If we spill the story, not only are we in immediate danger, but Cru and Prentice, not knowing that information is out, could walk right into a trap."

"We don't have a lot of options," Montrell remarked. "Okay, we got two more days to hatch out a plan; we better come up with something."

* * *

Prentice, Hoa, and Crucianelli enjoyed a warm, hearty breakfast compliments of Base Camp York. Exhausted, they were shown to a bunker where they were allowed to rest. The three slept well into the afternoon.

Prentice, rising first, refreshed himself with a long-needed shave and a shower. He decided to place his trust in Captain Glover and solicit his help regarding Master Sergeant Richards and the dilemma they were in. He sensed in Glover not only a good an honest man, but a man who had the inner strength and courage to do what he wanted to do . . . to do what needed to be done. Prentice knew that he would have to tell

Glover about the whole operation and that once he did that, there was no going back. Glover could turn him in, ignore him and send him on his way or worse yet, contact base operations at Phu Cat and tell them what he had heard. But Prentice was ready to take that chance.

After ensuring the night patrols and watch were in order, and the training schedule was on track Captain Glover made time for Sergeant Prentice's request for an audience and welcomed him into his hooch. He assigned the patrol the additional task of looking for the two other airmen from Prentice's crew, who were still out in the bush.

"Scotch?" Glover asked Prentice, producing two glasses.

"I've been known to have a touch of vodka now and then," Prentice replied. "Not much of a Scotch drinker but thanks anyway."

With that Glover went back to his footlocker and returned with a quart of Smirnoff's.

"I'm really starting to enjoy this little base camp of yours, Captain, You might have to evict us out of here," Prentice joked.

"You are welcome here as long as you wish and your OIC allows, Sergeant, but you may have to pull a few patrols carrying a little more gear than you air force boys are accustomed to. I've instructed my patrols to activate a search for your other two men," Glover replied. "Now how can I be of service to you?"

Prentice took a somber mood and a deep breath. Fortified with vodka, looking intensely at Glover, he delved into the situation they were in. He told him about the Kansas NCO and his many operations and connections, as well as his own complicity in it. It took the better part of an hour, with Glover stopping him now and then for clarification or additional detail.

When he was finished, Prentice added, "I want you to know that Crucianelli, along with Montrell and Redmond, who are the two men waiting for us back at the bunker have only been involved in this at the very bottom level, acting primarily upon orders from senior NCOs. They should not be held culpable in any way for the activities they were directed to perform. That goes for the men who were killed on this mission; Salas, Hardy, Canty, Childs and Becker."

Glover sat with his head in his hands for a few moments, deep in thought, looking up at Prentice every now and then, as if to validate what he had heard.

"I appreciate your candor, Sergeant Prentice. It is hard for me to digest all that you have divulged here today and harder to imagine all of this occurring with the complicit approval of senior level non-commissioned officers and staff officers as well. Here we are in the middle of hell, killing and being killed, believing we are the cutting edge of an honorable military effort to help these miserable people. I hear a story like this, and it makes me feel that we are just fools out here risking our lives while others sneak around gaining illicit profit from this bullshit fucking war." He sat there shaking his head, looking at Prentice from time to time.

"I'm sorry," was all Prentice could think to say. "I truly am sorry for my part in all of this, Captain Glover."

"To become a senior NCO you must have been a good man at one time, Sergeant Prentice, but somehow you lost your way. Nonetheless, I believe out of guilt, fear, or a combination of both, you are trying to find your way back. The fact that you went out and joined the men at Pleiku tells me you wanted to make good on your mistakes. I believe you. I believe you and I will help you."

Chapter 35

"Our brightest blazes of gladness are commonly kindled by unexpected sparks."

Samuel Johnson

"We need a well-placed friend," Montrell said, talking to himself but within earshot of Red.

Red looked at Montrell, "You mean we need a big chief on our side. Yeah, that would help," he replied. The two had agreed that if Prentice, Hoa and Cru didn't show up by the next day they would move out on their own. They planned on going out in stages, looking for their three brothers in arms. The trip would take them out one day, where upon they would return to the bunker, wait and plan, then head out a day in a different direction; probably east. If after three days they hadn't found their companions or the 1st Cav…they would head back for Pleiku and take their chances. They had plenty of food, but the problem was ammunition. They didn't have enough clips between them for any kind of sustained fight.

"Why not just keep on going when we're out there? Why come back to the bunker?" Montrell wondered.

Red explained, "If we don't find them or their sign, they may have gone a different direction completely. If they find trouble they'll head back to the bunker. We might miss them if we just keep on going. We'll come back twice to ensure we don't, giving them the benefit of the doubt."

"Ok, I guess," Montrell replied, though not entirely comfortable with the plan.

"I should have grabbed some of the AKs and ammo from the men Hoa killed," Redmond chided himself.

"Damn, Red, you were in no kind of shape to even think about that," Montrell reminded him.

"I was weak," Red replied. "A warrior overcomes pain and confusion."

"Well, you think we can find our way back there?" Montrell wondered.

"I can find my way back, but it's out of our way, and could be dangerous. The second day, maybe we should head that way. I don't feel comfortable being so low on ammunition. Unless . . . ," his voice trailed off.

"Unless what?" Montrell asked. "What the hell are you thinking, Red?"

Red smiled slyly, looking at Montrell and said, "I'll tell you what I'm thinking. Remember those crossbows we saw on those Yards on that one convoy near Vinh Thanh?"

The men had gone out on an official convoy that week, which took them into the territory of the Montagnards, or Yards as the GIs called them. The Montagnards were even poorer than the Vietnamese, and didn't get along with them, staying to themselves and depending on the countryside for all of their needs. They had few manufactured weapons and relied upon spears and crossbows for defense, not to mention a deadly array of Stone-Age snares, traps, and deadly spiked ambush sets, used on both man and beast. The crossbows, though unimpressive looking could easily pierce a flack vest, and the skill and speed at which the Montagnards wielded them was always a source of concern for any VC, NVA, or ARVN unit looking to take advantage of them.

"You're gonna make a bow and arrow?" Montrell said with doubt in his voice.

"No" Redmond replied, "I'm gonna make a crossbow; two to be exact. I learned to make bows and arrows back on the res, when I was a kid. They were accurate and effective; but here in this thick jungle we'll need something more compact. The Yard crossbows are perfect for this shit. There's a store of dried wood and twine in the corner of the bunker. We'll do some cobbling and see what we end up with."

The two worked most of that day sorting through the stores of wood and twine. Some of the wood wasn't dry enough for their purpose, but they found enough to make two crossbows. Within two hours Red had one completed. He tested it out back, using empty C-rat boxes stuffed with sand for targets. His first attempts were not accurate, but after working on

175

the twine rope of the bow, and heating and re-straightening the arrows, Red soon began to shred the targets with almost every shot. He showed Montrell how to use the weapon, and although not as proficient as Red, he was soon hitting the targets regularly. They had enough material for one more bow, which they completed. They made about 100 arrows and put them in two quivers, which they made from an old rucksack they found in the bunker. Now, if they ran low on ammo for their firearms, they could fall back on the crossbows. Red and Montrell were content in what they had been able to accomplish that day. They celebrated by feasting on the other hindquarter of pig.

*   *   *

"I don't have too many connections at Phu Cat," Captain Glover told Sergeant Prentice.

Glover then told one of his men to have his sergeant major join them in the command bunker. A crusty old soldier who had made his bones near the Yalu River fighting off wave after wave of Chinese soldiers who had invaded the Korean peninsula in an attempt to tip the war on the side of the North, Victor Manuel Lopez had been with Glover for five years now, two of those which included duty in the killing fields of Vietnam. Lopez had mentored Glover during his first tour of Vietnam, who as a naïve young 2nd lieutenant was fortunate to have the seasoned combat veteran help him navigate through the deadly mountains of the Central Highlands where so many young officers had fallen.

While Captain Glover depended on Sergeant Lopez to handle the mechanics of the day-to-day operation, Lopez depended on Glover for support regarding command, material availability, and direction; a complementary relationship that contributed to one another's success.

"Lopez?" Prentice half yelled, when the large NCO entered the bunker.

Lopez stopped dead in his tracks, "Prentice—you old fucking card cheat, what the hell you doing out here?"

Pumping Lopez's hand and laughing, Prentice told Lopez, "MACV sent me out here to see what the hell was going on. They said someone out here was draining the whole damn country of Johnny Walker Black."

"Captain," Lopez interjected. "I hope this bastard hasn't conned you into playing poker with him yet. He cheats and he's good at it."

Prentice shot back, "Hell, the only reason I cheat when I play you, is to get you so mad those extra aces you hide under your belt fall out, and give me a fighting chance."

Laughing, Glover replied, "Well, Sergeant Prentice, I see that you've played cards with Lopez before. It seems that you two crooks met your match in one another."

"Yes, Sir, that we have," Lopez added. Lopez went on to explain to Captain Glover the circumstances of their acquaintance, how during a fierce five-day running battle with combined forces of NVA and VC in Binh Dinh Province they had run dangerously low on ammunition and medical supplies.

"We reported to Qui Nhon for re-supply as ordered," Lopez said. "The fucking bureaucrats there hemmed and hawed, and shorted the shit out of us on everything we needed. 'How the fuck you expect us to fight a war by under-supplying us?' I asked the officer in charge. He threatened to have the MPs lock me up if I was insubordinate again and told us to leave the base immediately.

"We left and went to the only other large American installation in the area, the Phu Cat airbase. They tried to give us the bum's rush there too, but old Prentice happened to be on hand and he jumped in. He dismissed the young three striper who was hassling us, and asked what we needed. With our request in hand he left and came back in fifteen minutes, but not before he saw to it that me and all my men had chow and cold beers all around. When he came back, he told us to follow him in our vehicles. We got to a large warehouse where we were loaded up with everything we requested, plus enough C-rats and Black Label beer to last us a week."

Then Lopez smiled and added, "They quartered us overnight and even hosted up a nice game of cards." Looking at Captain Glover somberly, he said, "If Sergeant Prentice is in need of anything from our command, I would be honored to personally take care of it myself, Sir."

Prentice said, "Thank you, Sergeant Lopez, thank you."

Chapter 36

"Make voyages. Attempt them. There is nothing else."

Tennessee Williams

As they had determined the next morning with no sight of Hoa, Prentice or Cru, Montrell and Redmond left the bunker, which had become home, for a one-day exploratory foray, in an attempt to reconnect with their comrades. Along with food and water they took both their M-16s and crossbows, along with some emergency medical supplies and two poncho liners.

"I'll take point," Red stated. "We'll travel slow and quiet. We will follow their trail as long as we can. If we don't hook up by nightfall we'll find a hide in the jungle.

After several hours of following the other men's trail, they came to the point where their comrades had seen the smoke and moved east to veer around it.

"What do you see, Red?" Montrell asked after Redmond stopped and began scanning the area.

"They stopped here for a short time, then changed direction sharply. Something must have spooked them," Red replied.

Montrell looking around cautiously, said, "If they were being chased by someone, we could run right into them."

"Do you smell smoked fish?" Red asked.

"Smoked fish?" Montrell half-yelled. "What the fuck are you talking about?"

Red said, "One of my favorite memories back on the res was the odor of fish, smoking over a slow hickory wood fire."

"That's a great memory, Red, remind me to order us up some at the fucking deli next time we see one," Montrell replied sarcastically.

"Someone's been smoking fish not too far from here, and I'll bet they're the same people that caused our boys to change direction," Redmond explained. "We'd better follow their trail and keep it low and slow for a while."

Nervously fingering his M-16, Montrell followed closely behind Red for the rest of the morning. *Vietcong smoked fish, Special Forces smoked fish, and Richards's henchmen probably smoked fish as well,* he thought. Hanging around the bunker eating pig and sleeping for the past several days had lulled Montrell into a false sense of security. Now, inching through the bush, facing another potential life threatening situation he became depressed again.

Fuck, he thought. *I'll never get back alive. Odds are not with me, damn me for getting myself involved in this shit, damn me!* They kept moving until early afternoon where they stopped to rest and eat.

Red, sensing Montrell's mood, tried to put him at ease. "They would have moved on us by now," he said. "We're okay here. Let's just rest and relax for a while."

"Yeah, right," Montrell responded, but he felt no better.

*　　*　　*

After their reunion Prentice and Lopez sat with Captain Glover discussing Prentice's dilemma.

"So that's how you came up with all that shit we needed back at Phu Cat," Lopez commented.

Prentice looked at him and said, "I'm glad I was able to help you that day, Lopez. I have been able to help many others in need as well. Hell, murderer and scoundrel that he is, even Richards has helped many people in need. Frequently local villagers or other American or allied units who needed help benefited from the supplies of his operations. But I know that don't make it right. I'm not proud of what I did. I thought I'd cut a fat hog in the ass, but that damn hog's come back to bite me, and he ain't done yet."

"We aren't here to judge you, Sergeant Prentice. It may come to play that at some point you will have to face the uniform code of military justice, but our goal right now is to get you and your party into a safe environment and insure the murderers who have perpetrated these crimes are put out of business," Glover told him. "The way I see it, the biggest threat right now is from these rogue Special Forces roaming the countryside looking to take you out. Victor, do we know the whereabouts of the Special Forces in this area? And if so, what are the chances they are involved or even aware of this situation?"

Lopez thought about it for a minute. "Officially, we don't know their whereabouts, Sir... unofficially there are two different psy ops working in this area that we are familiar with. We bump into them on our patrols now and then, and we trade information as needed. These guys all know each other pretty well, so there's a pretty good chance they may be familiar with the ones who are after Prentice and his men. They're also pretty tight-knit and closed mouth, so I'm not sure we will get much cooperation out of them."

Glover put his hand on Lopez's shoulder. "Well, do some sniffing around and see what you can find out, Sergeant," he said. "I don't care how tight-knit these bastards are, if they're killing American GIs for profit, they've become a target of the 1st Cav."

"Yes, Sir," Lopez replied.

* * *

Redmond and Montrell headed back to the bunker after following the trail of their comrades most of the day. They took care to skirt the original trail, feeling whoever had been smoking that fish, would have been onto that trail as well. Back at the bunker, not finding their companions, they sat down to eat and discuss what they discovered.

"We have to assume they weren't attacked," Redmond stated. "They were definitely heading in the direction Hoa thought the 1st Cav would be. I think tomorrow we could take a short cut and just head straight for where we believe the camp to be. We probably will need most of the day to hit the camp, even with the short cut."

Montrell was doubtful. "What makes you think Hoa didn't know about that shortcut?" he asked.

"I think we don't understand the nature of the Vietnamese," Red replied. "Buddhists don't consider time the way Westerners do. I'm speaking from experience because my people, Native Americans, are of the same nature in that they may take a longer path, not to waste time but because they feel compelled to do so."

"Compelled by what?" Montrell wanted to know.

"Well," Red said, "in the spirit world, which is where we believe we really exist, what you may call instinct, we consider spiritual guidance. Hoa took the path, he felt provided that guidance."

Annoyed, Montrell said, "Okay, then maybe we shouldn't take the fucking shortcut either. Maybe it's trouble."

"It's trouble, all right" Redmond stated, "but not the kind of trouble you're thinking of. If I'm right, it will be grueling, thick shit, up and down steep terrain and hotter than fuck. But it will save us a half day, and it's unlikely we'll run into many, if any, people."

Montrell thought about it. "Well, if it means not running into anymore Goddam VC or hit men I'm in," he said.

"Okay," Red said. "We'll hit it first thing in the morning. I can't promise we won't run into anybody, but it will be less likely."

Chapter 37

"A wise man changes his mind, a fool never will."

Spanish proverb

The next morning, Lopez took the first patrol going out. Since assuming the duties of senior NCO at Camp York, Lopez found it difficult to get out on patrol, something that always gave him a great deal of satisfaction. Most small infantry units in Vietnam were still running "ambush" or "search and destroy" operations, as dictated by MACV, who now took their marching orders from General Creighton Abrams, who had taken over from William Westmoreland. Abrams had since introduced small unit "clear and hold" missions in an attempt to win the "hearts and minds" of the Vietnamese people. It was a good strategy and successful in the field, and soon most small infantry units in Vietnam would be employing this tactic.

Having cut his teeth in close combat Captain Glover had studied it, understood it, and believed in it. Lopez believed in it as well, and every time he had the opportunity to see an area cleared of VC and NVA, and subsequently turned over to what he considered an "honest" ARVN unit, he achieved a degree of satisfaction that not many military units in Vietnam had a chance to experience.

"Ok, move out," Lopez ordered. He was leading a twelve-man patrol, and they were heading north through an area of their responsibility that overlapped with an ARVN command and was also occupied by a Special Forces unit based in the area. The Special Forces unit had been making incursions into Cambodia for several months, prior to the official invasion of Cambodia ordered by President Richard Nixon. They had mapped areas of Cambodia for the purpose of determining suitable aircraft landing zones, as well as identifying NVA and VC strongholds and supply depots for bombing runs. Uncharacteristically this unit was not in the business of assassination or applying misinformation.

Lopez knew the CIA operative in charge as a no-nonsense stalwart character known only as "Scar" because of the many shrapnel and bullet wounds he had incurred as an air force para rescue team member in Vietnam, before adding more as a CIA operative. Scar could be depended on to do nothing more than he was told, and his integrity was only as good as any situation on any given day. He would do anything he felt necessary, given the circumstances he was in; he felt allegiance to no one out of his immediate sight.

Lopez knew all of this and he also knew that any information or deal made with Scar was susceptible to change based upon any variable which could possibly occur, of which there were many. Any agreement with Scar was similar to what used car dealers back in the States referred to as a "taillight guarantee." That is, the guarantee expired as soon as the taillights were no longer visible from the lot.

* * *

Montrell was panting heavily and his sweat had already soaked his fatigues through and through, but physical challenges were something he was familiar with and actually enjoyed. A high school track star and baseball player, Montrell still played softball on the field the men had made at Phu Cat, as well as basketball on the court they put up near the enlisted men's barracks. Despite working twelve to fourteen hours of physically grueling work in the steaming supply warehouse, he enjoyed an evening run now and then. Montrell knew he was not as mentally tough as Redmond. He wouldn't push himself into doing anything he didn't enjoy doing, but Montrell felt physically he could keep up with him. Redmond was sweating and panting also, but the look on his face was one of serene confidence and control. Monty envied Red's self-discipline; although Red drank and smoked pot, it never interfered with anything he undertook, unlike many of the other men in Vietnam.

For many GIs in Vietnam, alcohol and drugs became their primary source of refuge from fear and terror, searing heat, strenuous workloads, separation from family and friends, and guilt. Some turned to religion while some others dedicated themselves to volunteering and helping the local people through the work of chaplains and other ad hoc groups that may be involved. However a good number of servicemen took advantage of the low price and high availability of alcohol and drugs of one kind or another, as a solace to get them through the nightmare they found themselves in. Montrell was just one of the many.

"Wish I had some white crosses," Montrell said. The U.S. Air Force dispensed amphetamines or "speed" in the form of small white crossed pills. No prescription needed, no questions asked; just show up at the dispensary and load up. They were a favorite among overworked pilots, sentries, druggies, and even many straight GIs who figured if the military was dolling them out, it must be okay to use them, and by the way, as many as you want.

"Hell, with all the damn runnin' and shit you do, I figured you'd be to Cambodia and back by now," Redmond teased. "Put you on fuckin' speed and I'd have to fill your rucksack with rocks, just so I could keep up."

"Oh, I think you'll keep up," Montrell replied. "I saw you pull perimeter guard every night at Phu Cat after bustin' your ass all day throwing boxes of shit around in the warehouses. Most of us pass out after two days of that shit."

Redmond laughed, "Mostly sat around on my ass on perimeter guard. Lookin' around watchin' Flash sneak through the wire to get a piece of ass." Now they were both laughing.

"Yeah, I never saw anyone as horny as Flash. That sonofabitch would screw a snake if someone held its head," Montrell added.

After a moment Redmond mused, "Damn, I miss him. And Hardy and Salas, too."

Montrell, nodding his head in agreement, noted, "Well, we'd better push on."

* * *

Lopez and his patrol humped most of the morning without incident. After a short break they moved through an area in which they had successfully neutralized a village of VC by diligently working with the village chief in establishing a small medical facility for the people of the village.

The village chief convinced the local VC that this group of Americans was honest and able to provide them with many things they always lacked during the troubling times they were in. The chief had always believed the NVA were using the people of the south to take advantage of them, as were the ARVN. And although he wanted his land to be free of invaders, he felt the Americans were actually the lesser of two evils.

The 1st Cav soldiers who had come to their aid spoke their dialect of Vietnamese and did not look down their noses at them, as did the impolite men who came from the north. Uncharacteristically the VC left this village alone. Having tired of the heavy-handed way the people from the North behaved towards them, the local VC vacillated between allegiance to their rude, self-serving masters from the North and the sometimes boorish, but often charitable foreign invaders from America.

"Point's reporting dead villagers ahead," the young Spec 4 told Lopez.

When the man put the radio down Lopez inquired, "Fresh kills?"

"Didn't say," the Spec 4 replied. Within ten minutes Lopez and the rest of the patrol caught up to the point man, Spec 5 Robert DeAngelis, standing by the bodies of three Vietnamese.

"Looks like the work of VC, Sarge," the point man reported. Lopez inspected the bodies. Each had his throat slit from ear to ear and were stripped of clothing.

"Take a close look at these wounds, point."

DeAngelis removed the cigarette that was dangling from his mouth and stared curiously at Lopez, then peered closely at the wound of one of the dead men.

"Serrated," he remarked, somewhat surprised.

"That's right," Lopez replied. "These wounds were made by a serrated knife. Not too many VC carry serrated blade knives."

Perplexed, DeAngelis protested, "Only pilots and Special Forces use the serrated K-bars, the Marines and other grunts that use them have the standard non-serrated blade K-bar." Having said that, DeAngelis realized the implication of what he said.

Looking at him with a half-smile Lopez replied quietly, "That's right, Angel, these killings were done with Special Forces weapons."

* * *

After working their way through the thick cover for a couple of hours into the afternoon, Redmond motioned Montrell to stop and remain quiet. "We're being followed," he said.

185

"By whom?" Montrell asked with some panic in his voice.

"I'm not sure, I had the same feeling this morning but figured I just may have had the jitters, but now I'm sure of it," Redmond replied. "They were behind us for most of the day, but now they've flanked us on both sides. We're gonna let them come in, but we'll have a surprise for them. Get that crossbow out, but keep moving."

Redmond and Montrell moved about fifty yards until they came upon a deep ravine that was hidden by thick underbrush. Red motioned Montrell to get into the ravine. Looking around in each direction Redmond then slipped in as well. Whispering, Red directed Montrell to face the opposite way he was sitting, to arm his crossbow, and have at least ten arrows ready. Then they sat and waited.

Chapter 38

*"Victory is always possible for the person
who refuses to stop fighting."*

Napolean Hill

Lopez's patrol was back at Base Camp York by early afternoon. Captain Glover had received radio communication regarding the dead Vietnamese and met with Lopez as he and his men came through the gate.

"Everyone back okay, Lope?" he inquired.

Continuing on to the operations bunker while removing his pack, Lopez replied, "Yes, Sir, no casualties on our end."

"When you're done seeing to your men and the next patrol, we'll hook up," Captain Glover said. "I'm working with the engineer trying to get that fucking water pump to work for more than ten minutes at a time, so come on by and grab me."

"Will do, Captain," Lopez replied.

*   *   *

"Keep perfectly still, maybe they won't see us," Redmond whispered to Montrell. As he guessed, the men flanking them on either side had moved in to try and intercept them. They could hear the men moving through the thick brush above them and soon they could even see them as they worked methodically through the cover trying to flush Red and Monty out.

"Americans," whispered Montrell. "Fucking Special Forces, again."

There were two men on each side, crossing back and forth looking for signs and signaling to each other with hand gestures. One of the men, a

187

large scar-faced individual, seemed to be in charge. Sweating profusely, tense as piano wire, Redmond and Montrell could only look on in terror as the four men closed in on their position. The scar-faced man raised his hand and all four men stopped.

"Lost their fuckin' trail," the scar-faced man noted. "You guys have anything going over there?"

The closest man replied, "No, it's as if they just fucking disappeared."

The crevice that Monty and Red had found was only about fifteen feet long and three feet wide at the largest point. Red happened upon it purely by luck, and if he wouldn't have half stepped into it, he wouldn't have seen it himself. The men hunting them continued to scour the area, but none of them found the small crease that hid the two terrified airmen. After about twenty minutes they moved on. Montrell and Redmond lay frozen in position for another thirty minutes before moving.

* * *

After seeing to his men and informing the next patrol of what they had found and advising them to be alert, Lopez went to meet Captain Glover. When Lopez arrived, Glover and the engineer, a 2nd lieutenant, were struggling to pull the motor from the generator for the pump. A young enlisted man, Spec 4 Martin Dempsey, stood by holding a box of tools.

"Damn!" Lopez exclaimed. "Now this is what I like to see, a pair of officers actually doing a little work while an enlisted man gets a break."

Smirking, Glover said, "Well, if Dempsey here hasn't snookered us again! How'd that happen, Martin? I was holding the tools and you were doin' the grunt work. All of a sudden it's the other way around."

With a big grin Dempsey responded, "And I appreciate it too, Sir!"

"You damn goldbrick, get down here and help Lieutenant Ahrens get this motor off. Lopez and I are going back to the ops bunker," Glover said.

"Yes, Sir, no sweat, Sir." Dempsey replied.

Back at the ops bunker Lopez and Glover discussed what they had discovered on the morning patrol in detail. "And they were civilians, not VC?" Glover asked.

"I'm sure of it," Lopez replied. "One was an old woman who I've seen around the vil that's a couple miles from the ambush site, and one of the others was just a boy, barely thirteen or fourteen years old."

Glover answered, "We've seen plenty of juvenile VC, Sergeant. You and I both have."

"Yes, Sir," Lopez said. "But I don't believe this kid was a VC. The third one was a man around fifty, kind of old for a Vietnamese."

Glover frowned and sighed, "Yeah, not too many of these poor bastards get up into their fifties, do they?"

"No, they don't," Lopez replied in a low voice. "No, they don't."

* * *

"I think we can move now," Redmond stated as he slowly worked his way up and out of the small crevice they were occupying.

"What if they come back?" Montrell whispered, scared half out of his wits.

"We'll have to take our chances," Redmond replied. "This crevice we've been hiding in no doubt fills up with water with every rain. We have to move on and, if they show up again, we'll find another hide."

"They were Special fucking Forces," Montrell observed with anger and fear.

"Yes, they were, and it's in our best interest to beat feet out of here and find that 1st Cav unit ASAP. We can't be worried about the others right now. We'll have to hope to hook up with them further down the road," Redmond stated. "The direction of the men hunting us isn't the same direction we're heading, but we'll have to keep our eyes open for signs."

Montrell looked at Red quizzically, "Hey, you're the fucking Indian, Red; I couldn't track an elephant through a corn field."

Laughing, Red told him, "Okay, Monty, we'll both keep our eyes open, for people . . . and elephants."

* * *

When the second patrol of the day came in Captain Glover and Sergeant Lopez both attended their briefing in the ops bunker. The NCOIC reported making contact with a Special Ops patrol. They had hailed the men, but their call was not returned and the Special Ops team moved off quickly before further contact could be made.

"Was Scar one of them?" Lopez asked.

"We really didn't get a good enough look at all of them, Sarge," the man reported. "When they saw us they took off like scalded cats."

"I don't like it," Glover commented. "For some reason those guys didn't want to be seen by another American unit. I hope to hell they aren't out there killing more civilians. Lope, have a written report on the last two patrols. I'm going to contact Major Buckner."

"Yes, Sir," Lopez replied.

*   *   *

Montrell and Redmond slowly worked their way through the bush for the rest of the day. Redmond saw no other sign of the Special Ops unit they had encountered earlier.

"Let's start looking for a hide for the night," he told Montrell.

"Sounds good to me," Montrell replied.

After a half hour, Red found a dug-out in a hill surrounded by thick brush. Other than a few animal trails, there were no sign of recent use. They cautiously checked it out and then moved in.

"This should be good for the night," Redmond said. "It's well hidden and we should be able to hear anyone who may be trying to sneak in on us. We can't chance a fire tonight but we have enough rations left to carry us through tomorrow night."

Montrell was clearing the remainder of the debris out for their evening sleeping quarters. "Well, guess we can't have a pig roast every day," he said. "Sure as hell be nice to have a beer or a fucking joint though. My fucking nerves are about shot."

Going through his pockets Redmond replied, "I've got enough betel nut to carry us through the next couple days. You can chew on that."

"Damn, you're goin' Asiatic on me, Red," Montrell commented.

Redmond laughed, "Well, I am a damn Indian, so I didn't have too far to go anyway."

Not long after Red and Monty settled into their poncho liners for a night's sleep, Red sat up after he heard something or someone moving slowly through the thick cover within a short distance from their hide.

"I heard it, too," Montrell whispered, sitting up.

"Grab your crossbow and get an arrow ready," Red whispered, doing the same.

Montrell grabbed his crossbow. His hands were shaking so badly he could barely get the arrow into position. He took some of the betel nut Red had given him earlier and started chewing on it, hoping it would settle him down.

Red slowly moved some of the branches he had placed earlier to cover the entrance of the dugout. Peering into the dark jungle, he saw what he feared the most; two Caucasians in jungle fatigues with no unit markings. They were looking for signs and working their way slowly towards the opening that Red and Montrell occupied. He motioned Montrell over and had him peer out so he could see the men as well.

"Train your arrow on the man on the right; I'll take the other one," Red whispered. He moved to the left of Montrell, created an opening in the cover, armed his bow and waited.

"When they get within three or four feet they'll discover the opening, then they'll bring their weapons up and prepare to enter. That's when we hit them," he whispered. "Aim for the heart, they'll be close enough to hit it. After you fire, re-arm immediately, don't watch them or hesitate."

"Okay," Montrell whispered.

"Now!" Red whispered.

Flunk!

His arrow flew and on cue, Montrell shot a split second after.

"Hoosh!" The man Red fired at sucked his breath in, dropped his weapon, and grabbed at the end of the arrow now protruding from his chest.

Montrell's arrow found its mark as well. The man he hit spun around, hurt but not mortally wounded. He raised his weapon in the direction from which the arrow had come.

Flunk!

Red had re-armed his bow, noted his man was down, and fired his second arrow at the man Montrell had wounded. The man stopped moving as soon as the second arrow pierced his heart. His weapon slipped from his hand and both hit the ground.

"Fuck!" Montrell mouthed, hardly knowing it was him who spoke.

"Quiet!" Red ordered. "The others may be close by, rearm and sit tight. We'll wait at least fifteen minutes before we go check the bodies."

Chapter 39

"Good courage in a bad affair is half of the evil overcome."

Plautus

The next day just before Lopez and his patrol were to move out, the sentry reported men coming in. Lopez and Glover quickly moved to the gate by the perimeter to get a view of the men the sentry had reported.

"It's Scar," Lopez said, somewhat surprised.

Glover immediately slipped back to the bunker where Prentice, Cru, and Hoa were quartered. Informing them of the visitors, he moved them to the supply tent at the opposite end of the camp.

"You guys stay here till we come and get you," he told Prentice. "Don't come out for anything, and remain quiet."

"Right, sir, we'll stay put," Prentice replied.

Glover went back to the gate where Lopez and Scar were in conversation.

Lopez stopped for introductions. "Captain Glover, this is Special Operations advisor Ted Van Horn."

Then addressing Scar, "Mr. Van Horn."

"Ted," Scar interrupted.

Lopez continued, "Ted, this is Captain Glover, Officer in Charge of Base Camp York." The men shook hands. Two other men were with Scar.

"This is advisor Perry, and this is advisor Nikoloff," Scar said, introducing them. Glover suggested they move to the operations bunker, which they all did.

"The coffee's not always good, but it's usually hot," he told Scar and his men.

"Thanks," Scar replied. After the men were seated and comfortable, Glover asked them what they could do for them.

"We're tracking some renegades," Scar replied. "Some air force personnel involved in theft and murder. They took off with a load of high value goods out of Phu Cat Air Base a couple of weeks ago and disappeared into the jungle. They murdered the army enlisted men who were with them and tried to make it look like a VC ambush. They also murdered a couple of their associates who were in on it after they left Pleiku. Probably fighting over the loot, I'm guessing."

Captain Glover said, "Wow, these sound like some real bad characters. Do you have their names?"

Scar responded, "The ringleader's name is Prentice. He's a disgruntled master sergeant. We believe the other three are named Montrell, Crucianelli and Redmond. Supposedly they're in our area and they're considered very dangerous. Our orders were to bring them in dead or alive, so if you and your men should happen to run into them, give them no opportunity to kill or wound you. My advice is to take them out immediately."

At that Lopez gave Glover a quick sidelong glance.

Glover said, "We will definitely be on the alert for these bastards. Are you going to be in the area so we can contact you should we run into them?"

"Yes, sir, we'll be around," Scar replied.

*   *   *

After waiting fifteen minutes, Redmond and Montrell slipped out of their hide. Red moved out past the two bodies and checked for sign of others. When he returned he reported, "There were three others with them, but they didn't come in this close. I'm guessing they think these guys are still operating. We'll drag them back into our hide then I'll go out and cover up as much of their trail as I can."

"You mean we gotta keep these bastards in here with us?" Montrell questioned.

Looking impatient, Red told Montrell, "It's that or get our asses caught by their partners. Now drag him in and bring his weapon. Don't forget to wipe off the blood from the grass and bushes and make sure the arrows come back in with him."

"Right," Montrell replied in a resigned tone.

"Well, you sure made some crossbows," Montrell said, once back in the hide. "Three arrows, two dead men!"

Thinking about it Red remarked, "Yeah, well they were mighty close, and we were mighty lucky."

They had pushed the two bodies into one end of the small hide. They took everything out of the dead men's pockets, which wasn't much.

"What kind of weapons are those?" Montrell wondered, inspecting the two short-barreled automatic weapons the men carried.

"They're PPS-43 submachine guns," Red replied. "They're Russian made. NVA use them as well, I'm guessing they took these off of dead Vietnamese soldiers they killed. They'll do the job."

Balancing the weapon in his hand, Montrell softly commented, "I'm sure they would."

* * *

The 1st Cav at Base Camp York followed the movements of the Special Forces men for about an hour after they left. As Lopez suspected, they had doubled back and watched over the base for about a half hour after they left the perimeter. Only when Glover and Lopez felt certain they were long gone did they go back to retrieve Prentice and his men.

"We're going to keep you near the interior of the base for a while," Glover advised. "We'll dig another supply bunker which you and your men will occupy.

"I'm sorry for dragging you and your men into this, Captain Glover," Prentice said.

"Don't worry about it, Prentice, it isn't your fault. You made some bad decisions, but your man Richards is responsible. He and this piece of garbage we call Scar, would have gotten some other poor bastard to do their dirty work if it wasn't you. We're gonna take them down, together."

* * *

"How soon you think we can get the fuck out of here?" Montrell asked. The two dead bodies had already begun to decompose in the sweltering heat.

Redmond knew Montrell wouldn't like his answer. "Monty, these guys are professionals. They have all the time in the world and they will try to wait us out. Sooner or later they will miss their two companions here, and will start seriously following up on their trail, trying to find them. We can try to sneak out and get past them, or we can sit it out. Let's both think on this, hard." Red told him.

Montrell, frowning, knew they were in another life or death situation. Well, he wouldn't go down without making his pitch. "If we don't get rid of these fucking bodies, they'll be able to smell their way in here."

Red agreed, "Yeah, we're gonna to have to deal with them. I think in a couple of hours, when it's totally dark we'll have to move the bodies out, far out from here. We'll have to hide them as best we can, and cover our trail both ways so it's impossible to track."

About two hours after dark, Red went out for a look around. After about fifteen minutes he returned and told Montrell it appeared their antagonists were gone for the night. One at a time, they carried the two dead men about a quarter mile beyond their hide. They made a great effort to make it appear as if the men were ambushed at the position where they left them. Red spent an hour covering their trail each way. He knew it was a gamble; these Special Forces guys were highly trained and seasoned. If they bought it, they'd be lucky. At the least, they bought themselves about two hours of get away time.

It was almost morning by the time they were finished. Montrell was exhausted, but as tired as he was he knew they had to get as far away as possible. After covering their hide out and trail as best they could, they moved out slowly, listening for others, and removing all possible signs of themselves as they went along.

Chapter 40

"La lanh dum la rach."
(The good leaves protect the worn out leaves.)

Vietnamese proverb

Captain Glover decided to do something he missed and hadn't done in a long time; he intended to go out on patrol the next morning. During the previous afternoon, a patrol had gone out shortly after Scar and his men departed Base Camp York, in an attempt to shadow the Special Ops men without alerting them. They were unsuccessful, and after only one hour they completely lost the trail of Scar and reported back to base camp with no information.

"I'll take point," Lopez stated. Back when he and then 2nd Lieutenant Glover ran patrols together as a team, Lopez's skill at point and identifying sign was legendary.

Glover liked to say that Lopez could track an ant up a tree and return with the insect exhausted and tethered. He briefed 1st Lieutenant Dawson, his second in command, and let Prentice know his plans as well.

"Hoa believes he can help and wants to go with you," Prentice informed Glover. Glover looked carefully at Hoa, then at Sergeant Lopez.

After thinking about it, Lopez commented, "Might be a good idea. We will be contacting the locals to see what they know about the activity of Scar and his men. We speak the lingo, but they would probably open up more to a fellow Vietnamese. And from what Prentice tells me, Hoa knows the area at least as good as we do."

"Okay," Glover said. "Hoa will accompany us on patrol tomorrow morning at 06:00. Sergeant Lopez, equip him with a canteen and rations." Looking at Prentice and Hoa, he added, "No weapons."

"Yes, sir," Prentice replied.

197

"Right, sir," Lopez added.

* * *

Red only felt it was safe to move faster after two hours of travel, moving away from the previous night's hide.

"I think we lost 'em," he told Montrell. "If we stay on this tack, we should reach the area Hoa thought the 1st Cav was camped by late afternoon.

Montrell, more than happy to hear that, replied, "I just want to get out of this fucking bush and back on an American base. I don't care if they arrest me and throw me in the slammer for ten years."

Clenching his chin, Redmond replied, "I don't think jail is the biggest problem we got back there, Monty. Much as I admire the men of the 1st Cav, who's to say there ain't one of Richard's associates with them? When we do get there, we'll have to be very careful, with eyes in the back of our heads."

As if suddenly remembering the dilemma they faced, Montrell moaned, "Yeah, shit, I guess we're fucked no matter what we do."

Looking at him sympathetically Red told him, "We'll get through it, Monty."

Moving more rapidly, by late morning Red had identified several trails that crossed each other frequently. They also heard the sound of a chopper coming from the direction they were heading.

"We're on the right track," Redmond told Montrell. "I'm guessing a couple of hours away from the base camp at most."

Montrell suggested a plan for their arrival. "When we get there we should ask for the OIC, and not budge an inch till he shows up," he said. "Maybe we stay just outside the gate under cover till we see him."

Thinking about it, Red replied, "That's a plan. The other thing we may consider is intercepting a patrol, taking our chances that nobody in the patrol is hooked up with Richards. We could explain our situation and have them bring the OIC out to us, so we aren't exposed too much."

After a moment Montrell replied, "How do we know the OIC isn't hooked up with Richards?"

Grimacing Red told him, "We'll just have to take our chances. We can't stay out here hiding for the rest of our lives."

They didn't have time to discuss the problem any further however, as automatic weapons fire from their right flank engulfed their position, shredding the surrounding vegetation.

* * *

"I hear it," Glover responded when Lopez radioed back to the patrol from his position of point. "Is it coming from the vil?"

Lopez responded with a low voice, "I think just east of the vil, those aren't AKs or 16s."

Glover quietly told him, "Move back to our position quick as you can, Lope." After several minutes Lopez returned and Glover gathered the rest of the men.

"Those sound like MAC-10s, Lope. I'm guessing our friend Scar and his men are firing those weapons. The question is, at who?"

"Don't know, Sir. No VC or NVA patrols been in the area for a couple weeks. Hope they aren't killing more villagers."

Glover said, "We don't know they killed those villagers, Sergeant."

Jaw clenched, Lopez shot back, "Then the villagers are warring with other nearby villages with American Special Forces weapons."

"Lope, let's divide our patrol into two groups. We'll move as quietly as possible and flank whoever it is on both sides, no sense sitting around debating who's killing who until we can find out for ourselves," Glover told him while gesturing the men in formation.

* * *

Redmond's instincts and training saved him and Montrell from instant death. The telltale sound of the MAC-10 weapons being locked on triggered his action of pushing Montrell down and dropping with him. No one heard Montrell's screaming as the weapons fired non-stop for over forty-five seconds. The crease they were lying in kept them just low enough for safety, although the debris from flying vegetation and the noise was terrifying. When it stopped Red readied his crossbow, shook

Montrell out of his stupor and made sure Montrell had his M-16 locked and loaded. Red was going hunting.

"Stay here and shoot anybody you can see," he instructed Montrell.

Creeping through the vines and grass, Redmond soon saw the men who were firing at them from their left flank. The men were standing tensely waiting to move in or begin firing again.

Flunk!

Red's arrow hit the first man in the throat. The man croaked sharply, attempted to grab the arrow, and slumped to the ground. In a split second the other man opened fire, spraying the area where he thought the arrow came from. Then Red's second arrow hit him in the belly just below his flack vest.

The man winced and half-doubled over but kept firing, yelling to the others, "Crossbows!" His companions rushed up. They were about to reach Montrell's position when Montrell, who was lying in the crease almost directly underneath them, opened fire.

The first man, hit in the crotch, screamed and went down, twisting and turning in pain. The second man opened up on where he thought the sound came from, but Montrell's second volley hit him in the head; one round striking him in the upper jaw, the other right below the hairline. Though killed instantly, the dead man kept firing as he went down. One round found its way through Montrell's upper shoulder, cutting through the tendon and muscle.

Montrell's life was not in danger, and although he wasn't thinking about it at the time, the damaged tissue caused by the MAC-10 bullet ended any future chances the star pitcher from the University of Toledo Rockets had for a career in the major leagues.

*   *   *

"You copy, Lope?" Glover quietly but clearly spoke in his radio.

"Yes sir, I heard it too, Sir. Those last two volleys were from a 16," Lope replied.

"Right," Glover responded. "Are you in position yet?"

"Couple more minutes. I'll get back to you soon as I'm in," Lopez told him.

Glover and his men had worked their way into position just above a swamp where the shooting occurred. They could see movement and shadowed the men they saw until they heard screaming.

Soon Lopez radioed he was in position and was observing Scar and two other men moving in on a position.

"Stay on 'em," Glover barked. "We'll hook up soon. Tell everyone to watch the crossfire."

The Special Forces men, who normally would have been impossible to approach from a blind side, were too concentrated on their intended prey to notice Glover and Lopez moving in on their flanks. By the time they did Montrell and Redmond had already taken out four from their ranks.

"Freeze!" Lopez shouted at the three men he observed.

"Drop your weapons!" Glover shouted at the two he zeroed in on.

Like a wounded animal Scar reacted swiftly, attempting to salvage the situation. "What the fuck you think you're doing?" he screamed. "You fucking dogface bastards are interfering with a Special Forces operation and endangering our lives. Now get the fuck out of here before I turn you in to division!"

Glover, in a calm but firm voice, told him, "Don't you worry about that, Mr. Van Horn; we'll worry about division as needed. Now drop those fucking weapons or we'll engage."

Chapter 41

"What is life? It is the flash of a firefly in the night. It is the breath of a buffalo in the wintertime. It is the little shadow which runs across the grass and loses itself in the sunset."

Crowfoot, Blackfoot warrior

"Montrell!" Prentice exclaimed, upon seeing his young friend and charge, Douglas Montrell, being carried into the camp on a stretcher. Word had been radioed in that the patrol was coming in with WIAs, KIAs and prisoners and to get a dust-off chopper from Pleiku as soon as possible. Another patrol with a medic had gone out to meet the returning patrol and all were now coming in.

Looking weak, but conscious, Montrell looked up at Sergeant Prentice and said weakly, "Hey, Charley, I could use a shot of fuckin vodka right now."

Moving forward Redmond saw Prentice and yelled, "Hey, Sarge, glad to see you're still vertical."

Surprised even more, Prentice replied, "Glad to see the same about you, Red."

Hoa and Crucianelli weren't far behind Prentice and happily embraced Redmond and Montrell as well. As all of the men came in, Prentice met Captain Glover.

"Are you and the rest of your men okay, Sir?" he asked, concerned.

"Yeah, we're okay, but a couple of the cutthroats we were after are not thanks to those two wildcats of yours," Glover told Prentice.

Scar and four men, disarmed, tethered and guarded by two soldiers on each side, were escorted into a secured bunker that was locked from the outside. An armed guard was placed at the entrance. Three men were carried through the gate in body bags and the man Montrell shot in the groin was on a stretcher, unconscious and looking in poor shape.

"Sergeant Redmond?" Captain Glover inquired, glancing at Red with a concerned, but satisfied look on his face.

"Yes, Sir," an exhausted Redmond replied.

"Your NCOIC, Sergeant Prentice, has apprised us of your situation. It seems you have managed to solve your immediate problem. Be advised we are working toward a termination of the threat to you and your comrades in arms and fully anticipate getting the group of you back to work on the real and righteous effort of the U.S. military mission in Vietnam. Please give me a full report of the incident with the Special Forces unit that attacked you. We will ensure Sergeant Montrell receives the best medical care available. Bunk with Sergeant Prentice and your men and get some rest, get the report to me in the morning."

During his time as a Marine, and as an airman, Red had never been a cause of grief or disappointment to any of his non-coms or officers. He believed in and followed the rules and regulations and never broke the chain of command. Redmond was an ideal GI; he never questioned orders and seldom pitched a bitch. He did whatever he was told whenever he was told, until now.

Red had reached his breaking point. He refused to let go of one more friend. Flash, Hardy, and Salas were gone; snapped away so quickly by the demon of war he hadn't been able to acknowledge it yet. He would not leave Montrell under any circumstances. "I will stay with Sergeant Montrell, Sir," he said. "I will travel with him to the field hospital where ever he is taken, and I will stand by his side until he is able to walk out . . . with me."

Alarmed at how Red's outburst might be received, Prentice watched Glover with grave concern. Not used to having his orders disobeyed or questioned, Glover gave Red a stern look and then stared at Prentice even harder.

Prentice felt it necessary to intercede. "Red," he said. "The army will take good care of Monty, let them do their job."

The fury in which the stalwart young Ojibwa shot back at Prentice startled all those in the bunker. His face red with rage, blood pulsing through his temple, the quiet warrior spoke out, "Fuck the army! Fuck the air force! Is this the same army and air force that lets a senior NCO and his gang of thieves take over a base and run a goddamn black market business, making money on the backs of the starving Vietnamese and the U.S. citizens who sent him here? The same army and air force that allowed the son of a bitch to kill my friends, Flash, Salas, and Hardy, and try to kill us? The same army and air force that got us in a fuckin' war we don't belong in, and can't win?"

Red had worked himself up into a fever pitch. No one in the bunker moved an inch, watching and listening to the young Native American GI, who felt betrayed by the very same military he had sworn allegiance to.

Red shouted, "I'm going with him. You wanna try locking me up, lock me up. But when I get out I'm gonna go and find the last living friend I got in this shithole, and we're gonna get the fuck out; together."

Now Prentice was red in the face. He stood silently, alternately watching Redmond and Captain Glover. He feared for Redmond; unsure of how Glover would take this outburst, especially in front of an audience. But before Glover could speak, Lopez got up from where he was sitting and approached Redmond.

"Redmond, I've been associated with Captain Glover for over five years," he said "In those five years he has shown the highest level of integrity at all times, never forgetting the well-being of his men, yet fulfilling whatever mission he has assumed responsibility for. Captain Glover has said your man will be taken care of and all the men responsible for killing your other friends and threatening you will be found and dealt with. I assure you he will keep his word, and if you disrespect my captain again I swear by bloody Jesus, I will whip your ass here and now!"

Redmond and Lopez stood face-to-face glaring at each other for several seconds before Glover jumped in. "That won't be necessary, Sergeant Lopez," he said. "Both you guys, step back and relax. Thanks, Lope; let's see if we can resolve this peacefully."

Lopez looked at Glover, took a breath and backed away from Redmond.

Glover then turned to Red and said, "Sergeant Redmond, I can only imagine the loss of faith and hope you must have experienced throughout this entire ordeal, your entire group for that matter. Sergeant Prentice filled me in on most of it after he came into our camp."

Looking around Glover went on, "This is my second tour of duty in 'Nam, and things here have gone kind of haywire these past couple of years. What with confusion from our political leaders, hostility of the war from the U.S. citizens, and rampant corruption and chaos at all levels over here, it's no wonder that the subversion created by Richards has flourished under the nose of the upper echelon."

Glancing around at all of the men in the bunker Glover said, "To you and your fellow airman, you need to understand, this is the 1st Cav. We pay little attention to political swings, and less to the media, and even less to bored college students. We win. That is what our predecessors in other wars did, and that is what we do. If our politicians and civilians back home don't have the stones to get through the war, we do. Was the war ill chosen? Not for us to say. Don't ever speak that way in a 1st Cav compound again."

The men stood, quiet, as Glover continued, "I've heard all the stories about how our men are being treated when they go home. Spit upon and defiled by hippies and college students. Ignored and disrespected by the VFW, vets throwing their medals away and denying their military service, employers refusing to hire the 'crazy' Vietnam vets. But gentlemen, we swore to carry out our orders here and we will do that. What happens after we leave, we have no control over. But we will carry ourselves with dignity and honor, as always."

After a short pause, Prentice spoke, "As an NCO in the air force and a career military man, I have nothing but the highest regard for the 1st Cav. The great name they have carved for themselves has been honored and enhanced by the men here at Camp York. I would be deceitful if I said this war was going well, but as Captain Glover said, we are only responsible for ourselves, and for our unit's success. Whatever else happens you must know you have done your best as a U.S. fighting force."

"We can still make a difference," Glover said after Prentice spoke. To all the men he repeated, "We can still make a difference, all of us, and we will." He paused for a moment and went on, "Sergeant Redmond, you will accompany your friend back to Pleiku. Sergeant Prentice and I will be making that trip also. Upon insuring that Sergeant Montrell is properly attended to, Sergeant Prentice and I will pay a visit to the inspector general there. He, no doubt, will be very interested in the story of your odyssey and its history. My executive officer, Lieutenant Dawson, will handle my duties in my absence. Crucianelli and Hoa will remain here under the watch of Sergeant Lopez, who will make sure they are safe and well occupied." He looked at Lopez as he made the last statement. "Lope, you have anything to add?"

Lopez replied, "I'd like to go find out what else those bastards did to the other two hamlets, Captain. I think Hoa might be of benefit on that mission."

"Good idea. You agree, Prentice?" Glover asked.

"Yes, sir, I think Hoa will definitely be of help. Take Crucianelli as well, he's a good hand and if you don't, I'll have to listen to that crazy eyetalian bitch about it when I get back."

Looking sideways at Prentice Crucianelli went right back at him, "Hey, Sarge, if I didn't do any bitchin', all we'd have to listen to is hillbilly storytellin' all the damn day."

Laughing, Prentice said, "Ok, Cru, no stories today."

Glover instructed the men to plan around the trip; the dust-off chopper would leave at daybreak the next morning.

Chapter 42

"Mountains can never be surmounted except by winding paths."

Goethe

The dust-off chopper landed back at Pleiku around 09:30. Red accompanied Montrell to the dispensary while Captain Glover and Sergeant Prentice headed for base ops. Glover had asked the officer in charge at the hospital to allow Red to stay with Montrell, at least through the initial exam. The special ops man who Montrell had shot in the groin was unconscious and taken to surgery almost immediately, under guard.

Upon reaching base ops, Glover and Prentice signed in and were told to expect to see the IG no sooner than eleven hundred, as he was detained at the ammo dump.

Colonel Ted Worley was at the ammo dump checking on the compliancy reports the air force had adopted, partially upon his suggestion, after the ammo dump fire and explosions that rocked the air force base in Danang in April 1969. At the time of the fire and subsequent explosions, Worley was a lieutenant colonel working for the head of the Inspector General's office at the large air base, which was responsible for most air support operations in I Corps, which was the northern-most corps in South Vietnam. Worley's suggestion had proven its value, as no such fires had occurred on any base that had adopted the process. Although the ammo dump at Pleiku had an OIC responsible for the task of insuring safe and proper procedures were followed, Worley kept tabs on it as a result of his personal history.

Prentice felt strangely at ease even though disclosing Richard's operation, along with his involvement in it, to the IG would possibly leave him with a court martial and prison sentence. He felt unusually calm and confident of the impending actions. Prentice knew that much of his recent drunkenness, irritability and feelings of despair were caused by depression over his involvement with the illicit activities. He always knew that sooner or later he would have to pay the piper, and now that the time was drawing near he was somewhat relieved. The sword of Damocles that had been hanging over his head this past year was going to move, one way or another.

Prentice was snapped out of his thoughts when a spit-shined young lieutenant in crisp air force khakis entered the small waiting area and addressed them. "Captain Glover, Sergeant Prentice, Colonel Worley will see you now."

* * *

Back at Camp York Hoa and Crucianelli found Sergeant Lopez good to his word. He kept them busy on what seemed like every shit detail in camp. "I figured that Mexican fuck would throw the wood to us, but damn, he's got us on every fuckin' shit detail he can find," Crucianelli complained.

Spec 4 Melvin Hemmit just laughed. "The only thing Lopez hates worse than Spec 3s and 4s is rear echelon mother fuckers," he said.

"Well, Lopez can kiss my dago ass," Crucianelli interjected. "I've been out on the road and in the bush as much as most dogface grunts, and probably seen as much action."

Laughing Hemmit said, "He don't care. He just has to have someone to fuck with. He won't do it when Glover's around, but he's a real plantation boss when he gets the chance."

A voice in broken English quietly stated, "Maybe we should kill him."

Crucianelli and Hemmit both looked at Hoa incredulously. Looking nervously at Hemmit, Crucianelli stuttered, "Damn, Hoa, you been hanging around us GIs too fuckin' long. You're tellin' bad jokes already."

Hemmit stared at one then the other, not knowing what to think. "I don't think the fuckin' gook was makin a joke," he said. "I think he wants to waste Lopez."

Cru attempted to deflate the issue. "C'mon Hemmit, take a fuckin' break," he said. "Hoa don't mean that. He's just repeating what he's heard the rest of us sayin' all the damn time."

Hoa didn't care what Hemmit thought. He should probably be killed also for calling him the derogatory name of "gook." The Americans he was traveling with were pretty good people, he felt, and he had grown fond of them, especially Prentice who he came to view as an elder; one to be listened to and respected. But he didn't care for Lopez and some of the other soldiers here too much. It seemed they either patronized him or looked down on him, just like those bastards back in Saigon.

"I'm going for chow," Hemmit stated flatly, and left the work area.

Crucianelli pulled Hoa aside and said, "Hoa, I know these guys have disrespected you, but you can't just kill them because you don't like 'em, and you can't say you're gonna kill em! Hell, I don't like some of 'em much either, but we got to look at the big picture."

Hoa wasn't sure what Crucianelli meant by that. "What big picture?" he asked.

Pursing his lips, Cru explained, "What I mean is these guys, Captain Glover and these men that is, are gonna help all of us. They're gonna help Prentice, Montrell, and me get the fuckers who been tryin' to kill us off, and by doing that they're also helping you get to America. We might have to eat some shit to get there, so no more talk of killing anyone, huh?"

Looking at him with a frown, Hoa said, "Okay, Cru."

* * *

"Sit down, gentlemen. I've read Captain Glover's report. As a matter of fact, I've read it three times," Colonel Worley said, holding the report in his hands. "I'm not a naïve man. I realize the rules have been bent and pushed around over here, but never in my wildest dreams would I have believed that anything like this has been going on. And not only under the noses of higher echelons, but apparently with complicit approval and even involvement. Frankly, I'm flabbergasted. Sergeant Prentice, are you aware of the consequences of your activities in this . . . this operation?"

Sitting with his hat in his hand, Prentice said, "I am, Sir. Please know I am not proud of my activities. I have disgraced myself, and the U.S. Air Force. I take full responsibility for what I have done and will accept whatever punishment deemed applicable."

Worley sat silent for a minute, glancing at the report and looking back and forth at Glover and Prentice. "Captain Glover indicates you went above and beyond in getting your men out of immediate danger through your ordeal these past couple of weeks and have been candid and forthright in your involvement with the corrupt enterprise, and have expressed a sincere desire to take the enterprise down. Is that correct?"

Prentice grimaced, "I did my best to bring the good men assigned to me back. I was unsuccessful in that several of those men were killed. But I do wish to thank Captain Glover for his support. I do very much wish to play a role in putting an end to the corrupt operation, which I became involved with, Sir."

"Well, we'll see about that," Colonel Worley told him. "You have anything more to add, Captain Glover?"

"No, Sir," Glover replied. "But I do wish to remain involved, until such time as this Richards is taken down."

Worley had no trouble with that. "Captain Glover, at this time consider yourself reassigned to the Inspector General Command," the colonel said. "Make arrangements back at Camp York to have your second in command take over operations there until a replacement for you has been identified, or you get reassigned back."

"Yes, Sir," Glover responded.

* * *

Back at Base Camp York, things were heating up. Hemmit had felt it necessary to report Hoa's outburst to Sergeant Lopez. Infuriated, Lopez rushed to the bunker where Hoa and Crucianelli were staying and confronted him.

"You have something to say to me, gook?" Lopez sputtered just inches from Hoa's face. Before he could utter another word, however, Crucianelli jumped between them.

"Back off, Sarge, he didn't understand what he was saying."

Still enraged, Lopez got in Cru's face. "Get outta my face you fucking dago or take the ass whippin' for him."

Now, just as enraged as Lopez, with one sweep of his leg Crucianelli took Lopez down like a pole-axed steer. Lopez quickly got to his feet and delivered several hard blows to Crucianelli, most of which were blocked. Crucianelli sent a hard elbow to Lopez's midsection sending him to the ground again.

The look in Lopez's eyes was murderous as he glared at Cru from the ground. "I'll fucking kill you, you air force cocksucker," he said, and grabbed both of Cru's ankles and pulled him off his feet. He started pummeling Cru about the head and shoulders with his fists. Cru countered with a vicious knee to the groin, causing Lopez to roll off of him, writhing in pain. Hearing all the commotion, Lieutenant Dawson entered the bunker.

"Sergeant Lopez, Sergeant Crucianelli, I order you to immediately stop!" Dawson yelled. The two men looked to go at each other again, but Dawson yelled again, "First man to move loses a stripe!"

Glaring at Crucianelli, Lopez stood still. Crucianelli, glaring back, stood his ground but made no further move either.

"Now back off and explain this, Sergeant Lopez," Dawson ordered.

"Sir, Hoa threatened to kill me and when I confronted him, Crucianelli interfered," Lopez said.

"That's bullshit. You called him a gook and were lookin to kick his ass," Crucianelli countered.

"You'll get your chance, Sergeant Crucianelli. I'm speaking to Sergeant Major Lopez at this time," Dawson said, emphasizing "Sergeant Major" in his statement. "Lopez, I order you to stay out of this bunker and to avoid contact with these two men, do you understand?"

"Yes, sir," Lopez grudgingly replied.

Dawson went on, "Hoa and Crucianelli; you are hereby confined to this bunker. I also expect a written report on this incident by all those who were present. Dismissed.

Chapter 43

"Begin thus from the first act, and proceed; and, in conclusion, at the ill which thou hast done, be troubled, and rejoice for the good."

Pythagoras

"Who the fuck is Colonel Worley?" John Gustin, Colonel, United States Army 1st Cav, II Corps, Operations, wanted to know. Back at Qui Nhon, Captain Glover's direct Officer-In-Charge, Major Lance Brehm, had just informed him of the transfer to IG that Colonel Worley had issued.

"He's an air force colonel in charge of the IG in II Corps, sir," Brehm replied. Gustin wasn't happy.

"It's bad enough I've got ARVN generals pulling my units in and out whenever they get a fucking brilliant idea in their heads, but now I've got air force colonels jacking me around? Aren't there enough bicycles and water buffalos that need shooting without the air force fucking with us?" he asked, to no one in particular. "Well, I suppose if we don't go along with it the sonofabitch will whine to MACV and I'll have to write a hundred page report on the issue."

"That won't be necessary, Colonel," Colonel Ted Worley's voice, coming from the entryway of the office, was unfamiliar to Major Brehm and Colonel Gustin.

Brehm and Gustin both wheeled around, unaware someone else had entered the office. Gustin's face turned crimson when he saw Worley's nametag on his uniform.

"So you're the sonofabitch in charge of army personnel now," Gustin said angrily.

Colonel Worley approached the two men with his hands up palms forward.

"I came to explain my actions to you, Colonel Gustin," Worley said. "I felt it necessary to see you in person to explain the whole scenario and the necessity of those actions."

"Yes, please do," Colonel Gustin replied gruffly.

Major Brehm added, "May I suggest we take a table and get some coffee?"

Worley looked at Gustin, who cooled down, and replied, "Okay, good idea. Let's sit down and see what this is all about. How do you take your coffee, Colonel Worley?"

Worley, knowing he would have to do some fence mending, had a bottle of Irish Cream liqueur that he had brought in country after a short mission that took him to the Philippines. Pulling the bottle out of the paper sack, he told Gustin, "I take it black, and sometimes with a shot of this. Can I offer you gentlemen some?"

Gustin, grinning at the bottle, replied, "Looks like I was a little hard on our air force brother, Major Brehm. What do you think?"

Laughing, Brehm told him, "I agree, Colonel. We should hear this man out, and take our damn time doing it!"

$$* \quad * \quad *$$

Things weren't going so smoothly for Hoa and Crucianelli. The men at Camp York were angered at them for having bucked Lopez. Lt. Dawson thought it best to keep them separate and cool everyone off. He took Lopez back to his compound and queried him on why he thought it necessary to bully the two.

"I don't like VC," he said.

"Hoa is not a VC. Yes, he apparently ran with them at times, as a matter of survival, but he really is a loner who just got caught up in the worst elements of the war here. He does have strong survival instincts, so naturally he won't take being pushed too much. You are professional soldier, Sergeant Lopez, and your actions have belayed your stellar performance carrying out those duties. I don't think Captain Glover would be proud of you at this time," Dawson scolded.

At the mention of Glover, Lopez looked up sheepishly. He knew Dawson was right and now regretted bullying the tough little Vietnamese man.

Campolo

"You're right, Lt. Dawson. I let my emotions override my responsibilities. I am sorry for this distraction."

After a pause, Dawson said, "Listen, you want to confirm that Scar is behind the murders in the local hamlets, right?"

Lopez sensed where Dawson was going with this line of thought, "Yes, Sir, and we could use an interpreter, especially one who is familiar with VC tactics."

"Right," Dawson replied. "And when we get this patrol together, we'll take Crucianelli as well. He's got sand, and Hoa will feel better with him along."

"Will do," Lopez responded. "I'll plan the operation for tomorrow morning."

"We'll plan it together. I'm going along," Dawson commented, confident he could leave the young 2nd lieutenant engineer in charge. "And make sure your men are on board, we don't need any more intramural fighting on our turf, Lope."

"Yes, sir," Lopez agreed and left the bunker to prepare the patrol for the detail.

* * *

In the small operations office at Qui Nhon, Worley filled Gustin and Brehm in on the details pertaining to the transfer of Captain Glover. Shaking his head from time to time and frowning, Gustin listened as Worley filled them in on the perverted operation, head quartered at Phu Cat Air Base, but permeated throughout the whole II Corps. When Col. Worley finished, both men sat silently for a time, lost in their own thoughts.

Finally, Gustin spoke, "Wow! Every so often you'd hear rumors of a big black market op, and the finger always pointed to the air force. I never gave it much credibility . . . until now."

Brehm added, "You know, we often have truck convoys of material going back and forth from here to Phu Cat, and I often wondered to myself why they were always covered in canvas, and why they always had at least three men riding shotgun. Until now, I thought it was just an excuse for the airman to come here and hit the whorehouse by the front gate, but now things are starting to add up."

"Glover's one of my best men," Gustin stated looking at Colonel Worley. "I hate to lose him for any reason, but I will buy into this. If he can help you break this operation, use him as long as you can. Is he still at Pleiku?"

"No," Worley replied. "He's here, along with Sergeant Prentice. Their man in the hospital at Pleiku is doing fine; and he's in the company of one of his buddies, so they felt alright leaving them and coming here with me."

"Okay," Gustin interjected. "Let's get them both over here; we need to form a plan. Are there anymore IG personnel involved at this point?"

"My OIC at II Corps, and my aide," Worley reported.

"Damn, that's what I need, an aide," Gustin joked. "Okay, let's get those two over here and hatch a plan. We don't have much time."

* * *

Things were going better at Camp York as well. Sergeant Lopez and Lt. Dawson went back to Hoa and Crucianelli's bunker and discussed the patrol they wanted them to accompany. At first Hoa and Cru were suspicious, thinking it might be a setup to kill them and it took some time for Dawson and Lopez to convince them otherwise.

"I truly regret the way I treated you men," Lopez told them. "It was undeserved and unprofessional. You guys wanna help nail these bastards who killed some of your friends and comrades, kick in. I'll understand if you don't."

Looking at Hoa, Crucianelli said, "We want in. We'll pull our weight and you won't have to worry about us tryin' to frag anyone. We don't know what awaits us back at Phu Cat, and sittin around here pullin' shit duty ain't getting it done."

The rest of the afternoon involved discussion and planning with all the men who would be on the patrol. There were five hamlets in the area and they felt they could make at least three the first day. They intended to communicate to the hamlet chief through Hoa. They wanted to find out as much as they could about Scar's activities, and if there were any others like him also operating in the immediate area.

215

"Both Sgt. Lopez and I will be on this patrol," Lt Dawson told everyone. "We will split into two sub-patrols, with Sgt. Lopez heading one; I will head up the other. Sgt. Crucianelli will accompany Sgt. Lopez and will for all intents and purposes be engaged as another member of the 1st Cav. He is weapons qualified on the M-16 and also can operate a .50 cal; he's been in more than a few scrapes in the bush so he'll be of service as needed. Hoa will accompany my patrol and act as an interpreter and also help facilitate the interactions between the Vietnamese and us. Since Sergeant Lopez speaks the language he will of course handle that duty in his squad. We move out at 06:00, any questions?"

After some discussion regarding the specifics of what they were looking for, Dawson dismissed the men for the night.

Chapter 44

"Indeed one's faith in one's plans and methods is truly tested
when the horizon before one is the blackest."

Gandhi

Captain Glover and Sergeant Prentice reported to Qui Nhon base ops as ordered. Being an old acquaintance of Captain Glover's, Major Brehm met them at the entrance of the office. "Glover, you dog, are you still hiding from the brass out there in the boonies?"

Shaking his hand and laughing, Glover shot back, "You got that right, Brehm, and I see as usual your uniform is crispy clean. You should pass inspection just fine!"

"Hope to!" Brehm replied laughing. "This is Sergeant Prentice, I gather?"

"Sergeant Prentice, meet Major Lance Brehm, the biggest chowhound and chair polisher in the U.S. Army," Glover told him. The men moved to the back of the office by the small card table where the two colonels were seated. The two colonels stood for greetings and introductions.

"Colonel Worley, Glover's one of the best officer's in the 1st Cav, and I hate losing him, but I guess I can share him."

"Thank you, Colonel Gustin. I look forward to working with Colonel Worley," Glover replied.

"Looking forward to working with you, also, Major Glover."

With a quizzical look, Glover hesitatingly questioned him, "Major Glover?"

Colonel Gustin told him, "That's right, Glover, now that you're important enough to work for the damn air force, MACV decided you needed a promotion." He then handed Glover the two gold oak leaves representing the rank of major.

"Thank you, thank you sir," Glover said quietly.

Gustin went on, "You earned them, Major Glover, and I expect with the situation we now find ourselves in you will earn them several times over before this is finished."

"Congratulations, Thornton," Major Brehm added.

"Congratulations, and welcome to the service of the inspector general," Colonel Worley told him. "Now, gentlemen, we have much work to do."

* * *

The two Camp York patrols were scheduled to move out at 06:00. Hoa was to accompany Dawson's patrol and Crucianelli was to accompany the Lopez patrol as planned, but at 0:400, Lieutenant Dawson was awakened by the night duty charge of quarters.

Colonel Lawrence Johnson from MACV was on the radio and wanted to confirm what he had heard, that the airmen charged with the killing of several of their peers were at Camp York. Johnson, not knowing that Captain (now Major) Glover was in Qui Nhon, had originally asked for him. As second in command, Dawson took the call.

"Sergeant Crucianelli is the only one at this post, sir," Dawson informed him.

"Do you know the whereabouts of the other men?" Johnson firmly asked.

"One is at the infirmary at Pleiku, Sir. He was wounded in action. At this time I am unaware of the whereabouts of the others," Dawson reported.

"Where is Captain Glover?" Johnson demanded.

"Sir, he accompanied the wounded man back to Pleiku. I haven't had contact with him since he departed Camp York."

Growing more and more irritated, Col. Johnson issued Dawson orders, "Lieutenant, you put Sergeant Crucianelli on the first chopper out of York going to Pleiku. At Pleiku he will be interred until such time as he can be transported to Phu Cat where he will be charged, along with the

218

other associates involved in these murders. I understand these renegades have been joined by a Viet Cong, who has contributed to the mayhem. Are you aware of such a person?"

Dawson was unwittingly standing at attention while talking to the colonel, but he did have his wits about him. "No, Sir, I know of no such man."

Johnson was silent for several seconds, and then said, "You make sure Crucianelli is shackled, placed on that chopper, and at Pleiku ASAP, Lt. Dawson. Is that understood?"

"Yes, sir. Will do, sir," Dawson replied.

* * *

Major Glover got the radio call from Dawson at 05:00.

"Shit," Glover muttered. He immediately went to Colonel Worley's quarters, which was right next to his at the Barracks Officer's quarters at Qui Nhon. An early riser, Worley answered the door immediately.

Glover informed him of the situation and waited for Worley to collect his thoughts.

"Well, we had to realize this was going to happen sooner or later. Richards seems to have a damn contact under every fucking bush in Vietnam. Do you have any connections at Pleiku?" he asked Glover.

"Not really, Sir, being an air force base, I never had much to do with them other than asking for air strikes, supplies and transport on occasion."

Worley was thinking hard. "They're coming in on an army chopper," he said. "So army personnel will meet them on the tarmac, no doubt. We'll have to get someone there to meet the chopper or they might kill Crucianelli before he even gets off."

"If they don't kill him on the way in," Glover remarked.

Looking at him sharply, Worley then left to find Gustin. On the way out the door he told Glover to appraise Prentice of the situation and to prepare to depart for Pleiku on a moment's notice.

* * *

As soon as the chopper from Camp York landed at Pleiku, a chaotic scene broke out. Armed members of the 173rd Airborne arrived in jeeps just as two armored personnel carriers full of air force security police arrived. The men nervously eyed each other up, fingering the triggers on their weapons and waiting uneasily. A captain from the 173rd Airborne and a major from the air force security police stepped out of their respective vehicles and approached each other.

"We're picking up a prisoner, no need for your presence here, Major," Captain Thomas Davis informed Major Harold Lanard, assistant commander, base security, Pleiku.

"I'm sorry, Captain Davis, we are exercising our jurisdiction here, the prisoner is ours," Major Lanard replied.

"I have orders straight from MACV on this, Major. I'd check with your OIC if I were you," Davis replied.

"Why the hell would MACV be involved, kind of a small fish for them to fry?" Lanard commented.

"I don't know," Davis went on. "I do know that I'm also supposed to pick up two co-conspirators who are here at Pleiku. A Sergeant Redmond and a Sergeant Montrell."

Looking at him cautiously, Lanard made a proposal. "How about I call my commanding officer and ask him to look into all of this? When the XO gets back to me after checking things out, we'll decide who goes with who."

Irritated but not knowing what else to do, Davis accepted the proposal. "Fine, we'll all wait here and see what comes of it. I hope this doesn't take long as I have orders to get these perps back to Phu Cat ASAP."

* * *

Back at Qui Nhon, the two colonels and two majors, along with Master Sergeant Prentice, had been scrambling, arranging transport and alerting others of the situation, in hopes of sealing off the operation and keeping the airman at Camp York and Pleiku in a safe condition.

"Damn! Looks like we're too late," Colonel Worley told the group. They had reconvened at the tarmac with their gear, ready to board a flight to Pleiku. "Apparently Richards had soldiers from the 173rd Airborne meet the chopper carrying Crucianelli at Pleiku. Pleiku security challenged them and there was a tense standoff until some higher up in MACV interceded and ordered Pleiku security to stand down. The 173rd grabbed Crucianelli, along with Sergeant Redmond who was at the infirmary with Sergeant Montrell. They wanted to take Montrell as well, and would have if it wasn't for the chief surgeon there who insisted Montrell was not able to travel under any circumstances."

"Damn," Prentice said. "I'm guessing they took them back to Phu Cat, Sir?"

"That's correct, Sergeant, and the real bad news is the head of base security at Phu Cat is one of Richard's lackeys."

Adding more concern, Major Brehm spoke up, "Shit, with the 173rd and Phu Cat base security, as well as Richard's henchmen, we don't have much influence over there."

Gustin, listening to the discussion, suggested they go back to base ops and develop a new plan ASAP. "We've got to get some assets in there quick or there very well may be an attempted escape in which both Montrell and Redmond are killed."

As Gustin's statement sank in, Prentice lost his composure. "No! By God, no!" he said. "I won't let that bastard kill any more of my men! Colonel Gustin, I want a weapon and a jeep." Glover put his hand on Prentice's shoulder.

"Sergeant Prentice, we'll all go. But we must develop a plan, and we must keep our heads. The first thing we need to do, and we need to do it fast, is to identify the closest friendly assets we have and get them in there to stop or stall Richards before he can act."

Just then Brehm almost yelled, "Hey, the Tigers get their orders from Qui Nhon ops, don't they, Colonel Gustin?"

Excited, Gustin rose, "That's correct, Brehm. The command direction goes from II Corps Command, to Qui Nhon ops, then to the Tigers."

The "Tigers" they were referring to were the Tiger Division of the South Korean army. The U.S. government paid South Korea so much per man for each one they provided to fight in Vietnam. The Tiger division was a crack South Korean army unit, which was charged with the defense of several airbase perimeters, Phu Cat being one of them. They were a tough, no-nonsense fighting unit respected by all.

Campolo

"Get them on the horn, ASAP!" Gustin told Brehm "And find out when the next C-130 to Phu Cat is scheduled.

Chapter 45

"Adversity has the effect of eliciting talents which, in prosperous circumstances, would have lain dormant."

Horace

Crucianelli and Redmond's odyssey finally found them back at Phu Cat, only now instead of a bunk in a hooch they occupied a small cell in the brig at base security.

"Fuck," Crucianelli lamented. "These bastards are gonna find a way to kill us, Red."

Sitting on a bunk quietly looking at the floor, Redmond said nothing. The soldiers who had spirited them out of Pleiku had left the base and no one had spoken to the two, other than to confirm their identity since their arrival.

"How come those bastards let them take us? They had to know they were going to murder us?" Crucianelli asked.

Looking at him stoically, Redmond tried to comfort him, as one who was of a people who had been deprived, abused and neglected for ions, "One must resign himself to his fate, Cru. When a warrior has done everything in his power to overcome his enemies, the outcome makes no difference. You have fulfilled your obligation as a human spirit and can go on to meet your fate in good standing."

Looking at Redmond incredulously, Cru exclaimed, "Fuck that shit, Red. I'm not ready to die, especially before killin' that murdering bastard Richards. I just want a chance to take him out along with me." He then lapsed into silence. A moment later a shadow emerged from a darkened part of the brig,

"Watch out what you ask for, you may just get it," Master Sergeant William E. Richards, the Kansas NCO, then stepped out of the shadows.

* * *

Several hours later, Colonel Worley, along with Colonel Gustin, Majors Brehm and Glover, along with Master Sergeant Prentice hit the landing strip at Phu Cat in a C-130. Major Kim Junkee, Army of the Republic of Korea, Tiger Division, and a heavily armed platoon of his men met them at the airstrip. The presence of an armed South Korean platoon on the airfield did not go unnoticed. Phu Cat base security attempted several times to intercede with the South Koreans, but were met with stone faced indifference by their stalwart allies and when they attempted to block the runway the Phu Cat security team found themselves looking down the barrels of a dozen Korean M-16s and two .50 caliber machine guns. When base security alerted base ops of the situation, Major Junkee's superior in Qui Nhon was contacted. Junkee's superior was coy and the suspicious men at Phu Cat base ops then contacted the 173rd Airborne and asked them to return with a large contingent of armed troops.

A perfect storm was brewing at the Phu Cat airbase. Elements of the 173rd Airborne were rapidly approaching the main gate with the intent of dispersing the South Korean army contingent surrounding the base security brig there.

Realizing they wouldn't be able to hold their position long, Major Junkee had requested reinforcements from Qui Nhon; who were about to meet with the element of the 173rd they were sent to repel. The aircraft containing Worley, Gustin, Brehm, Glover and Prentice, along with a platoon of military police had just landed at Phu Cat. Unbeknown to Worley and Gustin, another contingent would soon enter the fray.

A flight of Apache gunships was bearing down from An Khe accompanied by a Chinook helicopter carrying Major General E. Dutton Smith, MACV Commander, II Corps along with his support staff.

Colonel Gustin was now in radio contact with the Commander of the Phu Cat Airbase, Colonel Walden Ballou.

"Colonel Gustin, I strongly urge you to stand down," Ballou warned. "A flight from An Khe with MACV authorities will arrive within the hour and we will sort this out upon their arrival."

"Why haven't they contacted us directly?" Gustin asked suspiciously. "Unless General Dutton Smith is on that aircraft with a good reason why we shouldn't retrieve those two men, their mission is pointless." Colonel Ballou did not respond to Gustin's comments.

E. Dutton Smith had entered the U.S. Army toward the end of World War II as a second lieutenant in field logistics. As the German military, along with its political, governmental, infrastructure broke down, the victorious nations found themselves facing a potential human catastrophe of enormous proportions.

While the Soviets were ambivalent, even seemingly happy at the thought of possibly tens of thousands of Germans perishing due to hunger and disease, the other major Allied powers felt compelled to prevent the impending disaster. In this toxic atmosphere Dutton Smith proved himself to be an improviser and an innovator.

Charged with assisting the civilian population during the transition from war to peace, Smith found himself wading through the endless bureaucratic maze in seeking supplies, food, medicine, and approvals. In a no-nonsense fashion, Smith fostered relationships with local merchants, businessmen, and entrepreneurs in developing networks to provide the materials where and when most needed.

He also ferreted out men in his own command that had shrewdly developed lucrative black market operations, providing anything of need to fellow military members, people back home, or the locals, as needed. Rather than stifle these activities he bought into them and supported them, so long as nothing of a harmful or sensitive nature was involved. Smith's success in smoothing the transition process did not go unnoticed, and he quickly rose to the rank of captain.

Forced to muster out or make a long-term commitment, Smith chose to stay in the military and hoped to continue providing goods and services to people wherever most needed. By the time the Korean War broke out he had attained the rank of major and was stationed in Guam, facilitating the provision of aid to the civilian population there as well.

As the situation in Korea slipped into a humanitarian disaster for Korean civilians Smith was sent along with the first waves of American troops with orders to prevent the potential deaths of hundreds of thousands of Koreans through lack of nutrition, medical supplies, and shelter. He was also tasked with coordinating logistical support for the American military units on the ground.

As in his previous assignments Smith was forced to work around the system in order to accomplish the mission. In South Korea Smith fine-tuned his skills of establishing local sources of needed materials, as well as using unconventional methods to obtain goods and services. When people were dying of malnutrition, exposure, or disease few questioned the people or methods who provided food, medicine, clothing and shelter. Within six months Smith was bumped up to lieutenant colonel and received two commendation medals along with several letters of appreciation accompanied by a host of medals from various authorities in the South Korean government.

In 1964 when U.S. boots seriously began hitting the ground in Vietnam, now Major General E. Dutton Smith was there. General Smith would play a major role in the planning and carrying out of the logistical support for the military through MACV, as well as the plans providing aide to friendly Vietnamese, Cambodians, and Laotians.

As the war progressed and the U.S role grew, Smith became one of the primary architects of the material plan in supporting the ever-growing effort. And as in the two previous wars, General Smith cultivated local sources of supply and services throughout the country, and employed the use of shrewd people both in and out of the military who knew how to circumvent the system, if need be, to acquire needed goods or get things done. General Smith's policy was success through the achievement of the mission, by whatever means necessary.

As the Vietnam War became more complicated and political, General Smith's job became more difficult. He had to support allies who were less than enthusiastic, and often corrupt. He had to come up with, and account for, weapons and supplies for a host of guerilla groups whose loyalty sometimes changed several times within a month's time. And he had to deal with the changing political climate back home.

When Richard Nixon assumed power he promised to end the unpopular war in Southeast Asia. He instituted a major transfer of the war effort from Americans to the Vietnamese and called it "Vietnamization." This effort, requiring the transfer of huge amounts of materials to the South Vietnamese military, drained the still present U.S. military of much needed supplies and equipment, as the Vietnamese were nowhere up to speed or effort in assuming their new role in the war. The unofficial networks of local sources of supply and labor became more crucial than ever.

Chapter 46

*"Leadership is the capacity and the will to rally men
and women to a common purpose and the character
which inspires confidence."*

General Montgomery

"**S**tand down!" The squawking voice coming over the hand-held loudspeaker was shrill and offensive.

Colonel Ballou himself was in the U.S. Air Force armored personnel carrier that had pulled up alongside five others. Ballou's voice, though raucous, was repeating the order to stand down.

Behind the five APCs stood several light infantry vehicles all manned by members of the 173rd Airborne. The infantry vehicles were armed with .50 caliber machine guns and one had a light artillery piece that was set up on the ground and ready to fire.

Facing this contingent was Major Junkee, a platoon of South Korean infantrymen, and a Sheridan tank from the South Korean contingent in Qui Nhon. Two jeeps carrying Gustin, Worley, Brehm, Glover, Prentice, and several armed infantrymen from Qui Nhon accompanied them.

"Release the two men to our custody immediately!" Colonel Gustin shouted back.

As the standoff dragged on, onlookers from the base edged closer and closer to the confrontation in an attempt to find out what was going on. Of all the things that happened at the base, this was probably the strangest. Two groups of armed American and South Korean forces confronting each other by the Security Police compound.

"Get those men back and keep em back!" Ballou demanded. Armed security police immediately set up a walking line and started rousting the gawkers from their positions. They cleared them back about fifty yards and positioned several sentries along the line to keep them from returning closer to the scene of the confrontation. The men reluctantly moved back, grousing and catcalling as they went.

"Hey you fucking apes, go pound sand up your asses!" These and other such remarks were showered upon the flustered security police.

Angered at having the Old Man yell at him, the young first lieutenant in charge took it out on the spectators who continued their raucous shouting and taunting.

"Fuck you, Louie shave tail, why don't you kiss my ass?" came from the crowd. The men, always looking for a diversion from hot duty, long hours, boredom, and moments of pure terror, happily added fuel to the already broiling fire.

The security police pushed a couple of the men who moved too slowly hard enough to knock them down.

"Police brutality!" the charge went up. Laughing and shouting ever harder it appeared nothing short of a water cannon would keep the men back. But out of the west, the entity that would soon render the boisterous crowd silent was on its way.

The first din of the incoming fleet of choppers was hardly noticeable. Conditioned to heavy air traffic going in and out of the base twenty-four hours a day, not until the five unusual helicopters were within a half-mile did the crowd pay attention to the incoming birds.

Slowly groups of men stopped what they were doing or focusing on, and turned their heads to the roar of engines getting closer and closer. Accustomed to the all too familiar Hueys, along with the very large Chinook, and some forward observation Loach's, the sight of these choppers had most of the people on the ground looking up with their hands above their eyes, straining to get a better look. The ACH-47 helicopter at the center of the group bristled with cannon and machine gun ports. The Chinook gunship was accompanied by four equally heavily armed AH-1 Cobra helicopters, having two on each side. The five choppers unceremoniously hovered above the brig where the confrontation was unfolding and slowly lowered altitude until they landed precisely, scattering on lookers and participants alike.

The officers involved in the confrontation warily stepped out of their vehicles, keeping a watchful eye on their antagonists even as they followed every movement of the now shut down chopper squadron that had just landed.

As each of the noisy choppers shut down, all those in attendance grew quiet and subdued. The emblem on the front nose of the CH-47 contained two stars, announcing a major general in the U.S. military. With the heavily armed Cobras in a circular defensive position surrounding the CH-47, the doors on the larger chopper opened. Seven army Rangers with commando automatic rifles and grenade launchers quickly exited the aircraft and took up defensive positions around the big chopper. It was clear that whoever was on that craft meant business and anyone foolish enough to engage in further hostile actions would face a deadly hailstorm of fire.

After a short time, Major General E. Dutton Smith followed by a small staff stepped off the chopper. Stone-faced, Smith stopped in front of the big bird and took in the scene. As he gazed in each direction he took in the sight of opposing forces of men he was responsible for . . . waiting for the right opportunity to kill each other.

Smith's aide, a lieutenant colonel then addressed the antagonists. "By the authority of Major General Smith, MACV commandant, II Corps, I order you to stand down your weapons and withdraw from this position. Furthermore, I order all officers present and involved to appear at base ops, disarmed, at 18:00. All other members of antagonists in this incident will be escorted to a neutral area of the Phu Cat Airbase by a team under my command. They will remain there, separated from each other until such time as new orders are issued to them by General Smith's command. You have five minutes to comply with this order."

Slowly coming to life, the crowd of antagonists started milling around cautiously, eyeing each other. They moved away from each other carefully. The tanks, jeeps, APCs and other large weapons, now empty, posed starkly; still confronting each other, though void of human occupants. The officers gathered together and moved to different areas on the base.

The two men under lock and key remained in their cell, but with General Smith's men now posted as guards instead of the Phu Cat security police detail. It was15:00. In three hours the officers would find out how the incident would be dealt with.

Chapter 47

"We all make mistakes. We know we make mistakes. I don't know any military commander, who is honest, who would say he has not made a mistake. There's a wonderful phrase: 'the fog of war.' What "the fog of war" means is: war is so complex it's beyond the ability of the human mind to comprehend all the variables. Our judgment, our understanding, are not adequate. And we kill people unnecessarily."

Robert McNamara

Pre-flight and post-flight orientations in Vietnam were taken up with any number of situations that arose in the air intensive conflict. The small conference room known as the flight room at Phu Cat base ops had a podium and seating accommodations for around twenty people.

The pilots and sometimes flight crews would learn about their missions, and go over the results (and mishaps) upon their return. If there was heavy enemy activity, including abnormal ground fire, or questionable weather conditions the meeting might take longer. If something went wrong with the mission, the meeting would extend beyond normal time frames.

Many things could go wrong with an air mission in Vietnam. The aircraft could get shot down, forced to divert, experience mechanical failure, experience weather related problems or misdirect ordinance. The flight room walls had witnessed any number of calamities in its time as the focal point of the mission of Phu Cat Air Base.

Of course, when aircraft were shot down, and the aircrews were killed or badly wounded, the meetings were somber and difficult. Today, however the flight room would witness something seldom heard or seen in day-to-day military operations. Today, the walls would hear something far different.

"Atten-SHUN!" General Smith's aide announced.

In addition to the entering General Smith and his staff, the conference room contained Colonel Ballou and his staff, Colonels Worley and Gustin, Majors Brehm and Glover, the commander of the South Korean military command in the Central Highlands, the commander of the 173rd Airborne in II Corps, the Binh Dinh province chief, Master Sergeant Charles Prentice—and Master Sergeant William E. Richards, the Kansas NCO.

"Sit down, gentlemen," General Smith told the crowd.

After looking around the room slowly Smith began. "I'm here today because of a rift that has caused consternation and open warfare right here, among us; the men in this room; mistrust, fighting, and murder, occurring among our own American forces, tearing at the fabric of our units. Gentlemen, how did it come to this?"

The men in the room listening were slowly and suspiciously looking at each other.

Smith went on, "I have asked Mr. Tan, the Binh Dinh province chief here to let everyone in this room know how important our mission here is. After Mr. Tan has graciously addressed us, he will leave us to sort out our issues."

Ban Ngyuen Tan then addressed the group. He spoke for fifteen minutes, telling the men what it meant to have the American support that provided security, as well as sustenance for his people. Tan's message was well received, with the men giving him a strong round of applause before he left.

General Smith then introduced Colonel Lee Kwong Sun, commander of the South Korean Tiger Division assigned to II Corps, Vietnam. He also spoke for fifteen minutes. Colonel Sun told the men how as a youth, Americans rescued him and his family from North Korean forces who had killed other members of his family.

He told them how proud he was to rise in the service of his country's military, go to Vietnam and finally have a chance to repay the Americans in some small way. Colonel Sun also received strong applause from the men in the conference room, after which he excused himself and left the room.

Walking slowly up to the podium, General Smith carefully eyed the men before of him. Then he said, "I asked Mr. Tan and Colonel Sun to speak to us today, so we would all be reminded of why we are here and what we have been doing, while here. Perhaps, in the confusion that surrounds us, we may have lost track of the purpose of our mission here. After listening to Mr. Tan and Colonel Sun, I have no doubt that we have been doing is what is right for the Vietnamese people, and for ourselves."

The men in the room, having been deeply moved by the previous two speakers, were looking at the floor and slowly nodding their heads in agreement.

General Smith continued, "Everyone here is aware of the confusion that is rampant in the war effort, both here and back home. We must now determine what led to the events that ended in the unfortunate deaths of several brave men at the hands of their fellow Americans. Everyone here must know we understand they were fulfilling their duty. I now ask all those here to stand, shake each other's hand, and consider this incident closed."

The men slowly stood and milled around shaking hands. Airborne, air force security forces, South Korean Tiger Division troops, all met and embraced or shook hands with each other.

"Now, men, please be dismissed and carry out your duty as you have been asked by your commanders," General Smith said. "Tomorrow morning, I, along with Colonels Worley, Gustin, Ballou, Majors Brehm and Glover, will meet at this office at 08:00. Master Sergeants Prentice and Richards shall also be in attendance."

* * *

Prentice was very frustrated. He had gone back to his barracks at the NCO compound and reconnected with some fellow NCOs. He briefly told them about the ordeal they had been through, and yesterday's meeting. "I always respected Colonel Ballou, and this Smith seems sincere and honest. I just can't understand how they not only tolerate Richards, but also are apparently involved with him. Where the hell is McKay anyway? I thought he'd be here to at least back me up if and when I need help . . . and I will need help."

The three men looked at each other then back at Prentice.

"What?" Prentice asked, returning their stares.

Prentice's friend from LZ English, Master Sergeant Morgan Shell, U.S. Army, who Prentice and Cru had helped on many occasions, was there with the two other senior NCOs.

"Charley, McKay was arrested last week. We haven't heard anything about him since. When we tried to get some answers we were stonewalled," he said.

Alarmed, Prentice said, "Sonofabitch, he must have discovered the drug operation and they snagged him to keep him quiet. Hope they don't find his body somewhere out in the bush."

Base security would not allow Prentice into the brig to see Crucianelli and Redmond. He had already contacted Pleiku regarding Montrell. His contact there confirmed that Sergeant Douglas Montrell had been medevac'd to Japan under guard. Prentice's contact assured him that the guards accompanying Montrell were legitimate and would ensure his safety.

"Thank God," Prentice said to himself.

The war was over for Montrell now. His wounds, though serious would heal fine and he would finish out his four years at Wright Patterson Air Force Base, not too far from his home back in Ohio.

That left Crucianelli, Redmond, and Hoa, in country and in danger. For now Prentice could do nothing about Cru and Red, but he had every intention of helping Hoa fulfill his dream and get on that plane to America. He went to find Major Glover.

* * *

"Okay, I'll get Dawson on the horn again."

Major Glover had listened to Prentice's concern about Hoa. If there were any more rogue troops out near Camp York, they could target Hoa for death, if for nothing else than for his close association with the men they were targeting for the past couple of weeks. Glover had been speaking with Dawson on a regular basis. The patrols to the villages revealed no new information.

Hoa had proved a good interpreter and a valuable tool in getting the villagers to open up to the Americans somewhat better than normal. When contacted again Dawson reported that Hoa was fine and no attempts were made on his life in or out of camp. He asked if Glover wanted him sent to Phu Cat.

"No . . . no. At this point he's safer there. I'll let you know when that changes," Glover told him.

Looking relieved, Prentice sat down. "Well, doesn't sound like we need to worry about him. I'm concerned about this meeting tomorrow, Sir. Do you suppose Smith is part of Richard's operation?"

Clenching his teeth, Glover didn't speak for a couple seconds. "I have known General Smith almost as long as I've been in the army, Prentice," he said. "By no means do I know him on a personal level, but I'm thinking, no. I always felt he was one of the good guys, and after yesterday I still do. Let's hope I'm not wrong."

Looking at Glover out of the corner of his eyes, Prentice responded, "Yes, sir, let's hope you aren't wrong."

* * *

"Attention!" The men in the conference room came to attention as Smith entered the room.

"At ease, gentlemen," Smith said. He strode to the podium and looked around. He noticed Prentice and Richards were sitting at opposite ends of the room, looking uncomfortably at one another. "Men, I'm going to suggest that we push two of the tables together and all sit together. Is the coffee pot on?"

The men then got up and moved the tables and chairs around so they could look at each other while discussing the issue which they had all been waiting to resolve.

Once everyone was settled, Smith spoke candidly, "Colonel Ballou and Sergeant Prentice, I am deeply sorry for the loss of your men at the hands of unscrupulous thugs and thieves. And I am very sorry for the hell they put you and the rest of your men through, Sergeant Prentice. As you know, the phase of the war we are now in called Vietnamization has put great stress on our military effort here."

Looking around he continued, "I don't believe President Nixon intended the process to be as such, but it has. Our Vietnamese allies were not and are still not in any way capable of taking up the load as the major player in the war. As such, we Americans have had to continue with as many patrols, sorties, bombing runs, naval bombardments, and every other task we carried out as before. Unfortunately the bureaucrats and politicians pulled the rug out from under us; they snookered us. The very day Vietnamization was announced the supply of materials and men started drying up.

"But . . . we were told the program had to succeed, the war effort must not falter. No excuses were allowed. No exceptions were made. When we faltered, heads rolled, high and low. We had to figure out how to make do. Well, we couldn't do much with the drop-off in troop strength, but we were allowed to let men extend their tours in exchange for shortening their overall military commitments. We also were given millions of dollars to pay the men to re-up, reenlist. But, we were given no slack regarding supplies and equipment. The flow of goods slowed down and we had to deal with it. And we did."

Every man in the room sat quiet and focused, intently listening to one of the architects of the war explaining the unconventional way the war was now being equipped and supplied.

General Smith continued, "Master Sergeant William Richards and others like him pulled our sticks out of the fire. They had local sources of supply as well as remote sources of supply. They had methods of moving the materials in and out. Gentlemen, as long as there have been marching armies; men like Sergeant Richards have been around, resourceful men who figured out how to get things done in crazy, insane circumstances. How to keep the army clothed, civilians fed and weaponry available. Did they do it for money or out of necessity? I think a little of both.

"Some fifty years before the birth of Christ, the Roman army in their province of Gaul found themselves under constant siege by Germanic armies crossing the Rhine. Julius Caesar had no way to expedite the supplies and equipment he needed to fight a war of attrition against them. Rome was as bureaucratic then as we are today, and actually much more so. Fickle senators debated endlessly on where, when, and who to provide men, materials and equipment to expand and protect the empire.

"Caesar came to rely upon men who accompanied his army for the purpose of ensuring a steady flow of whatever supplies were needed. These men made a profit, but kept the mighty Roman war machine in business. The men made their profit and Caesar crushed the German tribes impeding Rome. Caesar wisely courted these men throughout his career, and kept them near as he went from one military campaign to the other.

"Gentlemen, this is part of the history of warfare. Like many other parts, it may not be pretty, but war is not pretty. Know that I will continue to do whatever it takes to accomplish my mission. Now, I believe Sergeant Prentice has some concerns that need to be addressed."

Chapter 48

"This is the end
Beautiful friend
This is the end
My only friend, the end
It hurts to set you free
But you'll never follow me
The end of laughter and soft lies
The end of nights we tried to die
This is the end."

Jim Morrison, The Doors

All eyes were now focused on Master Sergeant Charles Prentice. Prentice, with a look of intensity and anger responded, "General Smith, I very much appreciate what you have had to do to continue the war effort over here. I understand your responsibility and obligation to the leaders back home, and everyone over here as well."

Looking directly at Smith, Prentice went on, "I have no quarrel with the use of any means necessary to fulfill those responsibilities and obligations. However, when the men carrying out those means perpetrate murder and drug peddling, I must respectfully and forcefully disagree, Sir. And the fact that a man in this very room was the perpetrator of those crimes is greatly discouraging." Prentice was now glaring angrily at Sergeant Richards.

"Charley, I didn't kill those men, and I didn't peddle in drugs," Richards said quietly.

This was almost more than Prentice could take. "Bullshit, Richards!" he said. "You think I have a bad memory? You think I'm stupid? I was with you when you were making the plans . . . you divulged them to me!"

Before Richards could respond, General Smith said, "Sergeant Prentice, Richards had no part in those murders, nor did he have any part in the drug operation."

Now Prentice stared at General Smith incredulously. And every other man in the room stared at General Smith as well.

"I understand your feelings, Sergeant Prentice, but you are wrong about Sergeant Richards. For your information I knew about the drug operation as well."

"Sir?" Prentice asked.

General Smith continued, "Long before the heroin operation, we knew there was a rotten apple in the barrel. Someone had been smuggling weapons, hashish, and even military pharmaceutical drugs out of the country. We tracked it down to someone who worked for Sergeant Richards. We narrowed it down to two or three people, but couldn't pinpoint the perpetrator; it was a very sophisticated operation. So we laid a trap."

Prentice couldn't contain himself, "The heroin pick-up in Cambodia."

Looking at Prentice, Smith said nothing.

"And . . . you, you thought I was the perp?" Prentice almost shouted.

"We didn't know at the time, Sergeant Prentice. You were a suspect, so Richards lured you into the trap." Smith calmly told him.

Prentice became livid upon hearing this. "Well it wasn't me, goddamn it," he said. "I don't know who it was, but if I find the sonofabitch I'll kill him myself."

"Not necessary, Sergeant Prentice, the man is in custody," Smith said, looking around at the whole group.

Prentice looked at him and asked, "Well, who the hell did it, Sir? The only one that had enough accessibility and information to pull off a stunt like that besides me and Richards was . . . " Sergeant Prentice's voice trailed off and he lowered his head with a look of sudden astonishment.

Half frowning, Smith looked at Prentice and said, "That's right, Sergeant Prentice, McKay — Sergeant Howard McKay had been stealing the weapons, drugs and goods and shipping them back to the States. He was also lured into the sting operation . . . and he got flushed out, as did his partner in this affair, Sergeant Denton, along with several others."

In his agitated state, Prentice had been standing while addressing the general. Now, with the look of a pole-axed bull, he slowly slumped back down into his chair.

Looking around, then back at Prentice, Smith continued, "I understand this is a shock to you, Sergeant Prentice. It was a shock to us as well. As the First Sergeant of the Supply Squadron, and a person with a long and well-served air force career it was difficult for us to accept the fact that Sergeant McKay had perpetrated these crimes.

"But unfortunately it is true; Sergeant McKay admitted to everything after he was taken into custody. We tried to locate you and your men at that point; however your whereabouts were unknown. As you and Major Glover discovered, Special Forces Operative Theodore Van Horn, the one you know as Scar, was also involved with Sergeant McKay.

"The two of you managed to take out most of his assets, but additional men are now at Camp York assisting Lieutenant Dawson in cleaning up any more renegades that may be involved and at large in that area. The only other involved person from Phu Cat, Clifford Canty, is as we know, dead at this time."

Prentice, who started to rise from his chair once again slumped back, with the look of a man with the air knocked out of him. "Flash?" He mouthed, barely audibly.

Looking at Prentice, General Smith replied softly, "Yes, Sergeant Prentice, Airman Clifford Canty, the one everyone called Flash. He was involved with Sergeant McKay, and carried out his role as a plant on your mission."

Again Prentice mouthed, hardly audibly, "Why?"

"Well, we can't say for certain," Smith went on. "But it appears Airman Canty had a very serious drug problem. He borrowed money from anyone he could to feed his habit. McKay lent him money, and supplied him with heroin as well. In turn, he required that Canty work for him and do his bidding. Airman Canty was very unhappy. The team that was sent to retrieve you and your men believe he shot himself."

After Smith's last statement Prentice whirled around, stunned. He was both flabbergasted and if possible, even more remorseful than before. "How can that be? Flash and the Vietnamese girl were killed in an ambush!"

General Smith's aide then responded to Prentice. "The recovery team reported muzzle flash on both of them. He apparently killed the girl, then turned the weapon on himself seconds later; probably wanted to use the ambush to mask his actions."

The room was dead quiet as Prentice now sat with his head in his hands, barely whispering, "Had I been a better NCO perhaps this all would not have come to pass."

"Not your fault, Prentice," Smith replied. "You made some mistakes, but Canty had big problems that only he could deal with. You did the best you could to get your men back safe."

Looking up, Prentice asked, "What about Crucianelli, Redmond . . . and Hoa?" What will happen to them?"

At that, Smith looked around the room, "Colonel Worley?"

"Yes, Sir." Colonel Worley, who was sitting almost directly across from Sergeant Prentice, now addressed him. "Sergeants Crucianelli and Redmond have been released from custody. They were being held for their own protection to ensure no more of Sergeant McKay's renegades were still at large, posing a danger. Hoa has been flown in and is bunking with Crucianelli and Redmond."

Prentice had more questions. "What will happen to them?"

Worley continued, "Sergeants Crucianelli and Redmond have agreed to stay on to assist in the critical fulfillment of materials, as in their previous positions. They will report directly to Sergeant Richards. Hoa will be assigned a mentor who will groom him and cut through the paperwork to allow him to immigrate to the United States."

This information uplifted Prentices spirits, which was the only thing he had left to salvage, after placing his career and self-esteem in jeopardy. Seeing those three come out of this nightmare alive and with a future was his only hope. It now seemed that that would occur.

"Good, thank you, Sir." Prentice said, relieved. Continuing to look at Worley, Prentice's expression changed. "What about me, Colonel?"

* * *

Three weeks later Sergeant Charles Prentice and Ngyuen Than Hoa sat in the small air terminal at Phu Cat. They were awaiting transport to Cam Rahn Bay, where they would board an American military chartered Flying Tigers DC-8, filled with American GIs returning home from the war. Hoa was nervous but happy and anxious. Prentice was happy. He had been the mentor Worley mentioned that prepared and guided Hoa through his immigration process. It was a learning experience for both men, shortened considerably by the influence of Major General Dutton Smith. Crucianelli, Redmond, and Richards were now there to see them off.

"You men take care of yourselves," Prentice said, looking at each of them seriously.

"We will," Richards said. "We will."

"Take care of each other." Prentice said.

Again Richards answered, "We will. You guys take care of each other, as well."

Hoa, looking at Prentice, then back at Richards, Cru, and Red told them, "We will take care of each other also . . . and we will see you upon your return."

* * *

October 1970.

Sergeants Crucianelli and Redmond, along with Airman 1st Class Alan Ispara, better known as "Bear" reported to Master Sergeant William E. Richards after their deadly convoy delivering materials.

"Men, I'm sorry your convoy was hit," he said. "Our information indicated no VC or NVA in the area. I am deeply saddened at the death of the two men who were killed, but the shipment that you were moving and protecting contained badly needed medical supplies for a village in the midst of a diphtheria outbreak. The fact that you completed your mission

241

and delivered much needed medicine that possibly saved dozens, if not hundreds of lives. Well done, and thank you. You men care for a drink?"

The three men went to the small wooden counter that served as a bar in Richards' office. Richards gave them each a can of Budweiser and a shot of Seagram's Crown Royal.

"Thanks." Crucianelli and Redmond told him.

"This is the best stuff I've had in 'Nam," Bear remarked.

"Well don't get too damn used to it." Richards replied. The men all laughed, enjoyed their drink and had another. Then Richards got serious. "Cru, Red, you guys have been here long enough. You've been shot at too damn much for a couple of air force supply pushers." They were all laughing again. "Colonel Ballou has authorized your early return from Vietnam . . . you guys start out-processing tomorrow."

Redmond and Cru were dumbstruck. They stammered, unsure how to respond. Cru spoke up first, "What about our early-out agreement?"

"Don't worry." Richards told him. "The agreement is intact. You guys will be honorably discharged at your point of return in Seattle. You get on a plane for Cam Rahn in three days. Try not to get yourselves killed between now and then."

Looking away, and then looking back he added softly, "When you get back, look up Hoa and Prentice."

"Will do" Cru told him.

"Right, Sarge." Red added.

Richards then addressed the big Airman 1st Class. "Bear?"

"Yes, Sergeant Richards?" Bear replied.

"Make sure these men are treated in good Phu Cat fashion before their DEROS. Let's have one more drink then you three bums get the hell out of here."

The men had another drink, then they all shook hands and started walking to the door.

242

"Oh, and Bear?" Richards added.

"Yes, Sergeant Richards?" Bear said.

"You can party with them all you want, but you go back out on the road in five days . . . be ready."

Bear looked at the floor and shook his head, "Yes, Sergeant Richards."

Epilogue

July 1982, Washington D.C., at the newly erected Vietnam War memorial, known as "the Wall."

Redmond, Montrell, Crucianelli and Hoa are all sitting on a small rise some distance from the Wall quietly gazing at it, and the people passing along its walk way. Two days before, they had all arrived in D.C., and situated themselves at their lodging in a suburban hotel. Together they caught up and became reacquainted.

They reminisced about their experiences in Vietnam, and found themselves at times laughing, and other times crying. Like many Vietnam veterans Red, Monty, and Cru had received an indifferent, cold, and at times hostile reception upon their return from the war. And again, like many Vietnam veterans they reacted to this treatment by retreating into their own minds, what would come to be known as "compartmentalizing" the experience. The unveiling of the memorial, funded mostly by Vietnam veterans, allowed many of them to feel safe enough to come out of that shell which they had been in, since their return.

Hoa, who had become a successful clothing storeowner, had his own set of experiences regarding his entry and subsequent life in the United States. On their second day in Washington D.C., they gathered the mementos they had brought and boarded the bus which would take them to the mall. As the bus wheels hummed, the men casually watched the scenery passing them by. They spoke little as they made their journey to the silent, striking memorial.

The day was warm and slightly breezy, with scattered clouds passing overhead. The four quietly walked past Arlington Cemetery observing those rows and rows of dreams gone by. They stopped at the small welcome hut near the Vietnam memorial and each received a guide pamphlet of the wall, which would tell them, among other things, where to find their friends who didn't make it back.

The disabled vet in the wheelchair handing out the literature gave each of the vets a knowing nod and smile. He paused at Hoa, and then gave him a nod, a smile, and a handshake. "Welcome home to all of you," he commented.

The little group wished him well in return and moved down to the Wall.

Before they went any further, Crucianelli spoke, "Although this Wall is dedicated to the fifty-nine thousand Americans who died in the war, we are also here today to honor the three million Vietnamese, half million Cambodians, and half-million Laotians who also lost their lives in that senseless slaughter." Redmond and Montrell nodded in agreement.

"Thank you," Hoa quietly responded.

"We also remember the Australians, Thais, Koreans, and Canadians who gave their life in the war." Again, the others nodded and murmured in agreement.

After finding the names of several of their friends and peers who had been killed in standoff attacks, sapper attacks, aircraft crashes and shoot downs, the men moved on to find the people killed in their deadly ordeal associated with the Kansas NCO.

They found the etchings of Becker, and all said a little prayer. They then found the etchings of Salas and Flash. There they lingered for a long time, some praying, others sobbing a little. Eventually they broke away and found the etching for Hardy. At this point Cru, Redmond, and, most of all, Montrell found it difficult to maintain their composure.

Montrell now spoke. "No person should ever have to endure war . . . it is a terrible thing, and humans are far too frail for it. But Hardy, most of all should not have been sacrificed to that terrible monster. He was a peace loving, carefree man, who only wanted to take photographs and return to his home in Michigan. God bless you and goodbye my friend, I think of you every day."

"Goodbye," echoed Crucianelli, Redmond, and even Hoa, although he had never met him.

Before they moved to the little hill where they were to sit, observing the Wall silently for most of the afternoon, they moved to the center of the Wall where Montrell spoke again. "Although he isn't with us, and his name is not on this wall of valor, today we are also here to honor Master Sergeant Charles Prentice. "

Prentice had died two years earlier of liver failure; ten years after his return from Vietnam, and two years after he had quit drinking for good.

Montrell continued, "He guided us through our trial by fire as our leader, as our mentor, and most of all as our friend." Having difficulty maintaining his composure, Montrell could speak no further. Redmond and Crucianelli sobbed as well; Hoa wept openly.

Left on the little hill, in memory of all those mentioned above, there remained a Native American dream catcher, a crucifix, a small bronze statue of Buddha, a can of Black Label beer, a bottle of Smirnoff's and a bottle of Seagram's . . . with the short timer's ribbon torn off.

Glossary

122: 122 rocket; a pedestal-launched 122 mm weapon, about 14 feet long, frequently used by VC as a weapon in stand-off attacks on U.S. military installations in Vietnam; it has a range of around 15 miles.

1st Cav: First Cavalry Division; an American army unit originally formed in 1855, noted in Vietnam not only for their airmobile operations, but for their vigorous search and engagement of the enemy no matter what the condition.

II Corps: one of four U.S. tactical military zones in South Vietnam.

AK-47: AK; Soviet made automatic weapon used by the NVA and VC.

ARVN: Army of the Republic of Vietnam; soldiers from the South Vietnamese army are referred to as ARVNs.

APC: Armored Personnel Carrier

B-52: Buff, big ugly fat fucker, Stratofortress, long range USAF bomber launched from Thailand or Okinawa used in bombing raids all over North and South Vietnam; the most feared weapon of the Vietnam War.

Betel nut: mildly narcotic berry chewed on by Vietnamese, long-term use blackens the teeth.

BX: base exchange, (PX post exchange); small store on larger U.S. military installations where GIs can purchase sundries.

CHICOM: Chinese communist; a weapon made or received from the Chinese communists is referred to as a CHICOM.

DEROS: Date Eligible for Return from OverSeas; the date every GI in Vietnam longed for; the date they went home.

Dust-off: a military airlift flying dead and wounded men back to an area for treatment or processing.

FANGS: fuckin' new guys, new arrivals in Vietnam, also referred to as FNGS, new meat, Jeeps, cheesedicks.

Fifty Cal: fifty caliber machine gun; .50 cal, a heavy automatic weapon usually mounted on aircraft or vehicles.

First Shirt: first sergeant; first sleeve; top; the top enlisted man in an army, air force, or Marine unit.

Frag: the practice of killing an American GI by another one; named for a fragmentation grenade sometimes rolled into the billeting quarters of the intended victim.

Grunt: ground pounder; an infantryman, or ground fighting soldier; a reference to any GI humping through the bush; the cutting edge of any military fighting force.

H: heroin, horse, smack, thouc lam diu dau; a drug frequently used, bought and sold by U.S. military personnel in Vietnam.

Indian country: anywhere outside the wire, or main gate of a major U.S. military installation.

KIA: killed in action.

Lifer: a career military person; a much maligned group, but in truth the heart and soul of the military.

LZ: landing zone; a place for aircraft to land and take off; a forward outpost where small tactical military aircraft operated.

M-16: 16; automatic weapon used by the U.S. military and its allies in Vietnam.

MACV: Military Assistance Command, Vietnam; the organization responsible for all U.S. military activity in Vietnam.

MPC: Military Payment Certificate; currency printed by the U.S. military and used in an effort to control black marketeering; also referred to as "funny money", or scrip; the Kansas NCO's operation made huge amounts of money manipulating the currency.

NCO: non-commissioned officer, an enlisted man of a higher rank.

NCOIC: non-commissioned officer in charge.

Ninety-Day Wonder: a person commissioned as an officer in one of the armed services after ninety days or a relatively short length of training.

NVA: North Vietnamese Army; troops from North Vietnam were referred to as NVA. They normally wore pea green helmets and uniforms.

OIC: officer in charge.

Phu Cat: an American Air Force base in II Corps, Vietnam, near the village of Phu Cat. A tactical combat support airbase, the base employed F4 Phantom jet fighters, Shadow and Spooky gunships, several types of cargo aircraft and several types of helicopters.

Piaster: Vietnamese currency; also referred to as "P."

Poncho liner: a small camouflaged blanket, used to insulate a raincoat, and more often used as a blanket.

Ration Card: a card each GI received on a monthly basis controlling liquor, cigarettes, and other such goods. As the goods were purchased, the card was marked or punched. Banking of goods from month to month was prohibited, but common. Persons working for the Kansas NCO turned their cards over to him upon receipt. He provided the goods to them when needed and banked and sold the rest on the open market at marked up prices.

RHIP: rank has its privileges.

ROK: Republic of Korea; soldiers from South Korea are often referred to as "ROKs."

R & R: rest and recuperation; a one week period of time away from Vietnam which all in-country GIs were allowed, after 6 months of Vietnam service.

Short: short timer; a person in Vietnam who had less than 30 days before DEROS.

Short timer ribbon: the ribbon off the cap of a bottle of Seagram's VO; tradition had it that a short timer drank a bottle after they had less than 30 days remaining on their tour; (many drank more) the ribbon would then be attached to a shirt button hole.

Speed: uppers, white crosses, go pills, amphetamines; a drug used by many members of the U.S. military in Vietnam; the U.S. military doled them out like candy.

TDY: temporary duty assignment to a locality other than your permanently assigned base or post.

The Kansas NCO: William E Richards; Master Sergeant, USAF, head of the largest black market operation of the Vietnam War. He is referred to as the Kansas NCO as a method of cloaking his identity.

The Old Man: a reference to the commander of a large U.S. military unit, a man of higher rank, normally with many of years in service.

Thirty Cal: thirty caliber automatic machine gun, can be mounted or hand carried.

UCMJ: Uniform code of military justice, the legal framework of the U.S. military under which whose laws all members of the U.S. military are subject to.

USO: United Services Organization; the organization responsible for the entertainment of U.S. GIs all over the world.

VC: Vietcong; South Vietnamese communist guerillas; they normally wore solid black shirts and pants, referred to as black pajamas; they frequently wore the conical hat common in Vietnam.

Vietnamization: Richard Nixon's program to turn over responsibility for the war to South Vietnam; the program was for the most part unsuccessful.

Vil: village; hamlet; home of many Vietnamese in the countryside.

WIA: wounded in action.

2/20/19

2/20/19

CPSIA information can be obtained at www.ICGtesting.com
Printed in the USA
BVOW11s1704090914

366036BV00007B/118/P